PERSONAL PROTECTION

TIFFANY PATTERSON

Copyright © 2022 by Tiffany Patterson

All rights reserved.

No part of this book may be reproduced in any form or by any electronic or mechanical means, including information storage and retrieval systems, without written permission from the author, except for the use of brief quotations in a book review.

CONTENTS

Author Note	v
Chapter 1	1
Chapter 2	7
Chapter 3	17
Chapter 4	26
Chapter 5	34
Chapter 6	41
Chapter 7	50
Chapter 8	59
Chapter 9	70
Chapter 10	84
Chapter 11	91
Chapter 12	98
Chapter 13	103
Chapter 14	112
Chapter 15	121
Chapter 16	130
Chapter 17	138
Chapter 18	148
Chapter 19	156
Chapter 20	162
Chapter 21	171
Chapter 22	177
Chapter 23	183
Chapter 24	194
Chapter 25	204
Chapter 26	208
Chapter 27	215
Chapter 28	224
Chapter 29	232
Chapter 30	238
Chapter 31	247
Chapter 32	257
Chapter 33	266

Chapter 34	272
Epilogue	277
Keep in Touch with Tiffany	283
More Titles by Tiffany Patterson	285
Forever Series	287
Non-Series Titles	289
Tiffany Patterson Website Exclusives	291
The Nightwolf Series	293

Dear Reader,

Thank you for choosing to read Personal Protection. Please be aware that this book contains some violence, attempted kidnapping, strong language and lots and lots of high-heat love scenes. As always, there is a happily ever after.

Please enjoy!

CHAPTER 1

Brutus

"And you're sure everything is scheduled for the security detail for Aaron's trip next week?" I asked, staring at my second in command as we stood outside of the Williamsport Airport entrance.

Joseph's eyes glistened and wrinkled at the edges. My stomach tightened along with the muscles in my face. I knew his ass was on the verge of a wisecrack.

"No. Would you mind running the plan by me for the fiftieth time this morning? I'm not sure I wrote down the exact color of Aaron Townsend's tie on the third day of his trip," he replied.

I stepped closer and stared down at him from my six-foot-eight height to his six-foot-three frame. "Everything's a damn joke to you," I growled.

He sobered up but only slightly. "Brutus, this is your first vacation in what? Five years?" He shook his head before placing a hand on my shoulder. "You know we're capable of doing our jobs as well as you." He stopped when my eyes narrowed. "Well, almost as well as you. The Townsends are in skillful hands."

I gritted my teeth but stepped back. After all, Joseph was right. I'd personally vetted and trained all twenty-five employees on the

Townsend Security staff. As the head of Townsend Security, I oversaw everything from close and personal protection to thwarting cyber security attacks to investigating business rivals and current or potential employees.

Though with the family growing, that placed more demand on my team. We were slightly understaffed since I recently let go of one of our employees. Guilt swelled in the pit Fof my stomach at the notion that I was leaving the Townsends uncovered.

"We've got this handled," Joseph assured me again.

On a deep inhale, I reassured myself with the knowledge that I would only be a phone call away if they needed me. My handpicked staff was adept enough to adjust to any changes that may come their way.

"Don't forget that you have a three-thirty training session with Kyle, Kennedy, Cole, and Diego today," I added.

Joseph nodded.

"Don't let Kyle and Diego joke around too much. And remind Kennedy that her father insists she takes part in these self-defense training sessions. She'll try to con her way out of it to read instead."

He rolled his eyes. "I know. She tried it on me a few months ago."

I let out a sound, something between a chuckle and a snort. Kennedy Townsend, the oldest daughter of Aaron and Patience Townsend, preferred reading over just about anything, especially over the mandatory self-defense practice that all of the Townsend children partook in, under the mandate of their parents—mainly their fathers.

Truthfully, after the shit I've seen as head of security for this family, I one hundred percent understood why all of the adults wanted their children to know how to protect themselves in any scenario.

"Listen, if you keep standing here, thinking of the thousands of ways things could go wrong, you're going to miss your flight."

I frowned. "Thousands? Are you talking like a few thousand, tens of thousands, or hundreds?" I wondered out loud. I'd only thought of a few thousand ways that my taking a two-week vacation could go sideways, but Joseph's words caused another wave of anxiety to push through my stomach.

Was there something I hadn't thought of?

"Brutus, lighten the fuck up. It'll be fine. It's been five years since you've been on vacation. Go."

I glared at him one final time before picking up my carry-on and hoisting it over my shoulder. With the suitcase handle in my other hand, I nodded at Joseph and finally headed inside.

I guessed I was doing this. I was going on my first vacation in over five years.

* * *

Minutes after passing through the security check, which was a breeze with the travel security clearance I had, I decided to head to the lounge area to get a drink and some food before my flight.

As I started toward the lounge, my phone buzzed in my pocket. *Fuck, I bet it's work already. I knew taking this damn vacation was a mistake. It isn't the right time to take off.*

Those thoughts stopped swirling in my mind as soon as I pulled out my phone and saw the name flashing across my screen.

"Rick, shouldn't you be taking your second nap of the day?" I casually asked my father.

He grunted on the other end. "I was, but then I got hungry."

I snorted.

"I wanted one of those peanut butter and banana sandwiches you make for me, but can't find the damn peanut butter."

I stifled a grin at the hard grumble in his voice. I could picture his domestically helpless ass as he moved around my kitchen, ripping cupboards open, the refrigerator door hanging open.

Speaking of…

"That door of my refrigerator better not be open. Letting all of my food defrost."

"That's all you can think of right now? My stomach is over here touching my back, and you're worried about the damn temperature of the food?" he grumbled.

My frown deepened as I rolled my eyes. "So fucking dramatic." I left the man at least a week's worth of frozen food that I cooked, and I hired a personal chef to drop off freshly prepared food for the second week I'd be gone. And that's not to mention the stacks of takeout menus he had in his own kitchen, in the guesthouse where he stayed most of the time.

"How the hell did you run Townsend Security for almost three decades when you can't even make yourself a damn meal?"

"Don't get sharp with me. I did my job well. But cooking wasn't in my damn job description."

"Making a peanut butter sandwich isn't cooking," I not-so-kindly reminded him.

"If I need to be in the kitchen to do it, it's cooking."

My father loved my peanut butter and banana sandwiches, which I always toasted to add a little depth of flavor. My mother had prepared the same sandwich for me as a kid. Since my father wasn't around for my childhood, I'd introduced him to the meal a few years back when he moved in with me, and since then, he bitched and moaned if he went without them for too long.

"Sweet Jesus." I pinched the bridge of my nose. Maybe I was wrong in worrying more about Townsend Security than my father. "Do I need to send Joseph over there to make you a sandwich?"

"Try it and I'll kick your ass."

At that, I let out a bark of laughter. It must've startled some people because a few stopped to look my way. That won them a scowl. I smiled inwardly when one man's eyes doubled in size, and he hurried in the opposite direction, reminding me of one of those damn pesky squirrels who loved congregating in my backyard.

I knew the intimidating picture I presented. At six-eight, bulky as fuck, and with my often scowling face, I didn't look like the guy you wanted to fuck with. Because I wasn't. But even at my height and size, I knew how to blend in better than most.

Which was why, I supposed, that even as I stood off to the side of the airport's walkway, directing my father to the particular cabinet where I kept the unopened peanut butter jar, someone walked right into me.

An involuntary grunt parted from my lips, accompanied by a scent of sweet-scented air. A woman. It was a woman who bumped into me.

On instinct, I reached for the woman who'd collided with my body. Though she'd been the one to walk into me, she caught the worst of it. My hold prevented her from toppling over entirely.

"Oh jeez, I'm so sorry," she said in one long exhale. "Are you okay?" she asked in an apologetic tone. The woman brushed a hand down her jeans before standing up to peer up at me.

Our eyes caught, and I watched hers widen for the briefest of moments. Something in my chest shifted, but I didn't have time to notice that. I was too busy taking in her soft brown eyes that looked as if they danced a little. Staring into her eyes stole the air from my lungs.

"Um, thank you, but I'm fine," she said.

I blinked and shook my head. That was when I realized she was trying to pry her arm out of my hand. My hand that continued to needlessly hold onto her.

My eyes lingered on her full lips, noting the nervous smile that played on them.

You're making her nervous, the voice of reason spoke up, and thankfully, I heeded it. But reluctantly. Slowly, I withdrew my hand from her body.

"I'm fine," I told her.

"Good, good. I'm late for my flight," she explained.

Professional instincts kicked in, and I wanted to tell her never to give a stranger so much information about herself, but I bit my tongue.

She exhaled, blinked, and moved around me. "Sorry, again." She tossed me one final look over her shoulder before rushing off.

I had to force myself to remain where I stood. The desire to follow her almost overcame me.

"Are you still there? What the hell happened?"

Remembering that my father was still on the phone, I shook myself free of my stupor.

"Did you find the peanut butter?"

"Where've you been?" he quickly countered. "You were telling me how to cook this damn sandwich right so it tasted just like yours."

I heaved a breath.

I took one last glance over my shoulder, searching for signs of the woman that bumped into me. Our exchange was brief … too brief, but from what I did get to make of her, she was short, like shorter than average. Thus seeing over the crowds of people in this damn airport was likely a lost cause.

I wonder where she's going?

There was no use in wondering about that. Hundreds of flights went in and out of this airport daily. I'd probably never see that woman again.

I told myself that should've been okay with me. Still, even while I gathered my luggage, and instructed my father on how not to burn down my damn kitchen, I couldn't help but think about how soft her body felt pressed against mine for that millisecond she was there.

CHAPTER 2

Mia

"I can't believe I missed my flight," I whined to my sister, Sharise, over the phone.

"Sorry, hun, but at least you were able to catch the next one. And it's a direct flight," she reminded me in that always-looking-on-the-bright-side-of-things way of hers.

"And I upgraded to first class," I confessed.

"Yess! That's what I'm talking about. You deserve it."

A grin split my lips as I peered at the screens listing the departing flights and their times. I needed to triple-check that I was by the right gate. I was determined not to miss another flight.

"Why were you running late anyway? You're hardly ever late," Sharise asked as I made the decision to bypass the seating area and head to the little coffee stand in the middle of the airport.

I hesitated but eventually answered, "Vincent called last night. He had a—"

"Your former co-worker Vincent Davis?" Sharise shrieked. "Not the same Vincent Davis that you trained for a year, who then spent the better part of the past three years riding your coattails only for him to get that promotion that you deserved? That could not possibly be the same Vincent Davis you're saying caused you to miss your flight this morning."

I groaned. "Sometimes I think I share too much of my business with you."

"Not possible. I'm your big sister. I changed your diaper."

Laughing, I rolled my eyes. "Sharise, you're eighteen months older than me. We were practically in diapers at the same time."

"Whatever." I could almost see her waving a dismissive hand in the air. "What did his backstabbing ass want?"

"He—"

"Hang on. Yes, Christopher?" she called.

Though slightly annoyed at being cut off so abruptly, my heart swelled a little at hearing my five-year-old nephew's voice in the background. I even grinned when Sharise started arguing with him back and forth over how to properly cut his hot dogs.

"That boy," Sharise griped when she returned to the phone.

"Give my baby nephew a kiss for me," I told her as I moved up one spot in the long line at the coffee stand. My stomach rumbled when the smell of freshly baked goods hit my nose.

"Now what were we ... oh yeah, you missed your flight because of Vincent. Tell me more about that."

I shook my head at how good my sister's memory was. "He didn't make me miss my flight. I was up later than planned because he called with a few questions."

"Work questions?" Sharise asked.

"Yes, of course."

"Questions about a company you no longer work for," she reiterated.

I bit my bottom lip before answering. "Yeah."

"Why would you—"

"Anyway, he had a few questions regarding the Marvins account, and I answered, which led me to postponing my packing. Then I was too tired because I had to clean all day yesterday to prep my home for the renters."

"Which means you shouldn't have answered that man's phone call in the first place."

"Please, Sharise..."

I moved up until I was the next person in line.

"Hang on," I told my sister so that I could order a cinnamon latte and one of their cherry cheese tarts.

"All right," I started once I retrieved my order. "Like I was saying, I ended up oversleeping a little and still had to finish packing, then my Uber driver got impatient and left without me. That's why I was late and ended up missing my flight."

"Let's go back to the part about you answering the phone when you should've let it go to voicemail," Sharise continued.

Sighing, I placed my latte and pastry on one of the tables in a seated part of the airport gates. I was a few spaces down from my gate but could see it.

"Why do you keep harping on this?" I took a sip of my latte, and despite Sharise in my ear going on about how much I let my former employer and colleagues take advantage of me, I relished how the cinnamon enhanced the sweetness of the latte.

"I'm definitely doing cinnamon lattes at my shop," I murmured, placing my cup down in front of me.

"I'm serious, Mi-Mi," Sharise started, calling me the nickname she'd used since we were kids. "You worked your ass off at that job for years, brought in countless clients, and God only knows how many millions of dollars you made that company."

I scoffed. "Not millions," I mumbled.

"Mi-Mi," she intoned.

On a huff, I admitted. "You're probably right." I was an excellent employee of Corsica Pharmaceuticals for well over ten years. I'd started as a sales rep and worked my way up to national sales manager. But when it came time to promote me to business director, a colleague with half of my experience got the job.

"I'm not probably anything," Sharise replied, sounding just like our mother. "You know I'm right. But this time is for you. I'm so glad you decided to quit that job and finally take the sabbatical you've been talking about for some time now."

My heart swelled from the pride in her voice. Sharise was always one of my biggest cheerleaders. Along with my best friend, Carlene.

"And you'll come home and open your coffee shop, and it'll be a huge success," she continued. "Your former bosses will wish they'd done right by you."

Opening a coffee shop had been a dream of mine since college. A desire I'd put off while working up the corporate ladder. Now, that goal was just in reach.

"I love you, sis," I replied, meaning every word.

I took a bite of my cherry tart. As soon as I started chewing, I frowned. "Oh, I do not love that." I managed to swallow that first bite but pushed the plate with the rest of the tart away from me.

"What?"

"The cherry tart I just had. The crust wasn't flaky or buttery enough, and the cherries tasted a little metallic." I pulled a face. "Not to self: be careful of which vendors I go with for the pastries and baked goods at my coffee shop."

"See, that's what you need to focus on," Sharise pounced. "Getting your mind right to open Cup of Joy."

"You don't have to remind me why I booked this trip." I planned to relax in Tulum, Mexico, for the first month of my sabbatical before heading down to Colombia for two months to stay on a coffee farm. I wanted to understand better where the best coffee in the world came from. And with any luck, I would be able to make some contacts to partner with to purchase my coffee beans once I opened my shop.

"All I'm trying to say is that this time is for you and your dreams. Stop worrying about that job that obviously never gave a shit about you and put you first."

Sharise was always the blunt one out of the two of us. But her words hit their mark. I'd worked my butt off for Corsica Pharmaceuticals. I'd never done the calculations, but I wouldn't be surprised if all of the money I'd brought in from new clients and ongoing sales of older clients totaled in the millions.

Yes, I'd been compensated well for my time, but respect was a different issue entirely.

"I'm going to enjoy my time in Mexico and Colombia," I told my sister.

"Good. And you better bring me back some of that Colombian coffee," she insisted. "And make sure you bring enough for Boris. His behind is always drinking up the last of my coffee," she complained about her husband, but I heard the softness in her voice.

"I want something, too," Christopher said in the background.

"Boy, if you don't go finish that hot dog," Sharise said. "Hurry before your sisters wake up," she rushed him.

Overhead, I heard a last call and my heart hammered in my chest when I realized it was my name being called over the speaker.

"Shit," I yelped and rose to my feet. "I'm late again. I gotta go."

"Don't miss this flight. Love you, bye. Call me when you get in."

"Bye." Hanging up, I silently scolded myself for getting so wrapped up in my conversation with Sharise I almost missed this flight, too.

"I'm here!" I called to the airline attendant right before I made it to the door. "Thank you."

I sighed as I stepped onto the walkway that led to the plane. Though rushed, a calmness fell over me. Sharise was right. This trip was for me. I earned it, and I damn sure deserved it. My former job wouldn't get another speck of attention from me. I was on to bigger and better things.

* * *

Brutus

I HATED TALKING to most people. It was part of what made me so damned good at my job. People didn't expect to speak to security. My responsibility was to be as discreet as possible, and yeah, even at my size, I blended in well. The number of times people had passed right by me and didn't notice until I struck was countless. If I had a dollar for every time that happened, I'd have enough to retire.

Actually, I already had well beyond the amount I'd need for a hell of a retirement. To the Townsends, protecting their family and assets was the highest priority, and they spared no expense. As a result, I'd never want for another material possession in my life.

While I always chose to wear and look my best, I wasn't flashy. I didn't need to stick out or flaunt what I had. But I did seek out comfort. Thus, the extra leg room and larger seating were why I always chose the first-class ticket when I flew alone.

I'd spent enough of my life packed into spaces and places while in the military. Now, I wanted to be comfortable.

When I peered to my left and saw the empty seat, a satisfied parting of my lips occurred. It looked like I wouldn't have to share the row with anyone since we were nearing the last passenger boarding the plane. Everyone in first class had already boarded.

Yet, as I closed my eyes and leaned back in my seat, a woman's voice at the front of the plane drew my attention. My eyes popped open, and they zeroed in on *her*.

"Thank God, I didn't miss this one," she said, her voice carrying over to me.

Something tickled up my spine at the sound of the breathlessness in her words. The flight attendant said something to her, making the woman laugh, and the melodic sound traveled to my ears and eased over every cell of my body. Without thought, a tension I hadn't even been aware of eased.

"Excuse me," she said, approaching me.

I didn't realize she'd grown so close. As I looked up at her standing over me, a pair of hickory brown eyes peered down at me. This time I noted the flecks of gold in them. Her eyes were a few shades darker than the brown coloring of her skin. Her smile was wide and bright enough to light up the entire 747 we were on.

I panned down, letting my eyes linger on body. She wasn't tiny by any means, and I liked that. Probably too much.

"Excuse me." She pointed to the chair next to me. "That's my seat."

I reoriented myself, recognizing that she was asking me to get my big ass out of the way so she could take her seat. Moments earlier I was relived at the prospect of not having to share this row with another passenger. Yet, finding out that she would be my row partner didn't bring on my typical bout of irritation of having to share space with someone else.

I stood to allow her in. Without being asked, I easily lifted the light blue carry-on she had and placed it in the overhead compartment directly above us.

"You didn't have to do that," she said. "But thank you so much. I sometimes have trouble getting my bag into those things."

Looking her up and down, I agreed. She was short as hell. Probably five-four without the three-inch heels she wore. She was short but not petite. Her body was lush all over. Her thighs, hips, and breasts were enough for my larger-than-average hands to fill. And my fingers did something strange.

They started itching.

To touch her.

She eased into her seat next to me, but as she did, her shoulder bag caught on the arm of the chair, spilling its contents onto the floor between our seats.

"Damn. I'm a mess today." She laughed.

I rubbed my palm against my chest to work through the tightness that suddenly formed there. I bent over to pick up the tablet that fell out of her shoulder bag. Flipping the device over to see the screen it lit up. She was listening to an audiobook.

"*Outliers*," I murmured.

Her lips parted, and eyebrows lifted. "Have you read it?" she asked as I handed her the tablet.

With a nod, I answered, "A few months ago. Didn't enjoy it as much as *Talking to Strangers*."

"I think I prefer *Talking to Strangers* over *Outliers*, to be quite honest," she said simultaneously.

Our eyes connected. There was a shimmer in hers.

"You're a Malcolm Gladwell fan?" I asked.

"I don't trust people who aren't," she replied.

Damn.

Another round of laughter spilled from her lips, and I wanted to rack my brain in search of something else that would make her laugh but came up empty. I went with the next best thing.

"What's your favorite part of *Outliers* so far?" I could hardly believe that I asked a question as a conversation opener. I didn't do that type of shit. I liked quiet. And this woman, she didn't strike me as quiet.

She wasn't loud or obnoxious with her talking, but she clearly didn't have a problem holding up the other end of a conversation.

"I mean, anything Gladwell writes is fascinating," she started. "Right? The man has a gift."

I nodded in agreement.

"But I think the part about how culture impacts communication and the real implications that has on the world around us." She leaned in. "Take, for example, the way he discusses the number of plane crashes that could've been avoided but not for lack of competence when it comes to communication across languages and cultures."

I gave her a contemplative look and said, "Now's probably not the best time to mention plane crashes. Especially when this one is heading into international territory."

Instead of that comment garnering a laugh, she gasped and covered her mouth with her hand. Instant regret settled in my gut since I hated not being able to see her mouth. The urge to capture her wrist and pull it away from her mouth nearly overwhelmed me.

Hell, I was half a breath away from doing that when a male flight attendant appeared next to me. "Seatbelt, sir."

His tone was polite enough, even friendly, but I still scowled him down. My anger baffled me for a second before I realized it was because he had the nerve to interrupt me while I was speaking to …

Shit, I didn't even know her name yet.

Right as that thought crossed my mind, she started talking again.

"I didn't frighten you, did I? Do you have a fear of flying?" The cute way her forehead wrinkled told me that she was genuinely concerned that she'd stirred up a fear of flying by mentioning Malcolm Gladwell's example.

"I've been on thousands of flights. If I ever had a fear of flying it would be long gone by now." All of which was true. Between my time in the Army, serving abroad, and working for the family I worked for, getting on an airplane was as second nature as getting into a car.

"Good." She visibly exhaled.

"I took a flight once with a coworker who was terrified of flying. He held onto my hand for dear life the entire two-hour ride."

My gut twisted. *He?*

Who the hell was this man holding onto her hand, and more importantly, why did it piss me off so much?

"He sounds like a pussy," I groused.

"What was that?" she intoned in that sweet, almost innocent voice of hers.

"Nothing. I have to agree with you on *Outliers*. Lack of cultural competency often leads to miscommunications which can cause entire deals or planes," I waved my hand, gesturing to the plane we were in, "to come crashing down."

She tsked. "Tell me about it. I've seen some mess ups in my career due to bungled communication. But that's why *Talking to Strangers* is one of my favorite books. He sheds a lot of light on how our preconceived ideas overshadow how we approach others or people we deem others, right?"

"Agreed," I replied. "But often it's necessary to do that *othering* if they pose a threat."

"But that's kind of his point," she jumped in, adjusting her body to face me as she made her point. "When we 'other' someone, we automatically make them out to be the bad guy or the enemy. Not everyone is your enemy."

I snorted. "Not everyone is a friend, either," I countered. A hint of skepticism stained my comment.

At that, she frowned, and honestly, I enjoyed her frown almost as much as her smile. It wasn't a malicious downturn of her lips, but more of a contemplative, taking my statement under advisement before she spoke, type of frown.

And goddamn it when she pulled her bottom lip in between her teeth, that itching feeling in my fingers started again. I wanted to drag that plump lip from between her teeth and suck on it. I felt the need to pinch her chin between my thumb and forefinger, holding her in place while I attacked her juicy lips with my own.

Fuck, this woman had me rattled already.

We made it halfway through our three-and-a-half-hour flight before I realized we hadn't stopped talking the entire time. By that time, I'd found out that she was also from and lived in Williamsport and her final destination was to Tulum, Mexico. Same as me.

I didn't talk that much. I hated talking too much, but with her, it was easy. Hell, more than easy, it was something I wanted to do and keep doing. Right until the time our plane landed.

CHAPTER 3

Mia

"I seriously had higher hopes for you," I told Brutus as we exited the walkway that led into the Cancún airport.

A deep chuckle passed through his lips, and I had to force my body not to visibly shudder at the smoky sound.

"I'm serious," I teased, turning in his direction. "How could a person read just about every Malcolm Gladwell book and then turn around and say *The 48 Laws of Power* was their favorite book of all time?" I grimaced at the thought.

He pinned me with those deep set, hazel eyes of his. I felt my body's temperature rise a few notches. This man was huge, probably like double my size in height and at least two-fifty. And it was all muscle. The gray T-shirt he wore clung to his body for its dear life. And Lord help me if it didn't look good doing it.

He had a head full of dark brown hair that he kept short at the sides and back but longer on top, with a beard to match. A beautifully sculpted jaw on a man was one of my weaknesses. And Brutus had it.

He was handsome, no doubt, but honestly, intimidating too. His size, combined with the way he sometimes scowled, I think any average person would do well to stay clear of getting on his bad side. Yet, something almost gravitational felt as if it pulled me to him.

"I never said it was my favorite book of all time," he replied. His voice reminded me of silk and smoke and late nights.

The kind of late nights that were bound to get a woman into trouble.

"I said the author made some good points."

I threw my hands up into the air. "That's the same thing."

Another rush of euphoria passed over me when the crack of a smile appeared on his lips. But it quickly disappeared. I noticed that throughout the flight. A smile would creep onto his mouth like the sun peeking out from behind the mountains in the morning. Then he'd tuck it away even quicker, not wanting to give too much away.

It made me want more.

"Hardly the same thing," he said. "You can't tell me there weren't some valid points in that book about power and influence."

I stopped right in the middle of the airport and the traffic of people, folded my arms across my chest, and pursed my lips.

Brutus stopped short, his eyes widening in surprise.

"I can and will."

He shook his head and then moved to my side, placed a large hand at the small of my back, and pressed me forward. And yeah, I went willingly. My body moved under his silent command.

As we walked, I expected him to drop his hand from my back. But he didn't. I thought about stepping out from his hold because, after all, this guy was a stranger. But I didn't. I remained right where I was, walking alongside him, as we debated the merits of that damn book I loathed.

Despite my not knowing this man from a can of paint only a few hours earlier, it didn't feel weird or awkward to be walking and laughing with him through the airport.

"Do you have bags to claim?" He peered down at me with those intensely blazing hazel eyes of his.

Why does one look from him make me feel like I'm the center of the universe?

I shook that thought loose. "Team carry-on," I answered as I patted the handle of my carry-on suitcase. "After one too many instances of getting my bags lost or things stolen out of my suitcase, I refuse to travel with bags that I can't carry on the plane," I further explained.

He dipped his head. "Smart woman."

I tamped down the butterflies dancing in my belly in delight from his compliment.

"Um." I pointed ahead to the sign that directed passengers toward the rental car area. "I need to pick up my rental to drive the rest of my way to my destination." I bit my tongue in the nick of time. To keep from telling him that my final stop was in Tulum, only to roll my eyes at myself internally. I'd already disclosed as much during our conversation on the flight.

"Same here." His deep and smooth voice sent chills down my spine. "What rental company are you with?"

"Uh …" I paused to remember. I snapped my fingers and answered, "Expertise Rentals."

His smile widened, and the slight crow's feet around his eyes deepened. I swallowed the lump in my throat.

"What a coincidence," he said, and damn that baritone distracted me.

I blinked, to again find myself the center of that stare. "You also have Expertise?"

He nodded and pulled out his phone. "I'll walk with you over. Give me a second." He waved his phone in his hand. "I just need to make contact to let a friend know I arrived."

My heart sank with my shoulders, but I fought hard not to let him see it. When I caught his eyes again, I could see they were narrowed on me. A slight frown appeared on his lips, but he schooled his features.

"You know what," I started, "I'm going to run to the bathroom. If you need to meet your friend or something, I can just head out from here." I hoped my voice sounded normal because the idea of parting ways so soon had a tightness filling my chest.

He peered over my head and nodded in the direction of the ladies' room behind me. "I'll meet you right here," he said firmly, as if telling me he wasn't going anywhere.

Honestly, I didn't know if I should've been elated or a little concerned.

"Okay," I told him before heading to the restroom with my bags.

While out of his presence for a few minutes, I let my mind wonder about who the "friend" was that he mentioned. An image of a smiling woman, ready to wrap her arms around his broad shoulders, welcoming him to wherever he was going, came to mind.

Not that I was jealous or anything. I was on this sabbatical for myself, to relax. Not to meet a man. Besides, I was a talker by nature. He was far from the first person I'd chatted it up with during a flight. A few of my closest friends I'd met that way.

But there was something different—a hopefulness I had to suppress, not to let it override my good sense.

After washing my hands and gathering myself, I exited the restroom. Hordes of people moved about the airport. But Brutus stood out. Yes, in part, it was due to his size. It was more than that, however.

His presence commanded attention, even with his head looking down into the phone in his hands. The urge to peek at the phone screen to find out if it was a woman he was messaging overcame me.

Every few seconds, he glanced up and scanned his surroundings. It was almost an instinctive move. He appeared to be on the lookout for something or someone, perhaps?

On one of his sweeps, his gaze collided with mine. His smile was instantaneous, and it chased away the doubts that'd clawed their way into my mind in our short period of separation.

"All set?" he asked.

I nodded. "You don't have to use the restroom?"

He shook his head. "I can go long periods without needing to go."

I tilted my head. "I don't think that's good for your bladder."

A deep chuckle broke free. "My bladder's good and trained." He grabbed my suitcase along with his. "C'mon."

Why did it feel like we were suddenly on a trip together?

We made our way to the rental car service, and he let me get ahead of him. I was almost relieved to get up to the clerk at the desk. With the keys in my hand to my rental, I would be able to get in my car and be on my way. Some time apart from Brutus would probably do me some good.

That's what I was thinking all the way up until the time the clerk apologetically informed me that somehow the car rental I'd set up weeks ago was no longer in their system.

* * *

Brutus

"That can't be right," I heard Mia say as she stood about five feet to my left, speaking with one of the car rental employees.

I squashed down on the satisfied feeling that passed through me. No, I didn't appreciate hearing the distress in her voice. What did titillate me was the awareness that the contact I'd reached out to while Mia was in the restroom held up his end of our arrangement.

He was able to get Mia's rental wiped out of their system.

"Mr. Prince," the employee handling my reservation called, "we have the smoke-colored Lexus SUV that you requested. She has just been washed and is all ready for your arrival."

"Perfect." I nodded before quickly looking over at Mia.

"What do you mean I will have to come back?" she questioned, impatience making a hint of an appearance in her tone. She wasn't loud or shrieking. It sounded like she fought hard to keep her voice even and professional, but I had excellent hearing.

I bit back a smile. And while I should've felt some guilt at causing this minor inconvenience, not an ounce of that emotion made its way into my body. Quite the opposite. Satisfaction coursed through me knowing that I was one step closer to spending even more time with Mia.

I thanked the employee after he handed me the keys to the SUV and a map of how to get to Tulum. Not that I would need it.

"Is there a problem?" I casually asked Mia, approaching her from the side.

She turned, a displeased expression on her face. "My reservation somehow got canceled." She gestured toward the counter. "Or lost or something. And they don't have any more rentals available for the next week. How is that possible?" She turned to the employee behind the counter to ask.

Before he could answer, I interjected, "You're going to Tulum, right?"

"Yes, it's over two hours away." She frowned. "There is a bus. A pretty nice bus from what I'm told. I could always—"

"Ride with me," I finished for her.

Her eyebrows lifted, lips parted.

I almost forgot all of my training that told me to remain calm, cool, and collected when I'm on the verge of hitting my target.

In my thirty-seven years of life, I couldn't recall a time when I wanted something so much. Not for myself, anyway. I'd wanted a lot —to keep my clients safe, to fulfill my obligations to my teammates in the military, to take care of my mother when she needed me, but never a woman.

"I couldn't ..." Mia trailed off.

"I'm going to the same place," I reminded her.

"Same city, but not the same place," she came back with.

"Close enough. I wouldn't mind dropping you off."

Her mouth parted again, and a lesser man would've folded, I swear. She shook her head. Clearing her throat, she said, "I mean, us talking and stuff on the plane was great. But we're strangers. And it wouldn't be smart for me to get into a car with ..." she notably scanned the length of my body with her gaze, "someone I don't know."

I wanted to brush off her comment, tell her she was being ridiculous, but I was a security professional. I knew better than most the dangers that existed in this world. In all honesty, if she were someone related to me or one of the Townsend women, I would've run down all of the ways in which she'd already failed at keeping herself safe.

She'd already shared with me where she was going, the name of the rental car company she would be using, and her first and last name. Had I been someone with more nefarious intentions, she'd be up shit's creek without needing to get into my vehicle.

Ah, who the hell was I kidding?

I was the one with somewhat shady dealings, seeing as how I was responsible for getting her reservation deleted so that I could take her to her final destination. The idea of finding out her room reservation so that I could have that canceled as well did pass through my mind.

"You're right," I responded. "But I can assure you, you're in safe hands with me." I held up both hands in a surrendering fashion.

She smirked but folded her arms across her chest.

I blanched, mentally chastising myself. Of course that move wouldn't work. I knew how damn big I was. And Mia couldn't be more than five-four, though her demeanor made her feel taller than that.

"How about this?" I pulled out my phone and held it up. "You take out your phone. Snap a photo of me and send it to whoever you want. I'll give you my number, full name, and home address so your contact knows exactly who you're traveling with."

She squinted and gave me a wary look.

"You know you've done the same thing while going on a date with someone for the first time."

"Oh, so this is a date now?" she asked.

"It can be whatever you want it to be." Shit, where did that smoothness come from? I rarely talked more than two or three sentences to most people. This woman had me going far out of my comfort zone without her even trying.

"I have done it before," she admitted. She held up her phone and snapped a couple of photos. "And I'm sending your information to my sister and my best friend."

"Make sure you spell my name right. The last name is Prince."

She eyed me before following instructions. I gave her all of my information, including the name of place where I was staying.

Her sister's response was immediate.

Who the hell is that? I read the question before Mia started typing a reply.

"My rental's right out here," I told her.

She hesitated.

"You're still not sure," I guessed.

She shook her head as she bit her bottom lip. For a split moment, I wondered if she knew how fucking tempted she looked? More than that, I wondered if she knew the enormous amount of restraint I exhibited at that moment. Probably not, because if she had, she'd run as far away from me as possible. There would be no part of her that would even consider getting in the car with me.

"How about this?" I pulled out my phone again and dialed my father's cell. "You better answer, old man," I mumbled.

He picked up on the third ring. "You made it to your home away from home already?"

"Not quite. I need you to speak to someone for me," I said.

"Listen, boy. You know I don't like talking to people. Who is—"

"Yeah, yeah," I replied. "This is Mia. I need you to tell her that she's safe with me." I handed the phone to Mia.

Her forehead wrinkled as the cutest look of confusion crossed her beautiful face. "Who's this?"

"That's my father. Say hello."

"Wha– Hello?"

"Who's this?" my father's gravelly voice bellowed through the phone.

"Mia, I, uh, um ... a friend of Brutus'."

My lips dropped at that word, *friend*. It was too tame for what she was to me. But if asked to put a word to it, I couldn't come up with one. So, I guessed friend was as appropriate a term as any.

"We met on the plane. Sat next to each other," Mia explained.

I couldn't hear my father's following statement, but something he said caused Mia to burst out into laughter.

"No, sir, he's been a perfect gentleman so far." Her eyes sparkled as she peered up at me.

"He wants me to let him drive me to Tulum, since my rental got messed up." She quieted while he responded with something. "I have taken self-defense classes, yes." She peered at me again, a smile on those lush lips.

I both loved and hated my father right then. I loved him because he seemed to be doing exactly what I wanted, which was making Mia more comfortable with the idea of letting me drive her the two plus hours to our final destination. But I hated him because I wanted to be the one to elicit those smiles and bouts of laughter from her.

"Okay, hang on." She drew the phone a few inches from her ear. "Your dad wants to know where you keep the bananas?" Then she whispered, "You live with your dad? That's so sweet."

"He lives with me," I corrected. "And tell him ..." I held out my hand. "May I?"

She handed me back the phone.

"You've had enough bananas today. You know they have all of that sugar in them. Eat one of the salads I left for you."

"Don't nobody want—"

"Bye, Pops," I grunted and hung up on his ass.

Mia chuckled. "That was ... entertaining."

"Did it work?" I asked.

She eyed me for a few seconds, then rolled her eyes skyward. "You better not make me regret this." She pointed at me. "Yeah, it worked. Besides, now you have my sister and Carlene texting me up a storm."

Carlene was her best friend, to whom she'd also texted my picture.

"Let's go."

Satisfied, I took her luggage and started to roll it and mine toward the parking lot to pick up my rental.

CHAPTER 4

Mia

Lord, I need you to get me away from this man. I silently sent up the prayer as we pulled into the parking lot of my bungalow.

My plea had nothing to do with how full I was from the pork belly tacos I'd inhaled during dinner. Nor did I feel unsafe in Brutus' presence. I felt safe with him, which was dangerous and made no sense. I shouldn't feel so secure and protected with a man I'd known less than twenty-four hours. But I did.

After we left the airport, Brutus drove, and our conversation picked up right where it left off on the plane. I spent the better part of our first hour trying to convince him that *The Four Agreements* was one of the best books ever written. Though he didn't agree, he wasn't dismissive or do that thing that so many men I'd encountered did. The one where they behave as if their opinion holds more weight because they think it's built on a foundation of "logic" whereas mine just has to be based in emotion, since I'm a woman.

He heard me out, listened carefully, and even said he might consider rereading the book.

Once we reached the city limits of Tulum, I spotted a restaurant and mentioned how much I'd fantasized about pork tacos in the weeks leading up to my trip. That did it. Because a minute later, Brutus pulled over, parked, and soon led me to the restaurant.

It just so happened the restaurant was rated as one of the best in the area. It also turned into a semi-nightclub after seven. That ended with me showcasing for Brutus some of my salsa moves.

I couldn't remember the last time I had so much fun, laughing, dancing, and eating good food for hours. Above all of that, the company was stellar. Throughout our dinner, I would notice Brutus surveying the area around us. His gaze would linger on this person or that one for a brief moment before moving to the next.

"Wait for me to open the door," he said while clutching my arm.

My hand dropped from the door's handle. Only then did he relax and open his door to get out. Yes, it was the gentlemanly thing to do, and he'd done the same thing at the restaurant. But it also felt protective.

I watched him in the rearview as he moved to the back of the SUV to retrieve my luggage from the trunk. He was a hulk of a man, but his movements were so fluid. He didn't waste one extra ounce of action. He danced the same way. It had me daydreaming about the other ways in which he moved.

Squeezing my thighs together, I tried to force myself to calm down. This was likely nothing more than a vacation fling, if even that.

Lost in my thoughts, I startled when the passenger door opened.

Brutus' forehead wrinkled briefly before he held out his hand for me. I took it, and this time wasn't thrown off by the jolt of electricity that pushed through my body at our skin on skin contact.

I inhaled the salty seawater scent that lingered in the air. Perhaps that was what was making me so lax in judgment. The fact that I was on vacation ... no, not a vacation. A sabbatical. I was letting my guard down, and with it, the reminder that it'd been way too long since I'd had sex.

It'd been almost a year since my last relationship imploded. It ended because I worked too much and *"didn't know how to let a man lead"* according to Mike.

"This place is beautiful," Brutus admired as we scaled the stairs to my second-floor bungalow.

"Yeah, I decided to splurge for the first month of my getaway. Treat yo' self and all of that," I said, laughing.

"Good for you," he responded.

We'd gotten the key from the check-in counter, and I reached to insert it into the lock when his massive hand covered mine.

"Let me."

The expression on his face was unreadable. Gone was the smile and the laughter in his eyes. He'd taken on a business-like demeanor.

"What are you doing?" I asked as I withdrew my hand from the inserted key.

He didn't answer. Instead, he twisted the doorknob and entered. "Wait here."

My back went ramrod straight at the seriousness in his voice. I watched as he entered my bungalow and looked from left to right. He breezed throughout the living room space, flipping on and off the light switches, looking underneath the table and couch, and checking the locks on the sliding glass doors that led to the private pool.

"Um, Brutus?" I asked.

He spun on his heels, turning to me. "What are you doing inside? I told you to wait at the door."

I put my hands on my hips. "This is my place, remember? What are *you* doing?" I demanded.

He blinked before slowly pushing out a breath. His shoulders relaxed, but not by much. "I'm making sure your room is safe."

I burst out in laughter. When he didn't join in, the laughter fell by the wayside. "You're serious?"

"Why wouldn't I be?" He held up a finger before I could answer. "This unit has a second floor, doesn't it?"

I dipped my head. "For the bedroom and second bathroom."

"Wait here," he said sternly.

I ignored the way my nipples pebbled at the command in his voice. I had half a mind to follow him up the stairs. But something kept me rooted to the spot where he left me. That odd security that I'd been feeling in his presence came back tenfold.

"All clear," he said as he came barreling down the stairs.

"Good to know there aren't any serial killers hiding underneath my bed," I joked.

He didn't laugh.

In fact, his face hardened, and he peered up the stairs again as if he had half a mind to go recheck.

"Thank you," I said, to distract him from said mission. "For the ride all the way here, and dinner, and," I gestured toward the rest of the bungalow, "for checking to make sure everything's safe." I tilted my head to the side. "Speaking of ... what do you do for a living?"

We hadn't spoken much about careers in all the hours we spent together. That was a great thing. After more than a decade of leading with my job in most conversations with strangers, it was nice to talk about other things with someone new.

But the way he constantly scanned rooms, how he automatically took over as if it was second nature, the protectiveness that emanated off of him. There was no way this guy filled out spreadsheets for a living.

Shaking his head, he approached. He tipped my chin with his finger, making me peer up at him as he stood over me.

"No job talk, remember?" We had established that rule during our talk on the plane.

I shrugged. "I already told you I'm unemployed, though."

The corners of his lips bent upward. "No job talk. Have dinner with me tomorrow."

The switch in conversation was abrupt but smooth. My instinct was to say yes. I didn't have much planned for the next few days, save for a scheduled massage and hanging out at the beach.

"You can't. You're having dinner with friends," I reminded him. Another topic we'd discussed during the two-hour drive. Turned out the friend he mentioned in the airport was an old Army buddy. One of a few who were scheduled to meet up while in Tulum.

"I'll dump 'em," he quickly replied.

"You can't do that," I said.

His reply was cut off by the ringing of my phone. "Oh, it's Carlene," I said. "Hey," I answered, remembering that I'd forgotten to text her since leaving the airport.

"Put him on the phone," she demanded.

I didn't say anything. Instead, I handed the phone to Brutus. "It's for you."

His eyebrows lifted, but he took the phone. "Carlene," he answered. He remained silent for a beat. "Please accept my apologies," he said while keeping his gaze trained on me. "I became famished with all of the travel, and we stopped for some tacos at what turned out to be a nightclub of sorts. We lost track of the time."

He paused and listened to whatever Carlene said.

"I assure you, she's fine."

"I'm fine, girl," I yelled loud enough for her to hear me.

Brutus chuckled from whatever my BFF said to him.

"Okay," he said before covering the phone with his free hand. "Carlene says she's talking to me, not you."

I rolled my eyes and sucked my teeth. "She can get off my phone then," I muttered.

The lines around Brutus' eyes wrinkled as he looked at me. "Will do," he said before disconnecting the call. "She said she'd like for you to call her as soon as you wake up tomorrow and tell her all the details of today."

He handed me back my phone.

"How about breakfast then?" He didn't waste a moment returning to our previous conversation.

"Breakfast? We just had dinner." Truthfully, I wanted to shout yes, but I refused to let myself get carried away. It'd been a long travel day, granted, made a lot easier and a hell of a lot more enjoyable by the man standing in front of me. However, I couldn't let my tired senses talk me into something I would regret.

"You're persistent."

He moved closer again, taking my chin in his hand. "When I want something, I don't know how to take no for an answer."

I swallowed. "You know, given the situation, that could come off as a threat." My gaze traveled around the empty room. A reminder that I was in a foreign country, in a city I'd ever been to, with a man that, at this time the previous night, I'd never laid eyes on.

"I would never threaten you," he said low while staring down at my lips. He looked at me the same way I'd looked at those tacos right before devouring them.

"Breakfast might be too early. We'll do brunch," he proposed. "I'll give you some time to settle in." He obviously wasn't giving up. And I didn't want him to.

It'd been a long time since I was pursued, and even longer since the idea of a job or career wasn't paramount in my mind.

"Do you like waffles?" he asked.

I pulled a face. "Who doesn't like waffles?"

He chuckled. "Right answer."

"That doesn't mean I'm agreeing to brunch." I had to play a little hard to get.

He held up his phone right as it buzzed. "That's my father. He's called me twice and texted once since we left the airport. He wants to make sure I got you home safe. Don't let that old man down."

I guffawed. "Don't call Mr. Rick an old man," I said, since his father had given me permission to call him by his first name.

"The old geezer's a half a step away from keeling over due to old age. Your turning down my brunch invitation could be the thing that does him in."

I covered my mouth as I laughed. "You're using guilt to get me to agree to brunch?"

"That depends," he quickly responded. "Is it working?" He wiggled his eyebrows.

I dipped my head, lowering my gaze to the floor because right then, he could've asked me to have lunch with him in the middle of an active volcano, and I might've said yes.

"Fine," I agreed. "But not before eleven. I want to sleep in."

"Eleven-thirty it is."

He stepped closer, and that was when I became aware of the

erratic beating of my heart. Not until he wrapped one long arm around my waist, pulling me into his warmth, did I realize how much I'd looked forward to feeling his lips on mine, ever since I'd stolen my first look at them on the plane.

And dammit if he didn't disappoint.

Brutus used his free hand to tip my chin up, keeping it in place while he lowered to capture my mouth.

The kiss was so powerful and all-consuming that I had to brace my hand against his shoulder, clutching it to keep from falling over. When his tongue flicked against the corner of my mouth, a sigh slipped from my lips.

Brutus groaned before pulling back, still holding my chin in place. His hazel eyes had darkened to an almost brown. For nearly a minute neither one of us said anything. We did all of the communicating with our eyes, staring into one another's.

If I had to guess, I would've ventured to say that he was silently questioning what the hell this was that was so powerful between us.

And if he wasn't, I sure as hell was.

"I'll see you tomorrow," I finally said.

His hold on my waist loosened. He didn't say anything, but he nodded right before he pressed a kiss to my forehead.

I almost melted on the spot.

"Tomorrow." God, his voice was so deep.

He gave my waist one final squeeze before releasing me and stepping around me, toward the door.

"Make sure the door locks behind me," he instructed.

After shaking myself out of whatever trance his kiss put me in, I followed him.

I closed the door behind him and started to press my back against it. A knock on the other side startled me.

I pulled the door open to a frowning Brutus. "You didn't even check the peephole before you opened it." He sounded angry, but it didn't frighten me ... which it should've. Brutus was an imposing man. And with that wrinkle in his forehead, he did come across as scary as hell.

However, he was angry because he thought I'd done something to jeopardize my safety. So no, that look, nor his matching tone, didn't scare me.

I folded my arms over my chest. "Who else would it be? You stepped outside of the door two seconds ago."

His frown deepened. "You never open a door without checking to see who it is *first*," he insisted.

"Fine," I agreed only to get him to drop it.

"Good. Now make sure the double bolt is secured once you close the door behind me."

While I did as instructed, I could feel his presence lingering on the other side of the door as I secured the double bolt.

"Now check to make sure it's locked," he yelled through the door.

"Oh my goodness," I groaned, yanking on the knob. The lock held.

"Good. Get some rest."

It's crazy but I could almost feel him walk away.

I wanted to linger at the door, but instead, I pulled myself away. It was late and I probably needed to shower and get in the bed. However, what I did was strip out of my clothes, unpack my bathing suit, and immediately went to for a swim. I needed to cool off, and while a shower could've done the job, I preferred to use the private pool. It was the main reason I chose this place.

I hoped it would cool my hot ass down. And my temperature level had not a damn thing to do with the outside temperatures. It was all due to one man.

"Don't get carried away, Mia," I mumbled to myself as I emerged from the pool about fifteen minutes later.

I had to keep telling myself that this was probably only the start of a vacation time fling. It'd last a few days. A week, tops.

Then we'd go our separate ways. Just fun, nothing more.

CHAPTER 5

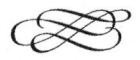

Brutus

"Are *The 48 Powers of Law* bullshit?" I asked right before taking another pull on the Cuban cigar in my hand.

Jameson, my longtime friend and former squad mate from the Army, lifted a dark eyebrow. "The fuck are you going on about?" he asked from across the small, wooden table.

We were having dinner at one of the local, outdoor restaurants. This one, like the one I'd eaten at with Mia the night before, doubled as a nightclub. It was shortly after nine, and in addition to the flowing cigars and tequila, the number of people on the makeshift, outdoor dance floor had doubled.

A few women looked my way and winked. And despite the fact that salsa was my favorite type of music, their enticing looks did nothing for me. All I could picture was Mia moving in my arms the night before.

"The book," I sat up and said to Jameson.

His forehead wrinkled. "You know I don't like to read."

I glared at him. "You told me you read it a few years back."

He shrugged. "Probably skimmed it or something. Why?" He spoke to me, but his gaze trailed off and followed a pretty woman wearing a frilly, black skirt with hair down past her ass.

She was cute I supposed but I only spotted her because that was my instinct. I kept an eye on my surroundings at all times. Even when I wasn't on duty. No one in the immediate vicinity was a threat or harm to me, but I still felt uneasy. It was the same feeling that had been with me ever since I dropped Mia off at her bungalow after our brunch and impromptu beach visit.

I wanted to be with her, not with guys I'd known for almost two decades.

"Something someone said to me," I finally answered Jameson. I folded my arms and pressed them into the table as I leaned in. "What if what that book teaches is all bullshit? Maybe it doesn't take into consideration the systems, traumas, and other dynamics at play in the world that impact us all."

Jameson's eyes narrowed and he sat back in his seat. For a long minute, he didn't say anything. Then he burst out into laughter. "What the hell?" He shook his head and whistled for our waitress. "Another round of beers for the table," he ordered in Spanish before handing her his card.

He pointed at me. "You need more alcohol and to shut the hell up with all of that philosophical nonsense."

"What's happening over here?" Will, another one of my friends and a former squad mate, asked as he left the dance floor.

Jameson stood and slapped Will on the back. "This motherfucker wants to talk about his feelings or whatever while there's prime pussy all around us." He rolled his eyes. "More beers are on the way. I need to drain the snake."

"Snake my ass. "More like a centipede," Will berated.

Jameson stuck up his middle finger before heading to the bathroom.

Will kicked his leg over the chair Jameson had vacated and sat across from me. "What are you talking about now?"

I shook my head. "Just asking some questions." I waved him off. I could take a ribbing just as good as anyone else, but I wasn't in the mood to talk about what led me to ask the question in the first place.

An almost overwhelming preoccupation with Mia had pummeled my mind for damn near the past forty-eight hours. I memorized every word she said to me. And if I hadn't had plans with Jameson and the rest of my friends already, I would've happily spent the entire day with her. As it stood, the only reason I didn't cancel on them was that Mia insisted I shouldn't cancel on friends.

"What was that?" Will asked.

I peered across the table, realizing that I'd grunted out loud at the reminder that I was spending the night with them instead of with her.

Maybe I should take her some tacos in case she's hungry.

"Are you still there?" Will's question caught my attention again.

"Yeah, I'm here," I answered begrudgingly.

"Shit, man. You're usually quiet. But even your taciturn ass is being unusually muted tonight. What's up?"

I snorted. "Nothing," I told him at the same time my phone dinged.

It was the company I hired, confirming that the excursion I scheduled for the next day was all set. Immediately, I started texting Mia to let her know our day of snorkeling, visiting cenotes, and parasailing was all set. A thrill shot through me that reminded me of that feeling a little kid gets the night before Christmas.

Instead of presents under a Christmas tree, though, I looked forward to seeing Mia dressed in only a bathing suit.

At that moment, I stood from the table as my fingers stopped mid-text. I wanted to hear her voice rather than texting her.

"Hi," she answered. "Are you still at dinner?"

My chest rose from the deep inhale I took before responding. "Yeah." I glanced over at the table I'd just vacated to see Jameson returning to the table with the woman from the dancefloor at his side.

Grunting, I turned my back to the scene. "Our excursion for tomorrow is confirmed. I'll pick you up at eight-thirty so we can have breakfast before we board the boat at ten."

Mia groaned. "This is my sabbatical. Why do I have to get up so early?" she whined.

My lips twitched into a smile. "You were the one who wanted the morning slot. I offered to get us the afternoon slot."

"No, by afternoon it'll be too hot and crowded. Besides, I like morning excursions. I'm just teasing."

"That's what I thought." The music in the restaurant grew louder, and the crowd swelled.

"What's that?" Mia asked.

I plugged my free ear and moved farther away from the fray to be able to hear her better. "Nothing."

"You're still out to dinner. You should go hang out with your friends."

"I'm doing exactly what I want to be doing." That wasn't the truth at all. If I were doing what I wanted, I'd be in her damn bed instead of on the phone with her.

In time, I reminded myself. Hell, it'd been barely seventy-two hours since I'd met this woman.

There was a hesitation on the other end of the phone. "Seriously, though. If you want to spend more time with your friends over going snorkeling with me—"

"I'll stop you right there. There are two things you should know about me," I said, a hard edge sinking into my voice. "I don't say anything I don't mean. And I don't volunteer my time for shit I don't want to do. If I said we're set for tomorrow, then we're set. You should make sure to have your pretty ass ready by eight-thirty."

Again, there was a pause on the other end. For a heartbeat, I wondered if I came on too strong. The last thing I wanted was to scare her away, but I'd be damned if I was about to let her get out of our day together. She wanted to go as badly as I did. I could sense it. I was a master at reading people. The skill had saved my life and the life of the family I worked for on many occasions.

"I guess you put me in my place."

"If I'd put you in your place, you'd be in my bed right now." *Shit.* I didn't mean to say that out loud.

"You're used to giving orders, aren't you?" Mia questioned.

I grunted. "Maybe."

"Hm," she murmured, and then pushed out a breath. "Has anyone ever told you you're intimidating?"

"More times than I can count." You don't get as big as I am without hearing that sentiment a time or a hundred. "I would never hurt you," I felt the need to assure her. "My father would break my neck," I joked.

She let out a breathless laughs and it felt better than a breeze on one of those famously humid nights in Tulum. It was soothing in a way that should be illegal when you've known someone less than three days.

"I can't let that happen, I suppose."

"Right? And who else will teach me about toxic masculinity and tell me my library of books is garbage?"

She gasped. "I never said *all* of them are bad."

"*The 48 Laws of Power*," I retorted.

"Well, that one is trash. Speaking of toxic masculinity …"

I groaned, and she giggled. "I'll save the lecture for tomorrow."

"I'm looking forward to it."

Suddenly, the twelve or so hours between then and the morning when I would see her was too much. I was typically a man of patience. In my line of work, there was often a lot of standing around, waiting for business meetings to end, and planes to arrive or take off. I knew how to occupy my time, stay aware of my surroundings for hours, and keep my clients safe. I had learned how to rein in my anxiousness.

But counting down the hours until I saw Mia again was a challenge.

"Get some sleep," I said before I could talk myself into showing up at her door.

"I'm going to go for another swim in my private pool before showering and going to bed."

I groaned.

"What's wrong?" she inquired, sounding more innocent than she should.

"If you want me not to abandon my friends at dinner and wind up on your doorstep before the night's over, I highly recommend that you don't tell me about your plans to put on a bathing suit and get all wet."

"I see how that could present a problem," she said with humor lacing her voice. "Good night, Brutus."

Fuck. The sound of my name from her mouth.

"Tomorrow, Mia," I said instead of goodnight. A promise lingered in my words, and I wondered if she heard it, too.

I pulled the phone from my ear and glanced over my shoulder. Will approached just as I turned.

"Was that work? Those Townsends can't get along without you, huh?" He slapped my shoulder.

I blinked, realizing that for the first time in … ever, work hadn't been a constant on my mind. A few hours earlier, I received a text from my second in command letting me know all was well back home. Aside from that, it hadn't even crossed my mind to check in with the office. Yeah, I was on vacation, but it was totally out of the ordinary to not check up on things back home when I was away.

"Everything all right? What? Does Aaron Townsend need you to fly back to Williamsport to go with him to some top-secret business conference or something?" he joked.

I shook my head. I never mentioned the details of my job, even with my friends. None of us did, even though we all worked for some high-profile and influential families and businesspeople. Will himself was on the security detail for an all-star athlete turned entrepreneur.

A part of me was still stunned that I hadn't thought about work in hours. Thoughts about Mia and our excursions the following day took up most of the space in my mind.

"I'm heading out," I told Will. "Early morning."

His forehead wrinkled, but he shrugged, knowing I wasn't about to give up any information I wasn't willing to share. "If your ass hops on a plane back to Williamsport, at least send a text this time," he replied before holding up a fist.

I pounded his fist and gave a noncommittal nod before waving over his shoulder at the rest of the guys. An uproar of, *'Where are you going?', 'That job's got you by the balls!',* and a stream of other nonsense followed me out of the door. None of it bothered me. Ribbing one another was a way of life for my group of friends. It was how we survived long, grueling missions in the military with one another.

Thoughts of my Army days and friends faded to the background as I headed back to my rented bungalow. Though I'd been hesitant to go on this vacation in the first place, I started to think that this trip was the best decision I'd made in a long time.

And it all had to do with Mia.

CHAPTER 6

Mia

"It's not serious," I told Sharise as I rushed around my bungalow to find the swimsuit cover-up I planned to wear for the day.

"And yet, this is the fiftieth time I'm hearing this man's name in what? Three days."

Stopping in the middle of my living room, I frowned. "I haven't mentioned him that much." I bit my bottom lip and thought back to the conversations I'd had with my sister since I arrived in Tulum. Sure, a few times I mentioned Brutus, but not that many.

"Who are you trying to play for Booboo the Fool?" she came back with, sounding just like our mother when one of us tried to pull one over on her while growing up.

"You know—"

"You better not try to tell me how much I sound like mama," she quickly replied.

I shrugged my shoulder. "Then I won't say it. That doesn't make it any less true." I hummed in satisfaction. "Oh, found it." I snapped up my bright, colorful coverall and thrust one arm in and then the other.

I ran up the stairs to the bedroom to check myself in the full-length mirror. I wore an electric blue, fishnet cami top and high-waist bikini bottom. The bathing suit hugged every curve to perfection and showed off my not flat tummy at the right angles.

"What do you think of this?" I asked Sharise.

"What?"

"I'm sending it now." I snapped a picture of myself in the mirror, modeling the bathing suit and cover-up.

"This bathing suit is new. Yess, come through legs, hips, and body-ody-ody," she sing-songed.

I burst out into laughter. "You're a fool. But really, do you like it?" I twisted and turned in the mirror. Typically, my plus-size didn't bother me any longer, not the way it did in my teenage years. But a smidge of insecurity rippled up my spine as I peered at my dimpled thighs.

"Absolutely," my sister answered. "That cover-up is fire. It's beautiful against your milk chocolate ass." She always gave the best compliments.

"Thanks, sis. Carlene helped me pick it out last month."

"Ah, she has such great taste. I think I need to recruit her to help spice up my wardrobe."

"You know she'd help you," I said. Though Carlene was my best friend, she and Sharise were friendly enough. And while Sharise was a full-time accountant, she had a side-hustle as a fashion consultant, just because she loved it so much.

"All right, I've gotta go. Love you."

I hung up with Sharise just in time. A knock on the door sounded, and I peered at my watch to see that it was 8:29. A smile tipped my lips. I loved a punctual man.

Just a fling. My subconscious chose that moment to remind me of what this was yet again. Brutus was on vacation, and I was on a sabbatical. We were two ships passing in the night.

This thing has an expiration date on it, I told myself as I stood in front of the door and inhaled deeply before pulling it open. And all those reminders went straight out the window when his hazel, brooding eyes landed on me.

My breath stuck in my throat as he let his gaze linger on my body, perusing it up and down.

Smoldering.

That can be the only word to accurately describe the gleam in his eyes. They visibly darkened. Any insecurity that might've crept into my mind earlier was thoroughly stomped out when his eyes remained trained on my thighs.

Suddenly, a curse violently ripped from his throat, followed by, "Christ." He appeared angry, his gaze turning stormy.

"What?" I asked, alarmed. "What's wrong?"

Instead of an immediate answer, Brutus' eyes floated closed, and he breathed in. He worked to calm himself, I determined.

When his eyes opened again, they were every bit as intense. "I knew you would look stunning in anything you put on for today. But I swear all eyes will be on you in this." He frowned. "I might have to beat some guy's ass for trying to get next to you."

Rolling my eyes, I waved him off. "Don't be ridiculous. Besides." I pointed a finger at him. "You better not be the caveman, barbaric type that thinks any guy who looks my way needs to get put on his ass."

His lips tightened, and he looked me over again. That same smoldering gleam appeared in his eyes. "I won't touch anyone unless necessary," he promised.

There was an edge in his voice that bordered on dangerous. At that moment, I was grateful for the padding in my halter top. Otherwise, I was sure the hardening of my nipples would've been glaringly obvious.

My stomach chose that moment to growl. I think that pulled Brutus out of his stupor. He blinked and stepped forward, taking my hand into his. Again, I held my breath as he lifted my hand to his lips. The kiss he gave it was so soft as he gazed into my eyes.

He moved forward and cupped the side of my face. "Let's get you fed," he stated before dipping his head. His lips devoured mine. Briefly, I lost interest in actual food or our plans for the rest of the day.

When his tongue traced my bottom lip, my knees weakened. I clutched onto his shirt to keep from falling.

He pulled back and laid his forehead against mine. "Yes," he murmured against my lips.

I wanted to ask him what he was saying yes to, but I stopped short. Somehow, I knew it was yes to everything happening between us. Things I didn't quite have the words for just yet.

"After you." He stepped back and aside, letting me close and lock up my bungalow for the day.

I couldn't wait for the activities that lay ahead.

* * *

"Oh gosh, that was amazing!" I screeched as Brutus helped me back onto the boat. Saltwater dripped from my body, and my hair felt like it weighed three pounds more than when I first awakened that morning due to my soaking braids, but I felt light as a feather.

We were in the middle of the Caribbean Sea, surrounded by other boats in the striking cerulean ocean. The first stop on our snorkeling adventure had been a spot to see the sea turtles.

"Did you see the turtle swim right up to me?" I asked Brutus with wide eyes. I bounced on my tiptoes. "He almost touched me."

Smirking, he nodded. "Even the wildlife can't stay away from you."

I laughed. "I think I scared the poor guy. And there was another one, too. They said it probably came back from laying eggs not too long ago. Wow." I gazed out toward the water. I felt Brutus come up behind me, his massive arms wrapping around my back.

I leaned back into his body. "Look!" I pointed at a shadow just beneath the water. "There's another one." Another giant sea turtle swam just below the surface.

"He's probably one hundred and eighty years old," our tour guide informed us from behind Brutus.

"Beautiful," Brutus whispered in awe.

I peered up at him to find his eyes weren't on the sea but on me. He leaned in and kissed my forehead.

"Next is the cenote," he reminded me. At the same time, he pulled me to have a seat along the boat's edge.

We spent another hour snorkeling among the colorful fish, taking in the coral reef and admiring the nature in the ocean before we moved on to a freshwater cenote. I kept squealing at all the natural wonder around me. And when I did, I always found Brutus by my side, taking it all in seemingly, but his eyes always appeared trained on me.

Part of me wanted to ask him if he had seen anything we came to see or if he was too busy staring at me the entire time. Honestly, I had to admit it felt good to have so much of his enamored attention. What woman wouldn't want to be underneath the watchful eye of a man like him?

While Brutus and I spent hours talking on that first day we met, something told me that he wasn't generally like that. He'd barely said more than a handful of words to the other snorkelers and people from other boat excursions. Even when our tours had coincided or met up with theirs.

He wasn't unfriendly, though, but intimidating. More than once, I saw men give him a wide berth when walking in our direction. And the man had a mean eagle eye. While I always felt and spotted his gaze lingering on me, I could tell he was constantly aware of our surroundings.

"This is the rock you can jump from," our boat captain, David, informed us as we pulled into a procession of boats along a path of rocks jutting out from the water. From where we were, I could see tour guides leading people from their boats along the rocks to the highest peak, which was about a ten foot drop down into the water below.

"Yay!" I cheered when two women from a boat up ahead took the plunge.

Brutus stared at me with wide eyes. "Are you crazy? You could be killed," he said sternly.

"Stop being dramatic." I swiped at his arm, but my fingers grazed across his chest. A shudder ran through me. Damn, his muscles were like granite.

His frown deepened. He looked over at our captain. "How deep is that water?" he asked in perfect Spanish.

"He said it was about twenty feet deep, right, David?" I interrupted.

Brutus narrowed his eyes on me. "You speak Spanish." Not a question, an observation.

"Si." I nodded. "As do you." I lifted on my tiptoes and turned my head up to his.

His lips brushed across mine. In the few hours we'd been on this boat, that was something that had become commonplace. I beckoned kisses, and he obliged without hesitation, even as he continued to frown.

He peered over my head, his long arm wrapping around my waist, pulling me into him. "Has anyone ever been killed doing this shit?" His voice came out in a growl.

"No," David quickly answered. "Of course not." He laughed as if the thought alone were ridiculous.

Brutus' body tightened. "Am I laughing? Do you know how many people die each year doing crazy shit on vacation?" he demanded.

I pulled back, but not entirely free from his body, as his arm held firmly around my waist. "Don't scare the man. He's our captain. And I'm sure he's done this hundreds of times. Right, David?" I peeked over my shoulder at our captain.

"Yes." He nodded vigorously. "Of course, of course. Very safe."

"See?" I turned to Brutus.

His frown disappeared but that warning in his eyes remained.

"I'm doing this jump," I told him, finally pushing out of his hold.

"Not without me beside you," he quickly asserted, taking my hand.

The smartass part of me wanted to argue. But my logical thinking side reminded me just how much I wanted him beside me at all times. Let alone when I would be cliff jumping. Technically, we weren't jumping off a cliff, but it was close enough.

I smiled up at him. "Good."

The tension in his body eased. We exited the boat and followed the line of other cliff jumpers, noting the instructions from the tour guides.

"Make sure your life vest is on securely," Brutus instructed while taking it upon himself to ensure my already secured vest was on correctly.

I swatted his big hands away and adjusted my vest. "This is going to be so much fun." I bounced on my toes, grateful for the water shoes that protected my feet from the jagged edges of the rocks.

"That's my group ahead," a man said from behind me. Before I could turn around, I was jolted aside, almost to the edge of the rock. My saving grace was a ledge of the rock that raised a bit, catching my foot, keeping me from tumbling over the side.

Brutus' arm was there, also preventing my fall.

"What the—"

"What the fuck is wrong with you?"

I gasped when I saw that Brutus had his entire hand wrapped around some man's neck. My hand clasped over my mouth as I looked down to see that the man's feet dangled a few inches off the ground.

"Brutus," I called.

"You could've knocked her into the damn ocean, you piece of shit," he growled. He shook the man by the neck, and I heard people behind me gasp.

"Brutus, please," I whispered, realizing this must've been the man who shoved me.

He looked over at me. "Are you all right?" His voice was so tender and full of care, as if he wasn't still holding a man like a ragdoll by the throat. He ran his free hand down the length of my arm.

"I'm fine," I hurriedly assured him.

That didn't appease him, as he didn't let the man go.

"Please, I'm okay. Let him go." I should've been freaking out. How he went from totally calm to threatening in a handful of seconds was alarming. To say the least.

But also, the guy did shove me and could've caused me to fall right off this rock at a spot that was pretty shallow. So yeah, it could have turned out badly.

"Apologize to her," Brutus ordered with a lethality I'd never heard from anyone before wrapping around each word. I watched as his hand tightened around the man's throat. "Apologize," he insisted through gritted teeth.

"I-I don't think he can speak," I told Brutus. "Your hand." I placed a palm against his arm.

His body noticeably relaxed. He loosened his grip on the man, and the color started to return to his face.

"I-I'm sorry," he stuttered.

"That's not enough," Brutus added, still holding onto him by the neck. "Ask her if she's all right."

The stranger's eyes darted from Brutus to me. "A-Are you o-okay?" He looked to Brutus.

"Don't look at me when you ask." He shook the man again.

"I'm great." I injected as much cheer into my voice as I could muster. "Terrific. Don't worry about it." I squeezed Brutus' arm.

Finally, he released the man. "Next time, watch where the fuck you're going. Dipshit."

Brutus wrapped his arm around my waist and escorted me around the man and past the few onlookers who watched the scene play out.

"I didn't scare you, did I?" Brutus inquired once we stopped at the spot we would be jumping from. He took my chin into his hand and turned my head up so that he could look into my eyes.

"That was a little intense," I admitted.

"You could've been hurt," he responded as if that made his outburst reasonable.

And, crazy as it may sound, to me, it did. It felt nice to have someone defend me.

"Maybe next time instead of immediately going to choking the guy, you just, you know, ask him to apologize nicely?" I offered with a wiggle of my eyebrows.

He planted a kiss on my cheek. "Don't count on it. Any motherfucker who comes at you wrong is going to get the same or worse than he got."

I shivered from the lethal tone in his voice. It occurred to me, again, to ask him what he did for a living, but I held back. I reminded myself that talking too much about home and our real lives would make this seem real. Too real.

"Are you ready?" David asked. He rattled off some last-minute instructions, checked our life vests, and allowed us to step up to the edge of the rock.

Brutus took a firm hold on my hand, causing me to look up at him. "Ready for the plunge?" he asked.

Why that moment felt more significant than it should've, I couldn't tell you. We were only jumping about ten feet into a rather secluded portion of the sea. Yet, with his hand over mine and his deep-set eyes peering down at me, it felt like time stood still.

Unable to speak, I nodded and smiled. His hand tightened around mine.

"Three … two …" someone behind us began counting down.

As soon as they said one, we both leapt, hand in hand. I pinched my nose with my free hand and let my body fall into the water. It was jarring at first, but then the warmth of the water surrounded me, and the buoyancy of my body brought me back up to the surface. The entire time, Brutus' and my hand remained connected.

I turned to him as soon as my head broke through the surface. He was right there, grinning at me, and I laughed out loud.

"We have to do that again," I insisted. Before he could protest, I started swimming for the rocks to climb up to jump back in. "And you're coming with me," I threw over my shoulder.

"As you wish," he said, right behind me.

Perfect day.

CHAPTER 7

Mia

"Aww, don't be a spoilsport," I teased Brutus, pulling on his arm, even though I knew there was no way I could get him to budge if he didn't want to. We were outside of the taco stand, where we had just had another dinner of amazing tacos. The place was only a short walk from my bungalow, and along the way, I stopped, noticing a fortune teller.

"Please," I begged. "For me." I playfully batted my eyelashes.

He folded his arms across his chest. "You're trying to use your trickery against me."

I guffawed. "What trickery?"

He deadpanned. "Your ability to make me say yes to just about anything."

I squinted. "I don't have—"

"You do," he admitted.

My smile widened. "Does that mean you'll do it?" I clapped my hands.

"I don't believe in fortune tellers," he insisted.

Turning my head up to the sky, I let out a groan. "But you do believe in *The 48 Laws of Power*?" I asked with my hand on my hip.

"Are we back to that again? It's a decent boo—"

"Eek." Covering my ears, I shook my head adamantly. "Don't you dare finish that sentence, not when I'm starting to fall for you. Don't ruin it."

I laughed and released my ears. But when I looked up at Brutus, his face was a mask of seriousness. I dropped the joking manner and wondered what had made him so serious all of a sudden.

He answered that question for me when he stepped closer and pulled my chin into his hold. God, but I loved it when he did that, capturing my chin so I had no choice but to look directly at him and only at him.

"What did you just say?" he asked in a low, but demanding tone.

I parted my lips and tried to recall what I'd said.

I'm starting to fall for you. I remembered the words that came from my mouth without me thinking.

"You have fallen for me, Mia," he said before I could repeat myself. "And I have fallen for you."

My mind was moving too fast to process everything. I wouldn't dare let myself think I had gone and fallen in love. That would've been ridiculous. It'd been less than five days since I met him.

But standing there on the sidewalk with him looking down at me like that stirred something profound inside of me.

He leaned in and whispered in my ear, "I've fallen for you, too," before kissing the corner of my mouth. "But no way in hell am I going into that fortune teller for her to rip me off."

I chuckled. "Fine. I need to get home and rinse this salt water off my body."

We'd spent all day out. An excursion that was only supposed to take us until to lunchtime turned into lunch on the beach, followed by kayaking and more swimming in the cenotes. And then dinner. By all accounts, I should've been exhausted.

But I felt rejuvenated.

Brutus wrapped an arm around my waist as he escorted me back to my bungalow. A part of my heart grew heavier with each step we took. I didn't want the day to end. I wondered if it would be too forward of me to tell him that?

Neither one of us spoke as we approached my door. When I went to turn the knob to let myself in, Brutus' hand covered mine.

I spun around to joke about him double checking to make sure no masked murderer was waiting in my bungalow, but I didn't get the chance. His lips crashed down on me and stole any previous thoughts in my head.

I surrendered to the kiss, allowing my bag to fall from my hand and then wrapping my arms around his neck. I gasped in surprise when Brutus took that opportunity to lift me, forcing me to wrap my legs around his waist. He was so broad that my short legs barely encircled him in his entirety.

Not once did Brutus let up on the kiss, though. He held me like I weighed little more than a trophy. And he held onto me like one, too. As if I was some prize that he'd won and he'd be damned if he let it go for the world. That feeling of security and safety enveloped me, and I clung to his shoulders while he plundered my mouth.

Before long, Brutus pulled back just enough to say, "I don't want this night to end." He stared me in the eyes, willing me to get his intent. "Invite me in, Mia. Let me wash the saltwater off of you."

I blinked. "Is that all you want to do?" I purred against his lips.

He nipped at my bottom lip. "That's only the beginning. I'll start by cleaning you off and end by worshiping your pussy all night long."

The muscles in my lower belly tightened. "Yes, I think I want that, too."

The sentence barely left my mouth before Brutus pushed through the door of my bungalow. He only stopped briefly to pick up the bag I'd let fall to the floor before ushering us both inside. How he still held me against his body while he secured the door and then quickly strode up the stairs to the second floor was a testament to his strength.

I marveled at how fluidly and easily he moved for a man of his size.

As we entered the master bathroom, I wanted to ask how he knew exactly where everything was. Then I remembered. "Did you memorize the layout of my bungalow?"

A sly grin slid across his lips, and my pussy wept for relief. He was in my apartment for only a few minutes that first night when he insisted on checking to make sure it was safe.

He moved to the marble countertop by the bathroom sink and set me down on it. "I sure as hell did," he answered before sliding his hands down my leg and removing my strappy sandal. He did the same on my other foot. "Don't move," he ordered, and then turned toward the waterfall shower.

Brutus turned on the shower and waited for a beat, checking the temperature of the water. He leaned in and planted a brief but heated kiss against my lips before sliding the cover-up I wore down my shoulders.

"You've tempted me all fucking day in this outfit." He locked his gaze with mine. "You do know that, don't you?"

I swallowed underneath his heated gaze and nodded. I ran my finger down the length of the white V-neck that clung to his muscles. "I wasn't the only one playing the role of tempter today."

That was the truth. I'd studied him almost as closely as he'd been studying me throughout the day.

"C'mere," he growled, pulling me from the counter and letting the cover fall free from my body. He brought me to the shower, and with precise movements, stripped me of my bikini bottoms, followed by the halter top.

I let my head fall back when he cupped my heavy breasts in his hands and began massaging them.

"They fit perfectly into my hands. You were fucking made for me." His words were almost pained.

A scream ripped from my lips when he pinched both of my nipples. "Shit," I cursed.

Brutus chuckled.

This man was going to tease me.

"You're trying to kill me," I groaned.

He laughed again. "You won't die, baby," he assured with a kiss to my lips. "Not before you experience all ten inches of my cock."

What the hell did he just say?

I didn't have time to process his statement before he undressed and then drew me underneath the spray of the water. He reached for my body wash and squirted some onto the washcloth next to it.

He lathered the entirety of my body, paying meticulous attention to my breasts. My nipples ached with need as he circled them with the soapy washcloth before moving lower to my belly. Never had I felt more cherished than when he lowered to his knees in front of me. He pressed a kiss to my belly, using his tongue to trace one of the stretch marks on my stomach.

"Spread your legs for me." The words came out low, but they were an order nonetheless. One that I followed diligently. "Good girl," he murmured.

Shit.

My pussy convulsed at the praise he just gave me. Not one inch of my body was left untouched by him. He lathered me up, and then just as thoroughly rinsed me off underneath the water.

I moaned when his deft fingers began massaging shampoo into my scalp, cleaning the salt water out of my braids.

In the recesses of my mind, I thought to ask him how he was so damned good at this. Did he have a wife or girlfriend stashed somewhere I needed to know about? But I couldn't even think straight enough to form the question.

He even went so far as to squeeze out the excess water from my braids.

"Thank you," I whispered before lifting to my tiptoes. He bent to meet my lips with the kiss I silently asked for. "Now it's my turn to wash you," I said, reaching for the extra washcloth I kept in the shower.

However, his hand closed around mine. "If you touch me right now, this night will end before it begins. And I'll be damned if I let that happen."

"You're driving me crazy," I told him through gritted teeth.

He chuckled, not seeming the least bit worried. "Let me help you with that," he replied and proceeded to sink to his knees and curving one of my legs over his shoulder. He lined his face with my pussy in a matter of seconds. Before I could ask what he planned on doing down there, he began eating my pussy like a man who spotted his first plate of food after a month's long famine.

I pounded my fist against the tile of the shower. This spurred Brutus on, and he groaned against my pussy, telling me without words how much he enjoyed his meal.

"Fuuuck," I croaked out. I cupped my breasts and pinched my nipples while grinding my hips against his face. It was as if a lifetime of desire flooded this one moment. It'd been over a year since I had sex with anyone. But even then, it hadn't been anything like this.

All of a sudden my brain went foggy, my eyes squeezed shut, and an explosion took place behind my eyelids.

When I finally opened my eyes, it was to see Brutus rising to his feet.

"That's number one," he said. "Let's see how many more we can get before the night's over."

* * *

Brutus

I carried Mia from the shower, only pausing to retrieve my wallet from the shorts I'd stripped off earlier. She had a glossy look in her eyes and a temptress smile tugging at her lips, which were slightly swollen from my kisses. They begged for the attention I'd just given her pussy. So, I obliged, kissing the shit out of those lips before laying her down on her bed.

She laid on the bed, arms stretched over her head, legs wide, offering herself to me like the beautiful, brown angel she was.

"Open wide for me, baby," I crooned. "Show me what's mine to take."

She did as I asked, parting her legs farther. I studied the way her pussy glistened, its wetness a mixture of my saliva and the physical representation of her yearning for me.

Slowly, her eyes traveled down the length of my body. She paused when they landed on my cock that was aimed directly at the entrance between her legs. She let out a gasp and sat up on her elbows.

"Aww, baby," I crooned, planting a knee on the bed between her legs so she couldn't close them, "don't get shy on me now." I leaned in.

"But you're big as hell," she said just above a whisper.

"Shh," I consoled, moving entirely in between her legs. I reached for my wallet and pulled out a condom, quickly sheathing myself. "It'll fit." I kissed her again. "You were made for me." Never had I been so sure of anything in my life.

I kissed her deeply, cutting off any protests. My hand moved to cup her pussy, feeling the heat from her core. I rubbed circles against her clit, getting her primed for my entrance. Mia inhaled sharply and arched her back. Her body went stiff, and within a few short moments she was coming again. Just from my hand against her clit.

"Number two. Just like I said. You were made for me," I told her at the same time I began sliding into her.

She tightened her thighs around my waist and stiffened.

"Let me inside, baby," I whispered into her ear before catching her earlobe between my teeth.

She relaxed, and I pushed the rest of the way in and stopped. I couldn't move.

"You're so fucking tight." My voice sounded angry even to me. "Fuck, I'm going to make this pussy mine, Mia." It came out as a warning.

"Please," she begged, to my surprise. "Make me yours."

Aw, hell. What the fuck was I supposed to do with that request other than oblige it?

I pulled almost all the way out of her before slamming my way back home. Mia cried out, but it wasn't due to pain.

"More," she pleaded.

I knew she was meant for me. Despite her earlier trepidation, she didn't run from my cock. So, I gave her what she wanted ... what we both needed. I pulled out and thrust my way home repeatedly, punishing her and her pussy for not showing up in my life sooner.

I became a man possessed, determined to write my name all over this pussy. To ruin her for all others, because dammit, that's precisely what she'd done to me. In time, her legs shook and her fingernails dug into the skin of my back. She was coming again.

She cried out my name over and over.

"That's it, baby. Give me number three," I demanded as she came, her pussy squeezing my cock. I rode her through that third orgasm, never once letting my thrusts falter.

When she opened her eyes and peered up at me with a look of amazement clouding her gaze, I almost came right then and there. But fuck that. I was determined to feel her walls clamp down around me at least one more time before I let my own release happen.

I rolled our bodies over so that she was on top of me. Mia lowered her head to mine, kissing me, even though she still panted to catch her breath. I squeezed her hips, loving the extra swell of her body.

She sat up, impaled on my dick, and pressed a hand to my abdomen. I lifted my feet to the bed and pressed her to lay back against my thighs. I raised my hips while holding her in place by her waist. I rode her from the bottom, keeping her trapped against my legs with my hand.

"Fuck, fuck, fuck," she croaked out as she wrapped her hands around my arms, holding on as if I was an amusement park ride she wanted to make sure she didn't fall off.

"So good," I groaned as I slid my cock in and out of her.

She felt so damned good. I wasn't sure how I had held on this long. But when her walls began to quiver again and her hips jerked against my thrusts, I knew she was ready for number four.

"C-Can't ... too ... much," she panted.

"Fuck that," I growled. "Take all of me, Mia. It's not too much," I insisted.

With that, she came apart again. A slew of incoherent murmurings fell from her lips as the fourth orgasm slammed into her. This time, my body couldn't hold out any longer. I came from the way she milked my cock for everything I had in me.

"So damn good," I groaned as the final spurts of cum shot into the condom. With a heaving sigh, I managed to roll our bodies so that we were on our sides, facing one another. We both panted, straining for much needed oxygen. And still, I refused to pull out of her.

In fact, I curled her leg over my hip, inserting my semi-erect cock inside of her even deeper. Mia moaned, her eyes half closed, lips swollen, and her skin glowing from complete satisfaction.

I couldn't take her again. Despite what my body was telling me. She was exhausted. I leaned in and pressed a kiss to her forehead.

Before I could pull back, she reached up and cupped my face. "Stay with me tonight," she whispered.

There was a plea in her voice that I was powerless to ignore, even if I had wanted to. As it were, I didn't want to. I wanted nothing more than to spend the rest of the night with her body curled in my arms.

"Tonight and every other night," I replied with another kiss on her lips.

Her eyes floated closed, and for the first time in … ever, something bloomed inside of my chest. It was the feeling I got while watching an early sunrise. The promise of great things to come.

I held onto Mia a little tighter and allowed myself to fall asleep.

CHAPTER 8

Mia

"Why a coffee shop?" Brutus asked, his lips grazing the back of my earlobe as he spoke.

We laid curled up in my bed after yet another round of sex. Seriously, the man had to be a damn robot. He woke me up at least two different times during the night. The first time it was with his head between my legs, bringing me to a full-on orgasm before I realized it wasn't a dream. The second time, I awakened to my legs resting on his shoulders right before he slipped inside of me. He counted every single one of my orgasms throughout the night.

We were up to twelve.

I should've been exhausted, but I felt better than I had in a long time. Like, fuck sleep when his dick and mouth were all I needed to fill my energy cup.

My lips curled into a satisfied grin as I faced the window across the room, the sunlight streaming through it. My back pressed against Brutus' chest while he stroked his fingertips up and down the length of my arm.

"I worked at a coffee shop throughout college. It was how I paid for all of my books and apartment the last two years in school. I loved it," I admitted. "It wasn't one of the big chain places. It had been around for thirty years before I started working there. Some of our customers had been there since the beginning. The coffee shop was like a second or third home for many of them."

I flipped over onto my back to face him.

"The atmosphere created in that little shop was so warm and welcoming. The customers would spend hours playing board games or bringing in their children and grandchildren to play in a spot the owner set up for them. It was a place where people came together.

"And it felt like no matter what was happening on the outside, in our little corner of the world, all was perfect. People got relief from their stress and got to relate with others over a good cup of coffee and delicious pastries. I want that again."

That was the first time I'd ever expressed out loud the entirety of what my time at that coffee shop meant to me.

Brutus stared down at me, the edges around his eyes wrinkled as he smiled. He lifted my hand to his and kissed my knuckles.

"Sounds like a hell of a place to work."

I nodded. "It was, and who doesn't love coffee?"

We both chuckled.

"That's why after this month in Mexico, I'm headed to Colombia for the rest of my three-month sabbatical, to live on a coffee plantation."

His eyebrows lifted. "Colombia?"

I nodded excitedly. "Yeah. They have the best coffee, and if all goes well, I plan to connect with some growers to be the suppliers for my shop. I have a list of contacts."

His lips pinched. "So, you're actually working. I thought this was time off for you."

"It is …" I sat up on my elbows. "I mean, yeah, it will be slightly work related, but it's something that I want. For myself. I'm not working for a huge, multi-billion-dollar company, only to be looked over when it's time for my promotion." I tried to keep the bitterness out of my voice, but it still made its way into my tone. "Anyway," I said before plopping my head against the pillow, "this is for me."

His expression became unreadable. He stared down at me, studying me for some reason that I couldn't discern.

"Have you checked out these coffee plantations? What are their safety measures? Do you personally know anyone who's been there? What are their references?"

I wanted to burst out into laughter from so many questions. But his face held stern. A wrinkle between his brows indicated that he wasn't joking.

A sly grin played at my lips, and I sat up, cupping his chiseled jaw, before kissing his cheek.

"That's so sweet."

His frown deepened. "What?"

"That you care." After all, this was simply a vacation fling. He didn't have to pretend he cared what I did after we parted ways. But there was a sincerity in his voice and expression that made me believe he was genuinely concerned about my safety beyond sleeping with me while on vacation.

"Of course, I c—" His comment broke off when his phone rang on his side from somewhere on the floor. He glanced over his shoulder, his frown deepening. "That's work." There was an apologetic note in his words.

A rigidness in his body set in. He still hadn't opened up to me about his career, and I hadn't asked. I assumed it was something related to security because he just gave off that aura.

"It's okay," I assured. Not that he needed my assurance to answer his own phone. However, once I'd said those two words, he nodded and then rolled over to pick it up. He stood from the bed, his naked backside to me.

My legs squeezed together, and the memories of what his body against mine felt like flooded my consciousness. I watched as the muscles in his ass tightened and relaxed with each step he took out of the room.

"Yeah," he finally said, by way of answer just as he stepped over the threshold and out into the hallway. His heavy footfalls trailed down the stairs.

Sighing, I leaned against the pillows, staring up at the ceiling. I didn't want to admit how after just one night together, my bed felt a little bereft now that he was no longer taking up space in it.

"Don't get too attached," I mumbled to myself. Good sex—no, phenomenal sex, absolutely should not be enough to make me fall hard for a man. Not at thirty-five years of age. I'd had plenty of relationships. And while none of them ended in marriage, I knew what it was like to be in love.

I also knew the sting of heartbreak, just like any other woman in her mid-thirties did. I wasn't opposed to getting into a relationship. Truth be told, I'd even found myself yearning for one more and more during the past year. Many of my relationships had fizzled out over the years because my career often took priority. And too many men I'd come across couldn't stand to see their wife or girlfriend making more money or exceeding in their careers beyond them.

I shook my head, shaking loose those thoughts. None of that applied to Brutus and me. This was a holiday thing. He was only around for another week and a half, anyway. I needed to just enjoy it for what it was.

Right when I'd gotten that settled in my mind and my heart, my phone rang. Assuming it was either my sister or Carlene, I picked it up. A number I didn't recognize flashed on the screen. I had half a mind not to answer, but Carlene had been known to call from unknown numbers since she made a habit out of leaving her phone in random places and often had to use strangers' phones to track hers down.

"Hello?" I answered.

"Mia? Thank God you answered," a familiar voice replied. "I've been trying to get in contact with you for days," Vincent Davis, my former colleague, finished.

"Vincent, why are you calling me?" I didn't bother trying to hide my irritation.

"I need your help," he replied unapologetically. "The Morris account is in trouble, and I—"

PERSONAL PROTECTION

"Vincent, I need to stop you right there. You do know that I no longer work for Corsica Pharmaceuticals, don't you?"

There was a brief pause.

"Yes, yes, but this is important." He brushed my words aside as if I simply said I was taking a three-day vacation instead of the very real reminder that I quit that damn company. "And if you're ever planning on coming back to Corsica, if you help me out this time, I wouldn't mind putting in a good word for you."

That had me sitting up in bed. "You wouldn't mind helping me out?" I asked slowly to make sure I'd heard him correctly.

"Yes, of course I would do that for you."

This fool was utterly oblivious. I thought back to an annual review I'd had early in my career at Corsica. I'd performed well in just about every aspect of the job. However, it was brought to my attention that a few of my coworkers cited my lack of smiling, making small talk with them, or not going out with them to happy hours as me being unfriendly.

After that, I bent over backward to ensure my coworkers saw me as a team member. I smiled bigger than I wanted, went out to happy hours when I would've rather gone home, and planned work outings that meant less time for my friends, family, and a relationship. I played my part well.

Almost too well, it seemed. Because Vincent believed that I actually gave a damn about his putting in a good word for me at a place I quit.

I decided to remind him, "Vincent, maybe you've forgotten, but I worked at Corsica longer than you have. I trained you," I pointed out.

"And I appreciate that, which is why—"

"Therefore, *if* I ever wanted to return to Corsica, I wouldn't need a word of reference from you."

He paused on the other end.

"This is pointless. I just have a few questions about the Morris account which would help me secure the account for the next ten years. They're threatening to go in another direction. That would be detrimental to—"

"Good-bye, Vincent," I said before hanging up on him. I knew from the moment I began training Vincent that he was a self-centered jerk. Sure, he came across as nice enough, but that was mainly because he wanted something. His complete dismissal of my free time and thinking that he could be some kind of savior for me if I wanted back in Corsica was enough to make me end the conversation before it began.

Vincent and that company would never get another ounce of labor from me.

With that, I tossed the covers away from my body and strode to the closet. I planned to throw on some loungewear and then head downstairs to prepare breakfast for Brutus and me.

This was my time.

* * *

Brutus

"There's a problem," Joseph, my second in command, said once I exited Mia's bedroom.

I paused at the top of the stairs. "What happened?"

"The family's fine," he said quickly. "It's not that big of a deal."

"Then why the fuck did you start with telling me there's a problem?" Frustration peppered my words. I knew Joseph had a slight tendency to be an alarmist. But that, combined with the fact that this call had pulled me out of Mia's bed, pissed me off in a way that few things did.

"It's Taggert."

I pushed out a breath while descending the stairs to the first floor of Mia's bungalow. The sunlight streamed through the kitchen window, bathing the living room in natural light. The first thought that came to mind was how I wanted to know what Mia would look like as I ate her out on the kitchen table while that light illuminated her.

Fuck. She'd look exactly like the angel she was. I turned and peered up the stairs, half a mind to disconnect this call and make that imagining a reality.

"He's been calling the Townsends, telling them that you unjustly fired him. He's threatening to sue," Joseph continued, unaware that I was only half listening.

I cursed under my breath. "That dumb fucker."

Taggert Billings had worked for Townsend Security for three years. I had to let him go six months earlier. He was good at his job, but then he let the lifestyle get to his head. I'd seen it before. Security specialists who worked for high profile clients sometimes got confused. They mistook flying on private planes, eating at exclusive restaurants, and having chauffeured vehicles everywhere as their way of life, instead of their clients.

The reality was, we were guests in our clients' worlds. There for a specific purpose, to keep them safe. But we weren't the high-profile clientele we served. Our personal lives tended to be simpler, with a lot less money. At least, for guys like Taggert.

Yes, I'd amassed a small fortune working for the Townsends and no longer needed to work. And, I supposed, my relationship with them was closer than the standard security specialist and their client. But that wasn't Taggert's case. And he'd forgotten that.

On a few occasions, women who he'd promised to fly private or show the inner workings of Townsend Industries, had shown up to our office demanding private tours and whatnot. He also sought to take on more and more hours. Which inevitably was to fund the phony lifestyle he'd created. Then, I discovered that he'd been using the Townsend name to get into exclusive restaurants, social clubs, and even to make a few business deals.

That couldn't stand, so he was let go with a warning to stay the hell away from everything Townsend. I also put the word out to my other security contacts not to hire him because he was a potential threat to the client. Essentially, he'd been blacklisted on my word alone.

"Did you remind the stupid fuck that he has no leg to stand on? And, in fact, since I kept all of the evidence against him, the

Townsends have more than enough ammunition to sue his ass from here to kingdom come?"

"Not in so many words, but yeah, I told him."

"And?"

"He backed off the lawsuit talk, but then he went on a rant about not being able to find another job and how you can't do that to him."

I grunted. "Fuck him. He made his bed. He'll die in it."

"He can't even find a job working mall security." Joseph chuckled.

I didn't give a shit about Taggert's whining. I kept a strict no bullshit policy for all the guys working under me. "Listen, keep an eye on him but he's probably just blowing smoke. Anything else?"

"Yeah, someone just came in that wants to talk to you."

I frowned.

"Hi, Mr. Brutus," Anastasia, Aaron and Patience's youngest child's, voice pushed through the line.

Despite my earlier irritation on the topic of Taggert, a smile tipped my lips. "Hi, Stasi," I replied to the three year old. "Helping your dad at work today?"

"Yeah." She giggled. "Oh, Daddy," she said before I heard rustling on the other end.

"Hello?" Aaron Townsend questioned on the other end. I assumed he'd picked up Stasi and taken the phone from her.

"It's me," I said.

"Brutus," he replied. "Are you back in Williamsport?"

I glanced up the stairs again. "Not yet." I paused for a moment, making a decision. "I'm going to need an additional week of my vacation."

I hadn't planned on extending my time in Mexico beyond the two weeks I scheduled initially. However, after one night with Mia, suddenly the fourteen days that felt like too much time away from work didn't seem like nearly enough.

"That's fine. Joseph's handling things," Aaron responded. "I suppose he told you about Taggert?" A thread of warning crept into his voice. He knew all about why I fired Taggert Billings.

"He did, and it's being handled. He won't disturb your family anymore."

"I trust you'll make sure he doesn't." There was a brief moment of silence. "Enjoy the rest of your vacation."

"Bye, Mr. Brutus," Stasi said before the phone was given back to Joseph.

"You know what," I said to Joseph, "send Mike and Jake over to Taggert's. Have them personally remind him why he should stay the hell away from the Townsend name and anything else security related."

"How badly do you want him to get the message?" he asked.

"No broken bones," I answered. "Just a reminder of how far and wide my reach is. Make sure he knows why it's not a good idea to cross me."

"Understood."

I nodded, knowing that Joseph would follow through on my order. I heard movement behind me and turned to see Mia coming down the stairs. Her breathing hitched when I fully turned to her.

Her long braids fell over one shoulder. She wore a pair of light-weight shorts and a matching, off-the-shoulder, button-up shirt. On her feet were a pair of fuzzy slippers that showed off the white nail polish on her toes.

She stood in the sunlight of the living room and her face glowed in the light. My body tightened with need.

"I need to go," I said, my voice thick with emotion. I quickly hung up the phone, not wanting Joseph to hear the rest of what was about to happen.

As I moved closer, Mia's eyes traveled down my body. She stopped, her gaze bulging when she reached my cock. I hadn't put on a stitch of clothing since leaving her bed. In fact, irritation prickled at the back of my neck to see she'd put on clothes.

I would have to change that.

"I was going to make us some breakfast," she offered. She visibly swallowed, obviously aroused.

"Yeah, it's definitely time to eat," I said, moving closer.

She gasped when I clasped her by the waist and brought our bodies together before slamming my lips over hers. As quickly as I descended on her for the kiss, I pulled away and stripped her of the shorts. I was pleased to see that she wasn't wearing panties.

"Good girl," I growled right before picking her up and carrying her over to the table. I placed her right where a perfect stream of sunlight fell onto the table.

"Lean back for me, baby. It's time for my first breakfast of the morning." I parted her knees and tossed her legs over my shoulders. "Keep your eyes open. I want you to watch me devour this pussy." And with my eyes locked on hers, I proceeded to eat like a man starved.

Mia fell back to her elbows against the table. Her eyelids lowered but she never took her gaze off of me. She watched while I took my fill, and I stared as her eyes became more and more glossy, her lips parted, and the most delicious sounding moans fell from her mouth.

Within minutes she was coming on my tongue. I lapped it all up and then some. I smiled against her pussy when her thighs tightened around my head. She could squeeze as hard as she needed to. I'd die a happy man with my face between her legs.

Fortunately, though, the orgasm let up, and her thighs slackened before I suffered any actual loss of oxygen.

"Shit," she cursed, her eyes still glossed over. She appeared exactly as I thought she would, staring at me dreamily, looking thoroughly satisfied, sitting there in the rays of the sun.

I leaned in and nipped her bottom lip between my teeth. "I'm going to go get dressed."

She nodded. "Do you prefer pancakes or waffles?"

I lifted a brow. Mia's gaze went over to the kitchen. There, I spotted both a griddle and a waffle maker.

"Surprise me."

Her smile widened.

Reluctantly, I left her and headed up the stairs. In just that short amount of time, I'd forgotten all about work and what was happening back at home. I'd bought myself seven more days with Mia. However, that thought was soon replaced by the reminder that I only had an additional seven days with her. In two and a half weeks I'd be back in Williamsport, working my usual long hours, and she would be preparing to head to fucking Colombia.

The way my chest tightened at that knowledge should've told me how deep I was in this after only a handful of days.

CHAPTER 9

Mia

"Oh, this place looks fun," I gushed as we pulled into the parking lot of the lounge where Brutus and I were meeting some of his friends.

I was two weeks into my sabbatical and just about every day had been spent with him. Tonight was the night that I was finally meeting his friends. Friends that he was supposed to have spent the bulk of his vacation with.

"Are you sure they won't hate me?"

"If you say that one more time, I'm going to toss you over my shoulder and take you back up to your bedroom and show you just how much I don't give a shit whether they like you or not," Brutus growled from the driver's seat. His eyes blazed with that usual ferocity of his.

Despite his heated look, my shoulders slumped. "I know what you said. It's just that I feel guilty for taking up so much of your time while you were supposed to be hanging out with your friends."

He leaned across the center console and took my chin into his hands. "I'm supposed to be doing exactly what the hell I've been doing. Which is *you*."

My nipples tightened at the resounding declaration in his voice. I sighed at the same time my eyes dropped to his lips. "Thank you," I said, surprising both of us.

"For what?"

"Extending your vacation." He was initially scheduled to leave the following day, but since he'd extended his trip by another week, we had more time together.

He smirked before leaning in and kissing me breathless.

Brutus climbed out of the car and strode around the front to my side to hold the door for me as I got out. Even after two weeks, I still hadn't returned to the Cancún Airport to straighten out the situation with my rental car. The rental company had refunded me the deposit I'd put down on the vehicle, and Brutus never once complained about driving us around. In fact, he seemed eager to do it.

We entered the lounge, and I instantly caught the eye of a tall man with dark brown hair and eyes. His smile grew as he looked over my shoulder.

"Son of a bitch. You actually showed up," he bellowed as he approached. He clapped Brutus on the shoulder and smiled before looking over at me.

"Mia, this is Jameson," Brutus introduced.

"Miss Mia," Jameson said with wide arms. He looked me up and down. "You are beautiful." He took my hand in his and kissed it. "Nice to finally meet you. This guy's been keeping you to himself." He nudged Brutus with his elbow.

"Because she's mine," Brutus responded, possessively taking my hand out of Jameson's hold. "So stop looking at her like she's about to be wife number three," Brutus warned. His voice sounded awfully similar to the time he threatened that guy who nearly pushed me off of that rock.

Jameson chuckled but he also took a step back with his hands up. "Did you come here to have fun or to bust my balls about my failed marriages?"

"I can do both," Brutus quickly replied. He wrapped an arm around my waist, pulling me in close. "Are you hungry?"

I nodded.

"Excellent," Jameson said. "This place has the best guacamole around, and the shrimp empanadas ... muah!" He kissed his fingers to indicate how tasty the food was.

Brutus kept his hand at my back as we made our way to the table where a group of other men sat. He introduced me to all of the men at the table, who I came to find out were all past Army buddies of his. I should've picked up on that. They all had that appearance about them. A look that read they could be lethal when and if they wanted to be. Even when they were laughing, there was a particular gleam in their eyes.

I first spotted that look in Brutus' gaze the moment we began talking on the plane. Every so often, he would scan the aircraft as if looking for possible danger, just as he did that night. Over the previous two weeks, I realized that it wasn't even a conscious act with him. It was an innate paper of who he was, to be protective, on the lookout.

"Want to split a basket of chips and guac with me?" I asked him.

His grin widened. "Make it two baskets. I'm hungry as hell tonight."

I laughed. Brutus wasn't big for nothing. All of that muscle required calories. And as much as he ate, he worked it off, too. Every morning since that first morning we ended up together, he either slept at my place or me at his. Most of the time I awakened to either his tongue, his fingers, or his dick inside of me, but after he delivered an orgasm that would send me back to sleep, he went out for a run along the beach.

He'd come back sweaty and smelling like salt water. Then we'd go another round in the shower, washing it all off.

"Mia, you've been keeping this guy busy," Will, one of Brutus' friends, said from across the table.

I chewed and swallowed the chip I'd just taken a bite of before answering. "Sorry about that," I acknowledged. "To be fair, though, I did try to convince him to hang out with you all more, over the past few weeks." I shrugged and grabbed for the mimosa that'd been delivered to the table. I swirled the straw around in the glass before cheekily saying, "I guess I'm just more entertaining than you all."

Will burst out laughing along with Brutus. "You're better looking, for sure," he added.

Brutus grunted beside me and tightened his arm around my shoulders. "I'll second that." His lips brushed against my temple.

I scooped up a tortilla chip, dipped it in guac, and held it up to his lips. He took the offered chip without a second thought.

A low whistle from across the table grabbed my attention. That was from Tony. "Yeah, we sure as well ain't feeding his big ass chips and guac like that. No wonder he prefers you over us."

I laughed and continued to joke with the guys at the table. Brutus was mostly quiet, interjecting here and there, but mainly he kept his hand stroking up and down my back, even when our meals arrived.

"That looks so good," I crooned, staring over at his plate. "I should've tried the shrimp empanadas." I pouted.

"Here, take one of mine," Jameson offered.

"I'll break both of your goddamn hands," Brutus growled, shocking everyone. There was no hint of joking or laughter in his voice.

Jameson's eyebrows rose to meet his hairline before he broke out into a hearty laugh. One of the guys sitting across from me whistled low, but I stared at Brutus' side profile. He glared at Jameson for a few more beats before lifting his plate and sliding one of his empanadas onto mine.

"Thank you," I told him.

He gave me a sly grin, utterly different from the stormy glare he'd just given his friend a few seconds earlier. "We both know you would've ended up with it on your plate anyway."

I covered my mouth as I laughed. Yes, I might have been known to sneak a bite or two off of his plate throughout our time together.

I shrugged. "It's not like you wouldn't have given it to me anyway."

"True," he confessed.

After that minor blip, we all got back to eating and talking around the table for a while. Once our main course finished, we had a round of delicious desserts that consisted of tres leches cake, churros with chocolate sauce, and flan.

"Uh," I groaned, patting my belly. "I need to dance this meal off," I said right as the music that had been slightly slower transitioned to more upbeat salsa music.

Without waiting for Brutus or anyone else at the table, I stood and made my way to the dance floor. There were already two women there dancing. They both ushered me into their small group, and we started dancing to Celia Cruz' "La Vida Es Un Carnaval". The women gave me surprised looks when I started singing along with the lyrics.

"¿Hablas español?" one asked.

"Si, claro," I answered before doing a spin around her.

She laughed and cheered, and we danced for the rest of the song. As Celia Cruz transitioned into a Tito Puente song, I felt a strong hand clasp my back. I didn't need to turn to know who it was.

"Can I have this dance?" Brutus said low in my ear from behind.

I spun around and wrapped my arms around his neck. "Do you think you can handle it?" I shimmied my hips in rhythm with the beat of the famous percussion player.

Brutus dropped his hands to my hips, taking control of my movements while grinding his front against my mid-section. We moved fluidly against one another, pushing and pulling to the music. It still surprised me how adept he was at moving his body for his size. He had no problem keeping up with me.

"Where'd you learn to dance?" he asked.

I paused, taking his hand so he could spin me in a circle, before I answered. "As a sales rep we had a lot of benefits and leeway to woo potential clients. One of my earlier accounts was an administrator at a major hospital. I courted her for months to build a relationship. Turned out she loved salsa dancing. So …" I shrugged, "I just so happened to sign up for classes at the same studio she attended."

"You didn't," he said.

I smiled, feeling proud. "I did. Not only did I win the client over, but I also fell in love with salsa, merengue, bachata, and even learned a little flamenco."

He spun me again in another circle, nearly stealing my breath. When he pulled me back into his arms, my breathing did hitch then. He stared down at me, his eyes blazing with their usual intensity.

"You do know how to get what you want, don't you?"

I grinned. "I wasn't the top salesperson in my job five years in a row for nothing."

"Five?"

I nodded and pushed out of his arms to spin in time with the music before he pulled me back into him.

"Sounds like you loved your job."

"I thought I did." I shrugged. "But then I kept getting overlooked. Sure, I'd get my annual raises and bonuses, and definitely the added responsibility, but moving up to management or executive level? Pssh." I rolled my eyes. "In some places that's still an all-boys club. And then I started to realize maybe I didn't love the work so much. But ..." I peered over his shoulder.

My rhythm slipped slightly. Brutus noticed and slowed his steps even though we were way off the beat of the up-tempo music.

"What?" he asked.

"I started to realize I was just working because that's what you're supposed to do. I—" I stopped just short of admitting that since I didn't have a husband and kids to fill my days, I fell into the belief that my job was the center of my world. However, I kept that part in.

"It became easy to make work my thing, you know? But the dissolution started to run out when I got looked over yet again for another promotion. My old dream of wanting to own a coffee shop caught up with me. For years, I saved and invested my sales bonuses to use the money to open my coffee shop one day after I retired or achieved everything I thought I should at my job."

I snickered. "I supposed retirement came earlier than I planned."

He peered down at me. "And the rest is history."

"More or less. I've put down the deposit on my shop's location and gotten approval for a business loan. I still haven't opened the coffee shop yet."

"But you will," he stated like it was a foregone conclusion. "You've already proven you know how to go out and get what you want. And the passion when you talk about your love of the coffee shop you used to work at is palpable. Almost as much as your love for *The Four Agreements*."

I tossed my head back, laughing. "It's a great book, and I am going to make you re-read it and fall in love with it," I promised.

"If you want me to, I'll give it another try," he agreed, sincerity lacing his tone.

A slow song came on right then, and he pulled me into his arms. He kissed my cheek. "Thank you for putting up with the guys."

I pulled back. "Are you kidding? They're a fun time."

He blinked. "I should've known. You can get along with anyone. They can be a little rowdy. They've toned it down tonight, though."

"I bet they have." I glanced over to see Jameson and Will both slow dancing with the two women I danced with earlier. Jameson was whispering something in the woman's ear.

"Has he really been married twice before?"

Brutus chuckled. "Would've been three but she bailed on him at the last minute. He's definitely working on finding number three."

"My parents have been married for almost forty years," I said out of the blue. "Sharise and Boris have been together for ten, married for seven. Nothing's guaranteed, I guess, but if I had to bet, I believe they'll go the distance." I caught the wistfulness in my voice and clamped my lips shut.

For so long I'd suppressed the desire I had to marry and have a family of my own. I'd even started to accept that it might not happen for me and was trying to learn to be okay with that. However, meeting Brutus opened up that old desire. It was becoming more difficult with each passing day to keep in mind that this was just a vacation thing.

"Hey," he said, tipping my chin up to look at him. "Let's get the hell out of here?"

"You lead, and I'll follow," I replied.

He dipped low to kiss my lips, and the next thing I knew, we were out of the door.

***

Brutus

Tonight was different. I sensed the shift in Mia's mood on the dance floor as she talked about her job and her family. I hated seeing her eyes dim with what I suspected were regrets. My only aim for the rest of the night was to take that dimmed look out of her eyes and replace it with pleasure.

As soon as I closed the door to her bungalow, I pressed her back against it and sank to my knees. Her pussy had quickly become my favorite meal. I could devour it morning, noon, and night.

Lifting her leg over my shoulder, I began licking her through the lace panties she wore. Her hand came down to cup the back of my head. She soon began thrusting her hips forward, hungrily seeking more.

Unable to deny her what she needed, I pushed her panties to the side and feasted on her. Her hips jerked at the first press of my tongue against her clit. But this wasn't enough for me. Not by a long shot.

Much to Mia's chagrin, I pulled back and rose to my feet. I barely took in her wide-eyed expression as if asking why the hell I stopped. Instead of answering, I spun her around and pressed her back to bend over the arm of the sofa. I lifted her dress over her hips and made quick work of removing her panties.

On instinct, I stuffed them into the back pocket of my jeans, before spreading her cheeks. I used my shoulders and upper body to widen her stance. With better access to her core, I continued to eat her out until we both were satisfied. Mia came apart after only a few minutes.

But one orgasm from her was never enough. Despite the fact that my cock felt like it was trying to hammer its way through my zipper, I held back. Even with the taste of her orgasm on my tongue, I continued to hunger for me. So, I took my fill again, lapping at her folds and devouring the pussy that I'd branded as mine.

"Brutus!" she cried out, her voice sounding a mix of anger, awe, and need. Her legs quaked and trembled and she came again.

Only then would I allow myself to take. I lifted Mia in my arms and made my way up the stairs to her bedroom.

She released an airy laugh when I tossed her onto the bed. "You throw me around like I weigh nothing," she cooed, sitting up on her knees.

"You don't," I replied.

She rolled her eyes in that cute way of hers before she reached for the hem of my shirt. I lifted my arms, allowing her to undress me.

"Fuck," I groaned when she reached inside of my jeans and began stroking my cock.

"I want you in my mouth," she whispered.

I went completely still. I wanted nothing more than to watch her wrap that pretty fucking mouth around my cock, taking all of me. I stepped back from the bed to give her room.

She undid the button of my jeans and helped strip me out of them before. She guided me to sit on the edge of the bed. I leaned back on my hands to give her enough room. The ends of her braids brushed against my thighs, tickling them. But that sensation was nothing compared to the feeling when she rimmed the tip of my cock.

I gritted my teeth and tightened my fists into the bed, forcing myself to hold back.

Mia looked up at me at the same time she slid her mouth fully around me.

Holy shit.

My entire body heated all over. When her braids slipped in front of her face, obscuring my view, I wrapped my hand around them. I held her hair back while she bobbed her head against my dick, sending waves to rippling pleasure up and down my spine. Not once did she take her eyes off of me.

I was forced to break eye contact as I lifted my head and groaned when she ran her tongue along the vein of my cock, before covering it with her mouth again. Fuck, I'd honed my patience over the years, but I grew antsy. And I didn't want to come in her mouth.

Before she could draw out my orgasm, I pulled free from that scandalous mouth of hers and tossed her on the bed. I quickly retrieved a condom from my wallet and covered my length before yanking her thighs to me. I removed her dress because I needed to see all of her.

And then I brought us together. We both sighed in delight. I thrust my hips forward while holding her waist firmly. When she jolted and screamed out, I knew I hit a particularly sensitive area. I hungrily watched how her tits bounced up and down with every push of my hips. When I hit her G-spot, Mia came apart in my arms yet again.

And still that wasn't enough.

Before she could recover from her second orgasm, I flipped her over onto all fours.

"Arch your back for me, baby."

I almost came at the way she beautifully arched her back, offering her backside to me. I reached down the length of her back and wrapped my hand in her braids again, pulling her head up to arch her back even more. When I slid inside of her once more, she groaned and cursed out her pleasure.

"Tell me what you want, Mia," I ordered while pounding into her from behind.

"More," she answered. "I want more, please."

Fuck. Did she have to beg like that?

I increased my strokes, pounding into her viciously. There were times with other women I'd held back, not sure whether or not they could take all of me like this. Mia took it and wanted more.

I fucked her so hard that the entire bed began to shake as the headboard banged against the wall. But I didn't give a shit about the bed or anything else—just the two of us. Mia screamed out, calling my name, which only spurred me on.

I tightened my hold on her waist and pushed in so deep that she and I became one. Over and over. I took and she gave, arching her back to the hilt, offering herself to me. Even as the bed rattled and shook, I paid it no attention.

Mia croaked out my name on a gasp right as her orgasm took over. Her pussy walls began milking me, and I couldn't withhold any longer. I stroked her through both of our orgasms. I didn't let up until the final spurts of my come jutted into the condom I wore.

Only then did I sigh before rolling over onto the bed, bringing her down with me.

"Oh my God," she screeched as we fell against the bed, quickly followed by a loud thud against the wooden floor. The bed jostled and shook as it fell to the ground.

"We just broke the bed." She stared at me, alarmed.

A brief moment passed before we both broke out into a fit of laughter.

"I can't believe we did that," Mia said in between gasps for air while wiping tears of laughter from her eyes.

"Believe it." I chuckled while noting the not uneven placement of the bed. We laid at an angle with our legs higher than the rest of our bodies.

"You're okay, right?" I sat up to make sure some random piece of the bed hadn't injured her or something.

She waved a dismissive hand. "Fine. I just wonder how much the owner's going to charge me to get a replacement."

Frowning, I pulled her in tighter to me. "He won't charge you a damn thing. This is on me. I'll take care of it."

"You can't—" I silenced her with a kiss to her lips.

"It's already done," I responded.

She rolled her eyes in that playful way I loved seeing. "This is some real life *How Stella Got Her Groove Back* mess." She laughed.

"Some what?"

She lifted her head, pressing her palm into my chest to bolster herself on her elbow. I captured her hand, keeping it against my body.

"You've never heard of that book turned movie from the 90s?"

I shook my head.

"It's by Terry McMillan. Her books and movies had a chokehold on our Black Mamas during the 90s." She smirked. "But she's often credited as an early pioneer of Black romance books during that era."

"And this, between you and me, is like one of her books?"

"A little. But in Stella the guy was like twenty-one or something. And she was forty, I think."

"The fuck does a twenty-one year old know about pleasing a grown woman?"

Mia guffawed before placing a kiss to my chest. "Someone sounds a little threatened," she teased.

"Threatened my ass." I sat up on my elbows to look at her more easily. "I'd snap the neck of any twenty-something who tried to …" I paused when I saw the way Mia's eyes bulged. "I'm not threatened," I amended.

She stared down at me for a few more beats. "What do you do for a living?"

"I work security for a family."

She angled her head and continued to look at me. I knew then that my answer wasn't sufficient.

"You're a security guard."

"We prefer the term personal protection specialist."

"But you're not just their personal protection specialist, are you?" she noted.

"I'm head of their entire security team."

"Head of security." Her gaze drifted over toward the far end of the room.

Briefly, I wondered if she was trying to figure out who exactly I worked for. The memory of her recounting how she finagled her way into a sales account by researching and taking salsa classes came to mind. Mia was resourceful and an extrovert who made friends wherever she went. I'd seen it countless times over the past two weeks.

Hell, she got me, who never liked talking or meeting new people, to open up. The fear that she could be using me to get to some other means welled up.

"Does your job put you in danger?" Her question interrupted my thoughts. "Could you be hurt?"

I searched her gaze for a long moment. She openly stared down at me, allowing me to see the very real fear in her eyes. I released a breath, my worries from a few seconds ago completely obliterating.

She wasn't trying to get to the Townsends through me. She was concerned about my safety.

I pulled her down to my chest where she rested her head against my shoulder.

"My job is ninety-eight percent strategy, going over details, and standing around just waiting," I reassured.

She curled her body into mine. "It's the two percent that frightens me."

My heart bloomed inside of my chest. The idea of having someone more concerned with me than the family I worked for was unfamiliar. It felt strange in a good way to have someone care about me.

"You don't have to think about that. I'm damned good at my job," I assured.

She wrapped her arm around my waist. "I don't doubt that."

It remained quiet for a few minutes as I stroked her braids. There was an ease. As we laid there on that broken bed, the air didn't need to be filled with anything more than our mere presence and our inhalations and exhalations.

"Tell me about your family."

I stiffened.

"Not who you work for. *Your* family," she reiterated.

Releasing the breath I held, I shrugged. "Not much to tell. It's just me and my father."

"What about your mom?"

"She died when I was nineteen. Who knew a two pack a day habit for over twenty years could lead to lung cancer," I quipped.

"I'm sorry." She kissed the center of my chest.

I started to say something dismissive like 'it was a long time ago' or 'I'm over it' but I couldn't. My mother was far from perfect, but she loved me, and I still missed her.

"You and your dad seem close," Mia said.

"He's a pain in my ass."

She laughed. "My parents can be a pain, too, but I love them."

"I didn't even meet my father until after my mother died."

"Seriously? Why?"

"My mother never told me who my father was until she was on her deathbed," I admitted. Very few people in my life knew that.

"How come?"

I shook my head. "They didn't have that kind of relationship. He wasn't the settling down type. She was angry at him for many years. I don't know her exact reasoning to be honest. Anyway, I sought him out after I got out of the Army."

"So, he didn't know about you? I'll bet he was shocked. Was he angry with your mom?"

I chuckled. "Hell yeah Rick was, but what could he do? She was gone. Plus, she wasn't perfect, but I don't let anyone talk shit about my mom openly and get away with it. Not even him."

I squeezed my free hand into a fist remembering the bastards my mother had dated. A few of whom I'd gotten in between when they tried to put their hands on her in front of me.

"Why am I telling you all of this?" I asked out loud.

"I'm sor—"

"No," I cut her off. "Don't apologize. I just mean ..." I ran my hand through my hair. "I don't talk about myself often. Not to anyone. I don't talk half as much about anything. But with you I'm a regular fucking chatterbox."

Giggling, Mia snuggled in closer to me. "I'm glad because I like the sound of your voice."

I snorted.

"No, really. If you ever want a career change, you should consider narrating audiobooks."

I pulled back to stare at her.

"I'm serious." She leaned over to her side of the bed and retrieved her phone. She brought up her e-reader app and opened it. "Start here." She handed me her phone.

"You want me to read *The Four Agreements.*"

"Out loud, please," she answered casually before laying her head back against my chest.

And Lord help me, I started reading. Simply because she wanted it.

CHAPTER 10

Mia

"Go away," I mumbled at the same time I flipped back over, curling into the warm sheets.

The loud noise continued, seriously disturbing the blissful dream I was in. I dreamt that Brutus was reading to me from one of my favorite books while his free hand stroked my hair.

Pounding from downstairs finally ripped me from the dream, and my eyes popped open. I blinked and looked around the bedroom. The other side of the bed was empty, the sheets crumpled. I knew Brutus was out for one of his early morning runs. It was then I remembered that I hadn't been only dreaming but it was an actual memory from the night before.

Brutus had read to me until I fell asleep after he made me see the stars with three orgasms, and then opening up about his family.

More pounding on the door startled me out of my reverie.

"Coming!" I called down. I quickly dressed in a pair of jeans, a bra, and a T-shirt that I had laying around. It was before seven in the morning. Who the hell was banging on the door this early in the morning?

"Señora Raymond?"

I nodded at the man standing before me. Behind him stood two more men, and they had a large, wooden bed frame between the two of them, along with a mattress.

"What is this?"

"We're here to fix your bed," the man stated. "I am Angel, the owner's repairman," he introduced in accented English. "May we?" He gestured toward the door.

"Yes, please." I forgot all about the broken bed even though I'd just awakened in it.

"We won't take very long," Angel assured as he and the three men headed up the stairs, carrying the new bedframe.

I watched wordlessly, wondering how they'd gotten a new bed and everything so early. The thing had only broken last night. Plus, I hadn't called anyone yet to tell the owner and arrange to have it fixed.

My thoughts trailed off when I heard the sliding glass door by the kitchen opening. I looked over to see a sweaty and shirtless Brutus coming in. My breathing hitched at the image he made. His face was slightly reddened from the exertion he'd clearly put forth, and his chest glistened from the sweat. He'd gotten a tan in the past few weeks, leaving golden skin covering his heavy muscles.

I allowed my gaze to travel down the V-cut of his hips to the gray sweat shorts he wore.

"What's that?" His question pulled me out of my lascivious stupor.

"What's what?"

His eyes moved skyward toward the ceiling. A few beats later noises from the bedroom sounded.

"Oh. The owner's repair guys showed up to fix the bed. Did you—"

"They're here?" His face took on a stormy, incredulous look. "You let them in?" He didn't bother waiting for my answer as he barged past me. I watched as he took the stairs two at a time.

I followed, wondering what the big deal was. By the time I got to the room, the three men had all come to a complete stop, tools in hand and everything.

"Who told you to come in here?" Brutus demanded in Spanish.

Angel's gaze shifted over to me. "Señora Raymond. We're just doing our job," he answered in Spanish as well.

"You were supposed to wait for me to be here." Brutus turned to me. "They weren't supposed to come until after eight-thirty."

"It's fine. They didn't disturb me," I quickly responded, even though I had been sleeping when the men arrived.

His frown deepened. He turned to the men, telling them they could continue and that we'd be waiting downstairs.

Abruptly, he spun to me and took me by the arm to lead me down the stairs. His grip wasn't punishing, but he held my arm firm.

"Why did you let them in?" he demanded once we reached the kitchen.

"They had a bed."

"You were alone. They could've …" He broke off.

"I was fine." I fisted my hips, feeling defensive. "They didn't do anything but their job."

"And what if they had tried to do something?" he insisted.

"I can take care of myself." Lifting my chin, I crossed my arms over my chest.

"Against three men?"

My confidence wavered a bit, but I didn't want to give him that satisfaction, so I didn't answer.

Instead, I replied with, "I'm not a client of yours or something. You don't have to take care of me."

"First of all, we both know that's bullshit. Second, don't ever open a door without knowing exactly who's on the other side. And third, call me. You should've never been alone with those men."

I wanted to argue but the truth was, it wasn't worth it. Brutus was a natural protector, and as much as I didn't want to admit it, he was right. Had I been at home, there was no way I would've let three men inside early in the morning without a previous appointment and at least my sister or Carlene waiting with me.

I knew better, but over the past two weeks I'd been lulled into a sense of security I never knew.

Instead of arguing, I sidled up to Brutus and ran my finger down the center of his chest.

"You're right. It won't happen again." I lifted to my tiptoes, and after a moment of pause he leaned in and brushed his lips across mine.

He cupped my face. "Make sure it doesn't," he said before kissing me again. "Once they're gone, I'm going to drag your ass into the shower and show you why you were wrong for letting them in without me being here."

My nipples pebbled from the promise in his voice. "Keep that up and I might decide to let strange men in here all the time."

That didn't garner the laugh I originally wanted. But it did earn me a hard smack against my ass.

"Don't play with me," he warned.

Damn this man.

* * *

Brutus

Damn that woman.

It was an hour later, and I was still slightly pissed off just knowing she'd let three men in the bungalow while I wasn't there. Sure, I'd already vetted the owner of the house and everyone who worked for him almost two weeks earlier. Just to make sure Mia was safe where she was staying.

However, she didn't know that.

The only reason I wasn't still fuming was because of the way she apologized in the shower once the men fixed the bed and left. She swallowed my cock like a damn pro. Kind of difficult to stay too mad after that.

"This place is so cute," Mia praised as we entered the small coffee shop that was a few blocks from her bungalow. "And it smells delicious in here. This was perfect for doing some research."

This was the third coffee shop we would have breakfast at in the past week. Mia wanted to check out all of the coffee shops in the area to get ideas and inspiration for her own shop once she got back home.

"I'm definitely getting the huevos rancheros," she said, peering up at me. "I worked up an appetite this morning. What're you having?"

"Probably the same," I answered.

"You must try the Cafe de Olla," an older woman said from behind us.

Mia whipped around to face the woman. "Is that your favorite?" she asked excitedly. Then whispered, "We had some at another café and it wasn't that great."

"Yes, the coffee here is delicious," the older woman responded.

That started a robust conversation between the two.

Before I knew it, Mia walked off with the woman, chattering about what she did and didn't like about the café. Next to me, a man chuckled.

"Your wife must be like mine."

I turned to face the older man with graying hair. He appeared to be in his sixties. "She can make friends with anyone." His comment was punctuated by a round of laughter from Mia and her new friend, as they stood beside another couple, talking.

I didn't correct him on his assumption about who Mia was to me. It felt too right.

I grinned. "Yeah," I said easily.

"It used to annoy the hell out of me. But after forty years of marriage, you get used to it," he said. His smile was casual as he glanced over at his wife.

"Brutus, can you get a few pictures, please?" Mia asked as she rushed over to me with her phone in her hand.

I took the phone and snapped some images of her with the older woman, whose name was Rose, and the two women who were a married couple that they'd just met.

"You all will have to come to Williamsport once I open my coffee shop," Mia gushed.

"Hun, can you snap some shots?" Rose asked her husband, Bill.

He laughed. "I never saw this one coming either. Thought I was done working once I retired." He grinned and looked over at me. "Now I'm an Instagram husband," he said before doing his wife's bidding and taking multiple pictures of her.

"Brutus, look, they have a chess set, too." Mia clasped my forearm, pointing at the table with the chess set. "It looks like it's made out of ivory. Remember I told you the shop I used to work at had a space where some retirees would come to play chess in the mornings?"

She took a few pictures of the chess set and the surrounding areas of the coffee shop.

"I have to have one for mine," she said.

She became so enthralled in the shop and talking with the customers as if she was one of the staff, she forgot all about her hunger. I ended up ordering the huevos rancheros for Mia since she continued to flutter around asking questions of customers and the employees alike. I got the tamales for myself and got us the traditional Mexican coffee along with a few others because I knew she would want to try them.

"Oh my, this looks perfect." Mia pressed her hand against her chest as she stared down at our breakfast on the table. "I'm so hungry."

"You've worked up an appetite running this place for the past twenty minutes," I joked.

She grinned as I held out her chair for her to sit. "Everyone here is so friendly. We definitely have to give this place another try sometime this week before you—" She stopped.

My heart tightened in my chest. Before I left, I knew that was the rest of her comment. Up until recently the fact that my vacation was coming to an end sooner than hers was always something in the distance. A thing that didn't need to be dwelled on at the moment. But as the days went by and my inevitable return to reality approached, the unsettled feeling in my chest grew stronger.

I hadn't been displeased with my life before this vacation. I often worked twelve or more hours per day with no complaints. Some might've called me a workaholic but fuck them. I loved my job and the family I worked for. Ensuring their safety felt like my mission. Nothing had ever rivaled that feeling.

Until I met Mia.

"Rose and Bill are going to visit the ruins today. They invited us to come along," Mia said, changing the subject.

"That invite probably came more from Rose than from Bill," I joked, doing my best to lighten my mood.

"Do you want to go? We talked about going to the ruins."

I nodded. "Let's do it."

I could put my feelings about my leaving on the back burner. There wasn't anything I wanted to get in the way of us spending time together. I'd have to figure out how to make this work between us even once I returned home, crazy schedule and all, because I was not about to let Mia go.

Somewhere along the line, I determined that. She was mine.

CHAPTER 11

Brutus

A week after our visit to the café, I rolled over in bed and wrapped my arm around Mia. I held her to me as she slept peacefully. I didn't want this moment to end. But in less than two hours I would be heading to the airport.

Most mornings since that first night I spent beside her, the sunrays that streamed through the window blinds had been a welcomed sight. Not that morning. I resented the sun for ushering in another day.

This day.

The day that I would be forced to say good-bye to Mia. For now.

I was headed back to Williamsport. And she would stay on here in Tulum for another week, before trekking down to Colombia.

I had to admit, I was proud of her ambition. I knew her shop would be a success because of how dedicated to the process she was. But I hated that I couldn't scoop her up and carry her ass on the plane home with me. No matter how badly I wanted to.

I lifted on my elbow, pushed the covers from over her body, and lightly trailed my hand over her back. She stirred a little but didn't wake up.

I ran my finger over one of the moles on her back and then kissed it. Then another, and another.

"Six," I murmured before kissing another one.

"What are you doing?" Mia's groggy voice questioned.

"Counting the moles on your back." I kissed one more. "Memorizing them all." Another kiss.

Moaning, she tried to roll over.

I pressed my hand to her shoulder. "No," I ordered. "I'm almost done." I slid my body down to kiss the final mole that was directly above the swell of her ass. I parted her cheeks and licked and kissed all the way down to her puckered hole.

Mia gasped and groaned, her hips lifting to meet my mouth.

I moved my hand underneath her hips, to her core which was already wet. I sank my middle finger in to the knuckle, and Mia let out a long moan.

"It sounds like you're ready for me, baby," I teased with my lips brushing against her cheek.

"Please."

"Shit. You know what it does to me when you beg." I sat up on my knees and pulled her hips up to meet mine. I pushed into her from behind. A wave of shock coursed through me.

"You're so fucking tight, Mia."

My devilish woman took that as an opportunity to tighten her pussy muscles around my cock.

I hissed. "You're going to pay for that," I growled.

Wrapping my hand around her throat, I pulled her up to me, placing her back against my chest. I squeezed just enough to keep her from moving but not enough to cut off her air supply.

"Brutus," she panted.

The sound went straight to my dick.

"Ride me, Mia. Show me what those hips can do."

She began bouncing her ass up and down along my rod. I watched as her cheeks jiggled every time they slammed against my waist. I could feel her slickness running down my cock.

I reached around between her thighs and stroked her clit. She cried out, and I tightened my hold around her throat. Her head dropped to my shoulder.

"Come for me, baby."

And she did. She came apart for me, right there in my arms. It was the most beautiful sight I'd ever seen.

My dick agreed because soon after I was coming. I came so hard and furiously, that it wasn't until after I pulled out that I realized that I'd neglected to put on a condom.

I waited for fear and regret to overcome me, but it never did. What did well up inside of my chest was hope. The hope that we might've just created something that will forever bind us together.

Not that Mia needed to get pregnant for me to know she was mine, but it wouldn't hurt.

"Did we ..." She trailed off as she turned and looked up at me. "We didn't use protection." She licked her lips.

"We've already discussed this." I cupped her face. "We both have been tested recently." In fact, we shared our test results with one another after that first night.

"And what about ... a baby?"

I swallowed and tried to push down how much that thought thrilled me. "Then we'll have a baby," I said firmly.

She folded her lips inward, her gaze falling to the bed.

"You don't want kids?"

She sat up. "No, it's not that. I do. I just ... it's been three weeks."

"The most life changing three weeks of my life."

"Mine too," she admitted, and then groaned, placing her forehead against my shoulder. "This feels absolutely crazy."

"Like you're Stella?" I joked.

She sat back with wide eyes. "You remembered?"

"I listened to the audiobook on my run yesterday morning."

Her mouth fell open.

"Baby, is that really what you romance readers listen to? That was straight up porn."

She giggled. "No, babe. What we just did was porn."

A deep chuckle fell from my lips.

God, I loved this woman. Yes, in three weeks I'd fallen in love. I didn't give a shit that it may not fit anyone else's timeline of how long it takes to fall. I knew my heart and my own mind. No one had touched me like Mia, not in a long time, maybe not ever.

It pained me to know that in a few hours we would be miles apart from one another.

I didn't have the words to express the heaviness that placed on my heart.

"We're going to be fine," I said out loud, more for me than for Mia. "Let's take a shower," I offered.

It would be our last one together for a little while.

* * *

"I NEED you to do me a favor," I told Jameson as he drove me to the airport. I'd left my rental car with Mia, after transferring the car in her name with the company. And I refused to let her drive me to the airport, since she'd already started to tear up at the bungalow.

All I needed was to see her cry and get emotional at the airport. My entire flight I would've been clawing the walls with worry that she'd become too emotional while driving and get into an accident on the way back to Tulum. I'd call her from the airport to hear her voice one final time before I boarded.

"What's up?" Jameson asked.

"You're still in between jobs, right?" I asked.

"Yeah. Client won't be back in California for another couple of months."

"I need you to stay on in Tulum for another week and then head down to Colombia."

He lifted an eyebrow and gave me a sideways look. "You want me to keep an eye on Mia." A comment not a question.

"Yeah." I nodded. "I can't be there to watch over her."

"You know Colombia is pretty safe. There are a lot of expats, especially down in Medellín where she's planning to stay."

It was my turn to give him a look. I glared. "I don't give a shit about other expats. Safe or not, I don't want her down there by herself without someone watching over her." I preferred to be there with her, but I had a job to do back home.

"You know ..." Jameson started.

I knew from his tone I wasn't going to like what he had to say.

"Just hear me out," he warned. "You seem pretty serious about this girl."

"She's not a girl, and I don't *seem* anything. I am serious as fuck about her."

"That's great and all. I can't remember the last time you were serious about a woman," he continued. "But have you thought about what it will be like when you're both back home?"

I didn't want to hear what he had to say, but I let him keep talking.

"I'm asking because I'm the one with two failed marriages under his belt." When we reached a red light, he turned to me. "You know more than anyone what this life of ours is like. You just had your first vacation in how long?"

"What the hell is your point?" I knew what his point was, but I wanted him to spell it out.

"You're far from stupid," he responded. "You know what I'm getting at." He leveled a look at me. "I can't tell you how many arguments Melinda and I had because I had to drop everything and fly halfway around the damn world for a client."

His lips pinched and eyes narrowed. I knew he was thinking about his first wife, who I knew, that despite a marriage and plenty of throw away relationships in between, he wasn't over.

"In our world, the client comes first. They have to because their lives depend on how focused we are on the job. One slip up means the difference between them staying alive and death. Our families can get left behind."

"That won't happen," I said firmly.

He glanced over at me again. "Relationships are hard enough to maintain without us having to work twelve to eighteen hour days. Are you prepared—"

"I said it won't happen." My voice came out harsh.

He quieted for a few beats.

"I'm just asking if you've thought about it all. Our life isn't a vacation."

"I hear you, but I've got this all handled," I told him. "Can you do me this favor or not?"

This conversation was over. I refused to admit it out loud, but Jameson was partially correct. He knew it and I knew it. The past three weeks with Mia had been a dream. A real-life dream. But back home was reality.

My very real life in which the bulk of my days and often my nights were dedicated to managing Townsend Security. Even with my highly trained employees, it was more than a full-time job. It was a lifestyle.

"Yeah, I can do it. It's been a while since I had real Colombian coffee anyway."

"Stay out of her sight," I told him. "She shouldn't know you're there."

"Do you think you're talking to some wet nose recruit? I know what I'm doing."

"Thanks, Jameson." I nodded.

For the rest of the drive to the airport we discussed logistics of his trip to Colombia along with other stuff that I could only halfway focus on. The unsettled feeling I'd had since I woke up that morning grew more intense.

Jameson's reminders of the difficulty of maintaining relationships in our line of work weighed heavily on my chest. Despite my shutting him down, I knew it was the truth. I'd seen more men than I could count wind up divorced or in failed relationship after failed relationship.

A wife or girlfriend would often be understanding in the beginning. But after one too many missed dinners, events at the kids' school, or wedding anniversary, it was all downhill. I'd lost a few specialists on my team because of the strain the job put on their homelife.

And I worked more than they did. Until then, my job had consumed my life. I hadn't minded that either, since it felt like my purpose, my calling.

But now?

What would it look like now?

CHAPTER 12

Mia

I sauntered back into my private room at the coffee farm, feeling physically exhausted. But the heaviness in my chest wasn't a result of the hours I'd spent working with and roasting coffee beans that day.

It was the same heaviness that'd traveled with me from Mexico. I expected it to lighten at some point, but it hadn't in the month since Brutus returned to Williamsport.

Though my sadness shrouded me like a cloud, my one bright spot of the day was in thirty minutes when he would be calling for our daily video chats.

I rushed to shower and moisturized myself before climbing into bed. After making sure my phone was charged, I saw that I had an email. I gasped when opening it.

A second later, my phone buzzed with the video call from Brutus.

"You didn't," I blurted out as I answered.

His smile widened, and the muscles in my belly tightened. "Didn't what?"

"Buy me the audiobook. I just checked my email."

"You said you wanted to read it next."

Those butterflies that I'd become used to over the past almost two months started fluttering around. Two days earlier, I'd mentioned that I wanted the audiobook version of Jennifer Lewis' *The Mother of Black Hollywood: A Memoir*. I wanted the audio because she reads the book herself and her voice is spectacular.

"Thank you."

"Have you started listening yet?"

I shook my head. "I just got in a little while ago."

"How was the coffee roasting?"

"Long. There are so many steps to making a great cup of coffee." I sat up on my knees. "But, babe, it's so worth it. We tried three different types today, and oh my gosh. So scrumptious." I groaned. "I definitely want to work with the distributor who buys from this farm. I have a meeting with them tomorrow."

"I'm so damned proud of you," he stated.

My breath caught. A part of me didn't know how to respond to a man being so supportive of my dream. Exes in my past were semi-supportive but up until a point.

"You're doing something you've always wanted to do and doing your damnedest to be ethical about how you go about it."

I swallowed. A week earlier I'd sent Brutus a copy of the business plan I drafted up months earlier. Long before I quit my job. He'd thoroughly read it over, gave me some feedback, and asked truly insightful questions about funding and growth potential.

"Your support means everything to me," I told the truth.

He scrubbed a hand down the side of his face.

"You look tired. It's after one a.m., isn't it?" I calculated the time difference between where I was and Williamsport to confirm that it was indeed closer to two in the morning there.

"Yeah, just got home."

"You work a lot. I know that life." The week before he'd been on the East Coast due to some business meetings his employer had over there. I still hadn't asked the name of the family he worked for because it didn't matter to me. But I did worry about his safety, even though he constantly assured me that the bulk of his job was quite dull.

I knew he downplayed the dangers to keep me from worrying.

"Have you eaten anything? When is your next day off?"

He chuckled, and I watched as he laid back against his bed. He'd given me a tour of his home on one of our other calls.

"I just had a peanut butter and jelly sandwich."

"That's not real food."

"Enough about me. Are you working too hard on that farm? I know you're researching for your business but that doesn't mean they get to squeeze you for free labor."

I laughed. "Nobody's squeezing me for anything."

"Good. I'm the only one who gets to squeeze you."

I bit my bottom lip.

He sat up. "What's that look?"

I hesitated before answering. "We, um, haven't really defined what we are. What this relationship is."

He squinted, his eyes crinkling at the edges as he gave me a stern look. "You want a definition?"

"No ... yes," I amended. "I mean, not if you're not ready. We're not even in the same country. So—"

"You belong to me, Mia. You're my woman. My girlfriend, though I hate that term because it's simply not enough to describe what you mean to me."

My heart melted, and embarrassingly, my eyes started to water. I wanted to blame the emotion on PMS or something but couldn't. I'd gotten my period a few days earlier. Brutus' face crumpled when I told him the news. And for a heartbeat, I'd wondered if he had hoped I was pregnant.

I didn't want to dwell too heavily on the fact that I was a little disappointed. I had to remind myself repeatedly that I'd known Brutus for less than two months. It was probably a good thing that he didn't get me pregnant that one time we didn't use a condom.

"I didn't get it," Brutus said, capturing my attention. That blazing look of intensity was back in his eyes as he stared at me through the phone's camera.

"What?" I asked, transfixed on that gleam in his eyes.

"I work for men who I've seen do some pretty outrageous shit for the women they love. I understood the need to be protective, but I didn't understand the lengths they went to. Not until right now. I'd skin a motherfucker alive for you," he declared.

I sucked in a sharp breath.

"Shit, I just frightened you, didn't I?" he asked, looking slightly chagrined.

"Yeah, kind of," I answered, truthfully.

"I didn't mean ..." He paused, "Shit, yes I did. I would filet a motherfucker for looking at you wrong."

I stared with my mouth agape. "You know that sounds insane, right?"

He nodded but there wasn't an ounce of remorse when he replied, "And I mean every word of it."

What the heck was I supposed to say to that? It sounded absolutely bonkers for a man to declare that he would openly commit physical harm to someone for me. And yet ...

"I must be a little crazy too because I'm turned on right now."

His hazel eyes sparked with desire. "Lay back against the bed and show me." His voice deepened a couple of levels.

A thrill of excitement shot through my body.

"Say please," I taunted.

He frowned, which made me laugh.

"You want me to beg?"

I nodded.

"If I do, you know that's a red ass for you as soon as I get my hands on you." It came out sounding just like the threat he intended it to be.

My nipples ached with need.

I unbuttoned the pajama shirt I had on, exposing my breasts. Brutus licked his lips.

"Show me the rest." His voice was thick with desire.

This wasn't the first time we'd had phone sex in the weeks since he'd gone back home. While it was better than nothing, it left me wanting. Each time I hung up the phone it got more and more difficult.

My days were filled with me learning about coffee beans and making connections for my business, but damn it, I wanted nothing more than to return to Williamsport. Just to be in the same space as him again.

What if it's different when I get home?

That old, familiar doubt crept in, despite how much I tried to keep it at bay.

By the time I got off the phone with Brutus that night, I felt torn in two. Half of me wanted to stay and finish what I'd set out to do. The other half of me wanted to get on a plane and be in his arms as soon as possible so I could prove that this thing was real. Not just a vacation fling that we were trying to hold onto for too long.

CHAPTER 13

Brutus

"You haven't heard anything else from Taggert, have you?" I asked Joseph as we stood in my office on the bottom floor of Townsend Industries.

"Not since you had us pay him a visit." He nodded. "I'm sure he got the message."

I closed the file in front of me. "Good. I'm headed up to Aaron's office for a meeting to discuss the security details for the upcoming charity gala."

Joseph checked his watch. "I'll be heading out in about fifteen minutes to meet Robert and Deborah for their flight."

The elder Townsends were going out of town for a few days. "Let me know if there are any issues."

"Always."

Instead of using the private elevators, I took the public elevator that all employees and visitors accessed throughout the day. I liked to take the general route to sweep the landscape visually. It was a simple precaution to make sure everything was running smoothly.

As soon as I entered Aaron's outer office, his assistant waved me in. "He's waiting for you."

I passed down the hall to Aaron Townsend's corner office on one of the top floors of Townsend Industries.

"Brutus," he greeted as he stood from his chair. He waved me in, that typical scowl on his face. It didn't offend me since he wore it with everyone. Save for his wife and kids.

"I need you to sign off on a couple of contracts for the additional security we're hiring for the charity gala," I said as I strolled over to the long, boardroom-length table at the far end of his office.

"You've vetted this firm we're going with, I assume."

"Of course. We used them last year for the Christmas party. A few of our guys will be out on vacation during the gala, which is why I thought the additional manpower would be best for this occasion."

Aaron's eyes narrowed as he stared, assessing. It was typical Aaron. He nodded.

I handed him the documents to sign. And just as he finished the final signature and rose from the table, a squealing noise sounded at the door.

"Daddy," three-year-old Stasi called out as she bumrushed the office.

Aaron bent down, scooping her up into his arms. She giggled as he tickled her underneath the chin.

"Dad!" Andreas, one of Aaron's younger twins, called out.

I peered down to find Thiers staring up at me. His light brown eyes already held more intensity than a five year old's eyes should.

"Hi, Mr. Brutus." He nodded and then narrowed his eyes.

I braced myself for what was about to come. Right as his little fist went flying toward my abdomen, I caught it in my much larger hand. Thiers frowned.

"Thiers!" Patience, Aaron's wife, yelled. "What did I tell you about that?" she admonished.

A deep chuckle fell from my lips. Thiers' little ass was always trying to catch me or one of the other security details off guard. He, more than any of the other children, took his self-defense training seriously.

"I'm sorry, Brutus." Patience grabbed him by the shoulders and pushed him farther into the office.

"Little man's just practicing," I told her.

She glared down at him and then looked up at me. "Practicing or not, he doesn't get to go around hitting people for no reason."

"I didn't hit him, Mom," Thiers replied.

"Only because Brutus is stronger and faster than your little behind."

"But—"

"Don't argue with your mother," Aaron's voice boomed from across the room, catching everyone's attention. All three of the children went silent for a beat. "Apologize to Mr. Brutus," Aaron told Thiers.

"Sorry, Mr. Brutus," Thiers mumbled.

"Save that energy for next training, kid," I told him, even though it wasn't a big deal.

"Hey, sweetness," Aaron crooned, finally greeting his wife.

I'd heard him give that same greeting to Patience thousands of times over the years, but this time, it caused an image of Mia to flash in my mind.

Silently, I watched as Aaron played with his kids, letting them have free reign over his office. He then pulled Patience into his arms, sitting her on his lap behind his desk. At the same time, she updated him on the kids' school projects, teacher reports, and the happenings at the community center that she and the other women in the family founded.

In the corner of Aaron's office, Andreas and his twin played a game on their tablets. I could tell from the arguing between them that it was some sort of battle game. Stasi flitted around the office with a doll in her hand that she'd pulled out of one of the drawers of Aaron's desk. I recognized it as the doll she'd left on her last visit to his office a couple of days earlier.

After about fifteen minutes, an alarm sounded. Patience hopped up from Aaron's lap. I noted the way he frowned at her withdrawal.

"It's time to pick up your sister from her riding practice," Patience told the children.

"And Kyle?" Aaron asked.

"He's having dinner at Chris' tonight."

Aaron nodded. "I remember." He peered at his watch. "I need another hour, and then I'll head home." He pulled his wife to him.

I glanced away, letting them have their private moment to say good-bye. But also because seeing their intimacy reminded me of what I was lacking. Never before had seeing any of the couples I worked for embracing one another or spending time with their children caused me to ache in a way that I couldn't explain.

Not before that moment.

Mia, a voice whispered in my mind. I curled my hands into fists at my side while mentally calculating the distance between her and me. It would be another few hours, at least, before I could even video chat with her. And those calls were becoming less satisfying by the day.

"Bye, Mr. Brutus." Stasi waved while Patience held onto her other hand.

Andreas also said good-bye, but his twin, Thiers, stopped in front of me. He looked up at me with those earnest eyes of his. "Sorry for hitting you, Mr. Brutus. I didn't mean it. I just wanted to practice."

Even as I crouched down, I still loomed over him by a few inches. "No worries, little guy. You just need to learn when and where to harness what you've learned. Got it?"

He nodded and gave me a small smile before waving again to his dad and running to catch up with the rest of the family.

I stood and turned to face Aaron, who stared at the empty doorway. Pride filled his gaze, and while most people wouldn't call his expression friendly, I knew the difference between a brooding Aaron Townsend and a satisfied one.

"Do they give your life a new purpose?" The question came out before I thought better of it.

I barely realized I'd even said it aloud until Aaron's gaze settled on me like a weight on a stack of papers.

His eyes narrowed and he tilted his head to the side.

"Never—"

"You have a woman," he responded, too damn perceptively for my liking.

Though his expression didn't change much, his hazel eyes lit up a bit.

"What?"

"You're seeing someone," he continued as he approached. "And it's serious." His hands slid into his pockets. The same move I'd seen him do hundreds of times in business meetings when he knew he had a rival cornered.

"Aaron," Joshua Townsend, his younger brother, suddenly interrupted with a knock on the open door. Josh paused, glancing between the two of us. "What's happening?"

Aaron kept his attention on me but answered, "Brutus has a woman."

"No shit." I heard the laughter in Joshua's voice without needing to look at him. "What's her name?"

He barged into Aaron's office and sat in one of the chairs across from his desk. He patted the other chair, presumably for me to sit.

I folded my arms across my chest and glared at both men. "We need to finalize the plan for the gala."

For the first time since his family left, a slight smile tilted the corner of Aaron's mouth.

"Hell no," Joshua spoke up. "You're not getting out of this conversation that easily. Who is she? What's she like? Do you have a picture?"

I had literally hundreds of pictures in my phone from our time in Mexico. Not to mention the pictures she sent me almost daily from her days in Colombia. My fingers itched to pull my phone out of my pocket so that I could look at her smile.

"Is she the reason you extended your time in Mexico?" Aaron asked.

Fuck. He wasn't the CEO of Townsend Industries by being anyone's fool.

"Maybe."

"Hell, yeah." Joshua clapped his hands, his green eyes sparkling with interest. "Wait," Josh said, turning to his brother. "He just told you he had a girlfriend?"

Aaron shook his head slightly. "He asked if my wife and kids gave my life a new purpose."

Joshua's eyes widened as he turned back to me. He whistled low. "Damn, this is serious. What's her name?"

"Mia," I answered before I could catch myself.

"Who's Mia?"

I turned to find the youngest Townsend brother, Tyler, entering the office. "Hey, Brutus," he called out with a wave.

"You'll never believe this," Josh said, standing.

"What? Kayla finally smartened up and left your ass for someone younger with more money?" Tyler joked.

Joshua's face darkened. He appeared utterly different from the joking, lighthearted manner of just a few seconds earlier.

"You think that shit is funny?" Joshua looked as if he wanted to knock his brother on his ass.

Tyler just chuckled. "No, but I still love getting a reaction from you."

"Yeah, the shit is real funny until I remind you that your wife is probably receiving emails from men who listen to her podcast as we speak."

Now it was Tyler's turn to frown. His face became downright stormy. "Don't mention my wife."

Aaron grunted. "How did you meet Mia?" he asked, bringing the attention back to me.

Tyler and Joshua eyed one another for a few more beats before directing their gazes my way. Previously, I would've said they were crazy as fuck for being so damned serious about their wives. Neither one of them were in danger of losing their spouse. Everyone knew how obsessed these men were with the women in their lives.

A man would have to be insane to think he could even attempt to get next to one of the Townsend women. I'd seen firsthand what happened when more than one man had tried.

"Screw that," Tyler said. "I want to see a picture."

"No." I shook my head.

"Come on, man," Joshua tacked on. "We share almost our entire lives with you."

"Because I need to know everything to protect you all."

"And that you do so well," Tyler said. "Let's see a picture."

The urge to take out my phone overcame me. Truthfully, I didn't mind showing them a picture of Mia. I wanted to show her off to someone.

Without too much hesitation, I found myself with my phone in hand pulling up a picture of Mia and me on the day we went snorkeling. In the photo, Mia grinned that effervescent smile of hers. I had my arm draped around her while we sat with our backs to the beach. Behind us, the sun was setting.

"Holy shit," Tyler said as he passed the phone to Joshua. He peered at me. "You've got it bad."

Joshua whistled again as he gave the phone to Aaron. "She's beautiful."

"And you look like a kid in a candy shop," Tyler added. "Hell, she makes you look a little less scary."

I snorted.

Aaron lifted his eyebrows half an inch. There was a glint in his eyes, though. "New purpose, huh?" He nodded.

"My phone," I said with my hand outstretched.

As soon as he handed it back to me, I took it. I couldn't help but stare down at the picture. In it, I wasn't even looking at the camera. I was staring at her. I trailed my thumb over Mia's face, remembering that day vividly.

Tyler's phone rang. "Speaking of purpose," he said before answering. "Babe, you'll never guess what happened," he started.

I could tell by his tone alone that it was Destiny, his wife, on the other end of the phone.

"Brutus is in love," he blurted into the phone, then laughed. "Yes, I'm serious."

I grunted and shook my head. All of the women in the family would know my damn business by the end of the day. These assholes didn't keep secrets from their wives. Not that I wanted Mia to be a secret.

It was that talking about her while she was so far away started to make me resent my job in a way that I never had before.

"That's an excellent idea." Tyler's eyes widened with excitement. He looked around the room before his gaze landed on me. "Destiny says you should bring her to the gala."

I damn near choked on my own spit. "I'm working the gala."

"You don't have to."

My eyebrows almost touched the top of my head to hear Aaron make such a statement.

He merely shrugged when I glared at him. "We have most of the details finalized. You have all of your staff in place."

"Right?" Joshua added. "This is like the hundred thousandth gala you've worked for us. We all know how it goes, and so does the rest of your staff. You can just supervise if there's an issue, but otherwise you might as well be there as a guest."

He looked between his two brothers as if the final decision was theirs.

"That doesn't make any damn sense," I pushed back.

"Makes total sense," Tyler said. "No, don't worry, baby. We'll convince him to bring her," he said to Destiny. "Love you."

He hung up and looked at me expectedly. "You can't let my wife down."

"She doesn't even know I work for you all," I told them.

"She'll find out soon enough." Joshua slapped me on the shoulder. "I'm looking forward to meeting the woman who captured your heart."

I started to wonder what Mia would look like in a gown. She would be back home a few weeks before the gala.

"Make it happen already," Tyler insisted.

I looked between the three of them. All of them wore welcoming expressions. Well, Aaron's was as close to welcoming as I'd ever seen.

"I need to make sure she's free that night," I hedged. Truthfully, it didn't feel like a horrible idea at all. I could easily picture Mia on my arm at any event. I wanted her on my arm. But I didn't know how the hell I would balance being as attentive to her as I wanted—as she deserved—and keeping an eye on all of the security details.

"I'll figure it out," I mumbled.

Joshua and Tyler chuckled and patted me on the back.

"I'll be in my office for another hour if you need anything," I told them before heading out.

When I exited Aaron's outer office, my phone buzzed. I pulled it out to see a text from Jameson.

Jameson: **Mia just checked out of her AirBnb.**

She checked out three weeks earlier than she was scheduled to. As I took the elevator down to my office, I wondered what that was about. Jameson had done a great job of staying out of sight, while also keeping tabs on Mia. It was the next best thing to me being there, I supposed. Though, I worried about her all the same.

I planned to call her as soon as I was back in my office.

But when I stepped off of the elevator, I already had a text message from Mia.

Mia: **I decided to return home early.**

A smile I hadn't smiled in weeks touched my lips.

CHAPTER 14

Mia

I couldn't take it anymore. That rational part of my mind constantly told me I was behaving like a lovesick puppy ... no matter how much I tried to tell myself that the reason I was returning home a whole three weeks ahead of schedule was simply because I missed sleeping in my own bed.

And to finally get started with my plan to open my coffee shop.

Those were part of the reason. But the main one was because I missed Brutus. And I was terrified.

Scared as hell that maybe what we shared had only lasted in Mexico. And over the phone. But what about once we were back in the real world? Would the fantasy evaporate?

Those unanswered questions spiraled inside of my mind and spurred me to end my sabbatical weeks earlier than I had planned. I had learned much of what I needed for my café. I connected with a few distributors who could ship products to Williamsport. My last few weeks were intended for relaxation and sightseeing anyway.

But it didn't seem as tempting without Brutus beside me.

So, as I stood on the sidewalk outside of the busy Williamsport

Airport, wringing my hands, waiting for my ride, I couldn't help but feel jumpy.

My phone beeped.

Brutus: **Pulling around the corner now.**

I looked up to see a large, dark SUV with the license plate number he'd texted me, pulling around the bend from the airport's entrance. Even without knowing the license and the physical description of the car, I would've known it belonged to Brutus.

It was large, sleek, and intimidating just like its owner. He pulled up directly in front of me and hopped out.

On instinct, I bent over, lowering the handle of my suitcase to lift it into the car's trunk. But strong hands wrapped around my waist, stopping me.

"What are you doing?" His deep, warm voice filled the air around me, and I unconsciously let out a sigh. "Give me that," he said without waiting, quickly taking my suitcase and shoulder bag from my hands.

I turned to face him. "Hi."

His smile widened and he lowered, brushing his lips against mine. Another sigh spilled from my lips. I heard some sort of noise, but was too focused on Brutus when he wrapped both of his arms around me for a deeper kiss.

PDA hadn't really been my thing in the past. I was more of a kiss on the cheek, maybe a little hand holding here and there, kind of woman. But standing there in front of the airport as who knows how many people passed around us, I didn't give one iota of a damn about anything else except his kiss.

"Hey, baby," he said when he pulled back from the kiss. "Welcome home."

A lump in my throat formed.

Home.

That word was so layered. I loved Williamsport. It was where my family lived, where I grew up and spent most of the years of my life. Yet, I also feared that home would be the very thing that brought my dream down to Earth. My fear of yet another crash and burn relationship that went nowhere loomed in the back of my mind.

Brutus took my hand and opened the passenger side door for me.

"I'll put these in the back," he said while lifting my bags to take them toward the back of the car.

I fiddled with the small pocketbook I still carried. Those butterflies that happened whenever I was around him fluttered in my belly.

As soon as Brutus climbed in behind the wheel, he took my hand into his. He lifted it to his lips and kissed each knuckle.

"Are you hungry?"

I nodded. "I didn't eat much on the flight." I bit my tongue, just shy of telling him that I was too nervous on the last leg of my flight to see him face to face.

He grunted. "Damn airlines," he griped as he expertly pulled into traffic with one hand on the wheel and the other still wrapped around mine, "and their delays. We'll get you something to eat."

I smiled at the little frown marring his lips. I should've been home hours ago. But multiple delays of my first flight caused me to miss my second flight. As it was, I had to stay overnight in Mexico City. I had planned to be back home a whole twenty-four hours earlier, but I hadn't gotten into Williamsport until after six that evening.

"I'll make you something," Brutus continued.

I started to ask him what he planned when his phone went off. He had to release my hand to check his phone. He frowned but didn't respond to the message.

"Work," he grunted out.

"Welcome home," I mumbled.

*　*　*

I turned to Brutus after he cut the car's engine off. "You know this isn't my home address, right?"

He smirked, and my stomach muscles tightened.

"You're hungry," he replied as if that was an appropriate answer. "I have a kitchen full of food. Let's get you fed." He didn't wait for me to respond before he got out of the car and strolled around to my side.

I rolled my eyes at the way he completely took over my plans.

Similar to how he had in Mexico. The tenant I'd rented my house to wouldn't be gone until the following week. I made plans to stay with my sister for the next week. Or at a hotel, if that became too much. I supposed Brutus had other ideas.

"You know I thought you meant stopping at McDonald's or something when you mentioned food," I told him as he helped me out of the car.

A deep V appeared between his eyebrows. "Baby, you don't actually believe I would feed you fucking McDonald's after hours of travel and weeks away from home, do you?"

Home.

There was that word again. I was sure he meant home as in the city where I lived, but standing there in front of his Tudor-style house, it felt almost as if he meant something more.

I focused instead on the house with its steeply pitched gable roof, stone siding, and masonry chimney. The home was large, at least four thousand square feet, which made sense. Brutus didn't do small.

"I've got sparkling water, freshly made iced tea, bottled water, and probably some sports drinks," he said as we entered through the wooden door.

"Iced tea sounds good," I said, glancing around.

He led me to a spacious kitchen. The inside of his home was completely different from its exterior. While the outside was a style from the late nineteenth century, the interior was a more contemporary design with its sleek countertops and appliances.

"Mm. This is delicious," I said after taking a sip of the iced tea.

"Brewed it this morning before work," he said with a smile. "Let me give you a tour while the oven warms up."

He turned on the oven before taking me by the hand. The house looked even bigger on the inside than it did from the outside. The main floor held the living room, dining area that was off from the kitchen, and a den, along with a full and half bathroom. Upstairs were three additional rooms, one the master bedroom, one for guests, and a third room that Brutus had turned into an at-home office.

"Downstairs is the entertainment room and the gym," he said as we came back down the stairs.

A buzzer sounded. "Time to warm up the eggplant parmesan," he said.

I sat on one of the black stools on the opposite end of the kitchen island, watching him. I slowly started to recognize that he probably had to have his kitchen and entire home outfitted to accommodate his size so easily. He moved fluidly around the kitchen like he was a natural.

I cocked my head to the side. "How come you never cooked for me in Mexico?"

He spun toward me, grinning. "I was on vacation."

I laughed. "Touché." I held up the glass of iced tea and took a sip.

"Plus, that kitchen was too small. This one gives me enough room to fit around it comfortably."

"Did you have it designed that way?" I asked.

He nodded as he slid his hand out of the oven mitt he used to put the eggplant parmesan in the oven. "Should be ready in about twenty minutes."

His phone buzzed once more. He flipped it over and frowned again before turning it back over.

"If you need to answer that, I don't mind," I told him.

"Come here," he said, rounding the island and lifting me to stand. Instead of mentioning anything about the phone, he cupped my face and devoured my lips.

The kiss nearly washed away all of my trepidations and worries. I wrapped my arms around his neck and lifted on my tiptoes, needing more of him. I spent weeks missing this feeling, and I wanted to soak it all in even if it might not last long-term.

"Baby, if you keep kissing me like that, you'll never get to have your dinner," Brutus said against my lips.

Both of us panted from the kiss.

I briefly closed my eyes and swallowed. "You're right." Taking a step back, I reminded myself to calm my runaway emotions.

When I looked back up at Brutus he was frowning.

"What's the matter?" he asked, a wrinkle on his forehead. "I wasn't putting a stop button on anything. I want to devour you whole, but I need to make sure you're fed first."

I sat back on the stool and turned away from him, again wringing my hands. I wasn't typically a shy or uncertain person, but these feelings I had for him had me feeling all off kilter.

"Look at me," Brutus said. But before he could continue, his phone buzzed again.

"You need to get that," I told him.

"It's fine." He never took his gaze off of me. "What's wrong?"

I shook my head before answering. "I just … what if we're rushing things?"

"Rushing?" he repeated as if it were a foreign word. "Rushing would've been me carrying my ass down to Colombia to bring you back home with me, kicking and screaming."

I let out an unintentional laugh. "You wouldn't have done that."

He gave me a stern look. "I had half a mind. The only thing that kept me from going crazy was how busy I was with work."

"Speaking of …" I trailed off and peered at his phone again.

"It's nothing." He stepped closer and pulled me, stool and all, closer to him. He dipped his head, diving in for another kiss. The idea of denying him or turning my head away didn't even come to mind. I guessed we'd have to table that conversation for another time.

Brutus slid his hand down my back and underneath the blouse I wore. Warmth spread through my belly at the feel of his fingers brushing against my skin.

"It smells good in here. What are you cooking?" a gruff, male voice interrupted.

Brutus whipped his head around. "Dad, what the hell?" he growled.

I stood and peeked around Brutus.

His father was instantly recognizable from the few video calls we'd exchanged while in Mexico. Brutus got his height and his build from his father.

"Mr. Kennedy," I greeted with my hand extended. "Nice to meet you in person."

Rick Kennedy frowned. "What the hell is with the Mr. Kennedy bullshit?" He grunted. "Come here, gal."

I gasped in surprise when he pulled me in for a hug. Then I laughed.

"I knew you would be back in town before those two months were up," he said. He turned and slapped Brutus on his shoulder. "I told you she couldn't stay away from ya."

Brutus' annoyed expression didn't let up. "Why are you here?" His voice was low but full of contempt.

"What the hell do you mean what am I doing in here? I live here," Rick said, looking appalled Brutus would even ask.

"You live in the guesthouse on the other end of my property."

"So what? I'm not allowed in the main house?" Rick turned to me. "Gave him half of my DNA and that's how he fucking treats me." He tutted and shook his head. "I saw your car in the driveway," he told Brutus, turning to him again, "and wondered what had brought you home so early. For a second, I thought the Townsends fired you, but we know they'd all be lost without you. The last time we played golf, Robert went on and on about how invaluable you are to them."

"Townsends?" I asked, looking between them.

"Yeah," Rick answered quickly. "He told you who he worked for, right? Hey," he continued, not bothering to wait for an answer, "what are you cooking? It smells delicious."

"That's for us," Brutus growled. "You've already had dinner."

"You can stay," I said, squeezing Brutus' arm. "Brutus made eggplant parmesan."

"Hot damn!" Rick declared. "That was one of your mama's best recipes," he said to Brutus. "She only made it once for me, but I remember it being good."

At that, the buzzer for the oven went off.

"Perfect timing," Rick said with a beaming smile. He took it upon himself to slide on the oven mitt and remove the casserole dish from the oven.

"What the hell—"

"It's okay," I said, tugging on Brutus' arm.

"He's interrupting," he said to me.

"He's your dad and he wants to have dinner with us," I told him.

His face softened.

"Ah, don't let my son bother you none," Rick said. "He might look scary as all hell …" He paused, a wrinkle in his brow. "Nah, he *is* scary, too. But for you," Rick pointed at me, "he's a damn teddy bear."

Laughing, I wrapped my arms around Brutus' waist. "I kind of figured."

"Yeah, you've got him wrapped around that pinky finger of yours," Rick continued while setting out three plates and serving up spoonfuls of the eggplant. "You might have to contend, some, with that job of his. He's like me in that way."

"Like you?" I asked at the same time Brutus made a noise at the back of his throat.

"A workaholic. That's why none of my relationships lasted. I never had time for anyone. Not for the long haul anyway. Who wants to be stuck with a man who can get called away for hours or days on end?"

Rick continued to talk as he brought the plates over to the kitchen island. All the while, Brutus grew stiffer in my arms.

"That's probably why his mama never told me about him. She didn't think I would make time for him while he was young."

"That's enough," Brutus said harshly.

Rick finally stopped talking, a stunned expression on his face, like he hadn't noticed how uncomfortable his son grew the entire time he spoke. He slid one of the plates in front of me along with a fork and a napkin.

My stomach growled as soon as the smell of melted mozzarella and tomato sauce hit my nose.

"Let's eat," Brutus said, but his phone ringing punctuated his last word. Instead of ignoring it, he answered brusquely, "What?"

I watched as his eyebrows spiked.

A curse ripped from his throat. "Where are they? I'll be there in ten."

My heart rate kicked up at the seriousness in his voice.

"Problem?" Rick asked.

Brutus looked at his father. "Code black."

"Holy hell," Rick replied, looking worried.

"I have to go," Brutus said, cupping my face.

"Okay, I can catch an Uber over to my sister's."

"No." He shook his head adamantly. "You'll stay here. Rick will keep you company until I get back." He looked over at his father, who nodded.

"Sure will."

"Take your time and enjoy dinner. I'll be back as soon as I can."

He kissed me firmly before pulling back. When he did, I saw regret in his eyes. He looked as if this situation was tearing him in two. He didn't want to go, and he felt guilty because he felt obligated.

"It's okay," I whispered.

He visibly swallowed before releasing me. I watched him grab his keys, give me one final look, and then head out the door.

I turned to Rick, who, surprisingly, stared worriedly in the direction his son had just left.

"What's code black?"

Rick's expression was grim. "One of the Townsend kids is missing."

CHAPTER 15

Brutus

I made it to Joshua and Kayla's house in under fifteen minutes.

"Where the hell is my son?" Joshua fumed at one of my staff as I entered the door. At least ten members of my security, along with all of Joshua's brothers, were there. Their wives had remained home with the children, but I watched Kayla sniffling on the phone and knew she was probably on the phone with her sisters-in-law.

"Brutus," she called as soon as she saw me. "He's here. I have to go."

Her eyes were red-rimmed, and my heart constricted in my chest. Hot anger rushed through me.

"What happened?" I asked Joshua and Kayla.

Joshua held Kayla, who leaned on him for support.

"Nothing," Kayla answered. "It was a normal night. I put the kids to bed and said goodnight to them. A few hours later, I went up to peek in on their rooms like I always do, and—" She broke off.

"Cole was gone. He'd remade his bed," Josh gritted out. "How the hell could someone get in or out with our alarm system?" he demanded to know.

"I already checked your security system. No one got in," I told them. With pinched lips, I took the tablet Bernie handed me and pulled up their security system's cameras. "Cole got out," I said grimly.

Cole was the couple's nine-year-old adopted son. He'd been with them for a little over eighteen months.

"Mommy."

All of the adults turned toward the staircase. There stood eight-year-old Victoria, the couple's firstborn daughter.

"What's wrong? Where's Cole?" she asked, rubbing her eyes.

Kayla rushed over to her, whispering something to her daughter.

"Where the hell is my son, Brutus?" Joshua demanded to know once Kayla carried Victoria back upstairs.

"We've got eyes out looking for him," I assured.

"That's not good enough. He's nine, and he shouldn't be out at night by himself." Joshua's stormy face told the depths of his fear.

"We've checked the school, most of his friend's homes, the park he likes to go to," I told him. My men were out prowling the neighborhood searching for the boy. "I need you to tell me if anything happened that might've pushed him to run away."

"Of course not!" he yelled.

His reaction didn't startle or anger me. If it were my son out there, God only knew where, I'd probably have a worse reaction.

"Son, calm down," Robert Townsend urged. He squeezed Joshua's shoulder. "We need clear heads if we're going to figure out where Cole went."

Joshua blinked, and then looked over at me. "The shelter?"

"What about it?" I asked while pulling out my phone.

"He mentioned something about it tonight at dinner." Josh shook his head. "He was quiet, and Kay asked him if something had happened at school. He said no, but before bed, he asked me something about the shelter." Josh thought for a moment. "He asked how far it was from here. Then asked how long it would take to walk from here. Fuck," Josh broke off, his voice becoming thick with emotion.

I used the locator app on my phone to map out the distance between Josh's home and the shelter that Cole once lived at. Uneasiness coursed through me when I realized it was over fifteen miles from the house.

"I'll call over there to let them know to be on alert. I'm on my way there now," I told Josh.

"I'll go with you."

"No," I insisted, stopping him.

"I'm not fucking staying here," he insisted.

"Listen," I persisted. "I know you want Cole home. I'll find him before the night is over. But you need to be here for Kayla, Victoria, and Alec," I said, mentioning their youngest son. "And for Cole. If he comes back on his own and you're not here …" I trailed off.

A bleak look appeared in Joshua's gaze. His helplessness was palpable.

"Look," I said, getting closer. "Ordinarily, I wouldn't try to stop you from coming, but in this case, it might do more harm than good. You need to be here with your family. Let me do my job."

"Bring him home."

"Already done," I assured before heading out of the door. I'd been in constant contact with my staff ever since I got the call that Cole was missing. My guys had scoured all the places we knew he had recent contact with. Joseph already related to me that some of Cole's clothes and his backpack were missing. Which meant the boy had left with intentions of staying away for a while if not permanently.

I made it to the foster care center where he'd lived right before Kayla and Joshua took him in. The main office was closed, but I'd had Joseph call ahead to wake up one of the social workers.

As I got out of the car to approach the brick building, an older woman was already waiting for me outside of the main door.

"You're looking for that little boy?" she asked, a pinch in between her brows. She wore the skeptical expression of a seasoned social worker who didn't intimidate easily. "Mr. Townsend contacted me."

I didn't bother to ask which Townsend she spoke with. That name carried weight, which was why she was up late, waiting for me.

"I'm looking for Cole Townsend." I showed her a photo of the boy on my phone screen.

She studied the picture, then shook her head. "He hasn't been here today."

"Are you sure?" I studied her and noticed when she took a slight step backward. "What aren't you telling me?"

The fear that entered her eyes let me know she was withholding something. Whether or not that something was relevant to Cole's disappearance would need to be seen.

"Ms. Fairchild." I stared, watching how her eyes widened. I assumed her surprise was from the fact I knew her name, though she hadn't offered it. "I just promised a family that I would bring their son home before the night was out. A nine-year-old boy who should not be out at night by himself. If there's something you're not telling me, I suggest you come out with it."

I stepped closer, crowding her space. That was when I smelled the alcohol on her breath. "It would be in your best interest to start talking. Now."

"I-I haven't seen him." Her gaze skirted away from me. "But …"

"Keep talking."

"I haven't made my rounds tonight. I, um, got sidetracked with paperwork."

I grunted. "Paperwork or a bottle of Jack Daniels?"

She gasped, and then scowled at me. "You don't know me. You have no idea what it's like working with these kids."

"I know it's your damn job to watch over them. To protect them." I made a disgusted sound at the back of my throat before brushing past her. I didn't push her, but my sudden movement caused her to stumble out of my way.

I barged through the main entrance of the home.

"Hey, you're not authorized to go in there."

"Shut the fuck up," I spun and growled at her. That instantly made her close her mouth.

I moved past the main entrance counter, noting the empty front chair. The halls were clear, so I chose to check each door, even if it was closed. I was as quiet as possible, hating to disturb the children, many of whom I knew suffered from their traumas. Out of the ten rooms, a few children slept, and some were still awake. But Cole wasn't in any of the rooms.

A hunch told me that this home was relevant to Cole's disappearance.

"Are these the only rooms?" I asked the woman, who continued to follow me. She suddenly had an interest in checking in on all of the children that stayed there.

"Yes."

I eyed her, discerning if she was telling the truth or not. When I decided she was, I headed toward the exit. Instead of climbing back into my car, I went with my gut and decided to check around the perimeter. Behind the home was a thick copse of trees that separated the home from a small neighborhood.

I followed a trail that led directly from the home, through the trees, and to the closed off end of the neighborhood. The lit streetlights allowed me to see enough into the distance to spot a park about a hundred feet from the clearing of the trees. In the park, on a swing, I could make out a shadowy figure.

My feet started moving before I fully deciphered the scene in front of me. The figure was too small to be an adult, and my gut screamed that this was Cole. When I got to within about ten feet, he looked up from the swing.

"Hi, Mr. Brutus," he said with his dark hoodie still covering his head.

"We've been looking for you."

He dropped his head and kicked a small rock underneath his foot.

I started to sit on the swing next to him but then thought better of it. Instead, I crouched low, directly in front of him. "How did you get out here?"

His blue eyes met mine. In his eyes, I could see years' worth of pain. I had to force myself not to show the anger that welled up in me. He wasn't even ten years old and had already seen more than any child deserved to see. I'd watched him open up little by little in the year and a half since Kayla and Joshua adopted him.

But he continued to carry the memories of what he went through before he made it to the Townsends.

"I saved up some of my allowances and walked out to the main street to catch a cab."

I blinked. That was so damned old school. I didn't think a kid his age would even think of it. Most would've turned to an app on their phone to call an Uber or something, which would've made tracing him a hell of a lot easier.

"I didn't want to wait for them to say good-bye." He kicked another rock. "I hate good-byes," he murmured.

"For who to say good-bye?"

He lifted his eyes to meet mine. "Mom and Dad." He shrugged, like I should've known the answer to my question.

"Why would you need to say good-bye?"

"Not me." He shook his head. "Them." He paused and turned his head away from me. I could see water welling up in his eyes.

"Cole, what is it? Your parents are worried sick about you."

"They don't have to be, okay? I know they're getting rid of me soon. So I bailed before they had to do it."

I stood, confused. "Joshua and Kayla aren't kicking you out. Is that what you thought?"

He swallowed. "It's been over a year. I've never stayed with a family longer than a year. They'll probably want a real kid soon. That's what all the other foster moms wanted, the ones who didn't keep me—" His voice broke off, but he sucked in a breath to prevent the sob from spilling out.

My eyelids drifted closed, and I took a deep inhale. I needed to control my anger. The last thing I wanted was for Cole to mistake my rage at the foster families in his past for being upset with him.

"Cole," I stated, crouching low again, "your parents love you. They aren't now or ever going to get rid of you."

"They could. Sean told me his parents got rid of his adopted brother because he had too many mental problems. They sent him to live with another family. And I get angry sometimes. Last week

Victoria and I got into a fight because I got mad at her for touching my stuff. Mom sent us both to our rooms."

"That's normal kid stuff. Your mom would never kick you out over an argument with your sister. Have you ever asked your dad how many fights he got into with his brothers growing up?"

He speared me with his gaze. "Dad fought with my uncles?"

Grinning, I nodded. "I didn't know them when they were kids, but I bet they got into some knock down drag out fights. And your grandparents never kicked them out, did they?"

"Probably not."

"There's no probably about it," I responded. I opened my mouth to tell him how worried his parents were when my phone rang. "I bet that's them," I said, pulling out my phone.

Sure enough, it was Joshua coming through with a video call. When I answered, the screen lit up, showing both an anxious-looking Kayla and Joshua.

"Did you find him?"

"We haven't heard from you."

They both spoke at once.

"He's right here." I looked at Cole. "Your parents want to talk to you."

I handed him the phone.

"Baby."

"Son."

Again, Joshua and Kayla spoke in unison.

"Where are you? We were scared to death when we saw you weren't in your room," Kayla told him.

"I'm sorry. I didn't mean to scare you. I..." He trailed off.

"It's okay, Cole," I encouraged, patting his leg.

"I didn't think you wanted me anymore, so I came back to the home." He looked over into the distance in the direction of the home, which couldn't be seen from the park. "But I couldn't go in," he confessed. "I don't want to go back there."

He finally let the first tear slip out. He broke down crying, confessing that he didn't want to leave them, but he thought they'd eventually take him back anyway.

I swallowed the lump in my throat for any child that had felt so unwanted and unloved. It pissed me off to know there were adults in this world who treated children like this. I listened while Kayla and Joshua continually told Cole how much they loved him, how much of a part of their family he was, and that there wasn't anything he could do to make them abandon him.

"I'll take you home," I said, holding out my hand for him to take, even as he remained on the call with his parents.

They stayed on the phone with him the entire drive, constantly reassuring him. I squeezed and loosened my grip on the steering wheel as I listened to Cole tell them how sorry he was for his tantrums.

Truthfully, it wasn't anything out of the ordinary. Especially for a child with the history Cole had. But somewhere along the line, this little boy had been taught that his normal, human emotions were unacceptable. And therefore, he was unsuitable.

A raw memory, one I thought I'd long suppressed, shot through my mind. It was so damn vivid that it stole my breath. For a half a second I became that scared eight-year-old boy I once was.

The only thing that brought me back to the present was hearing Kayla promise to make Cole whatever he wanted for breakfast. That was followed up by Joshua telling Cole that just because he got a special breakfast, didn't mean he wouldn't be grounded for the next three weeks.

When I glanced over, instead of a frown, I saw that Cole wore a semi-smile. Being grounded sucked for most kids, but for a boy who'd been thrown away, ignored, and mistreated, being grounded demonstrated that his parents cared about him.

This was all the more evident when as soon as I pulled into Josh and Kayla's driveway, their front door flew open. Kayla ran down the walkway, immediately scooping Cole up into her arms. Josh followed, hugging both of them to him.

The rest of the Townsend clan filed out of the house, one by one. Robert Townsend patted me on the shoulder.

"Thank you."

I could've sworn I saw wetness in his eyes, but he abruptly turned from me. He went over to Cole and kissed the boy on the head before whispering something in his ear.

"I'm sorry, Grandfather," Cole said, still firmly held in Kayla's arms.

Robert ruffled his hair and then gave me another nod of appreciation before heading to his chauffeured vehicle. Robert lived the farthest away, but it was less than a ten-minute drive back to Townsend Manor. Aaron, Carter, and Tyler lived within walking distance and soon made their exits as well, after ensuring that Cole was all right.

Once I checked and rechecked the security cameras and codes for all of the Townsend homes, I started for my car.

"Brutus," Joshua called out.

I turned just in time for him to wrap me up in a hug. I stiffened, surprised by the embrace. But then I returned it.

"Thank you. I don't know what …" He sighed, running a hand through his hair. "Thank you."

"Go be with your son."

He nodded, and Kayla, still holding onto Cole like she would never let him go, nodded my way. I returned the nod before climbing back into my car.

The only person I wanted to see was the woman I'd left in my kitchen. I just hoped she would be there once I returned.

CHAPTER 16

Brutus

Don't let her leave.

That was the message I'd texted my father right after I left my house to head to Joshua and Kayla's. I suppressed the guilt I felt having to run out on her like that. Especially since she just returned from Colombia. Jameson's warnings about the nature of our jobs flooded me.

Loathe as I was to admit it, he was right. I didn't work the typical nine-to-five. And the hours I worked were often erratic and seemingly never ending. That could cause havoc on any relationship. Let alone one as new as ours.

But I wasn't about to give Mia up. Not when we were just getting started.

I entered my front door and expelled a breath when I saw Mia emerge from down the hallway. Behind her was my father.

Her smile caused a reduction in the invisible band of pressure around my chest. She stopped a few feet from me, her eyes searching mine. I stood there, mesmerized by the fact that she was in my home. For the first time that I could recall, I looked forward to getting home at the end of a work shift or situation with the job.

"Looks like I'm no longer needed," my father said, his voice breaking the silence.

I gave him a short nod before he did the same. He patted Mia on the shoulder. "Pleasure to finally meet you. We'll have to finish that movie another time."

She let out a little laugh that sent a shockwave up my spine. "I knew you were a romantic, Mr. Rick. There's no fooling me."

I watched their exchange. My father tossed his hands up in a surrendering fashion. "Guilty as charged. Who knew Nicholas Sparks could write so well."

"Only everyone on the planet," Mia quickly retorted.

"What do they know?" My father headed toward the kitchen that led to the backdoor and the path to the guesthouse.

"What was that about?" I asked, approaching Mia. I let my hands skim up the sides of her body before cupping her by the waist.

"Your dad liked *The Notebook*."

I blinked and looked from her to the door where my father just exited. "Excuse me?"

She guffawed. "It's true. I think I saw him wipe away a few tears."

"Now that I don't believe." I snorted to keep from laughing as I pulled her into a hug.

I wrapped my arms around her lush body, reveling in the way she felt pressed against me. When she folded her arms around my shoulders, I let out a sigh. Everything about that moment felt right—more right than even returning Cole Townsend to his parents.

"Are you okay?" Mia asked, pressing a hand to my chest.

"I am now."

"You don't have to tell me the details, but the child ..." She didn't finish the question. The concern in her eyes called to me. I rarely, if ever, spoke about my job or the family I worked for with anyone. Especially not with the women I dated. But Mia wasn't any ordinary woman.

She was my wife.

Sometime between our time in Mexico and that very moment, I determined that she would be my wife. My life partner, the one I would have children with, go to sleep next to me at night and wake up the next morning. And as much as I was known for keeping secrets, not speaking, I had to force myself to bite down on the urge to claim her out loud.

She'd literally just returned home a few hours earlier. I would have to wait some time before I sprung the inevitable on her.

"He's fine. Home safe," I answered.

She let out a breath as if she'd been worried about it since I left hours ago. "Well ..." her eyes drifted to something over my shoulder, "it's late and you're probably tired. If you want me to call an Uber ..." Her voice trailed off when she caught the incredulous expression on my face.

"An Uber for what?" My voice came out eerily calm.

"To take me home."

Why did that feel like a spear to the heart? At least, what I imagined a spear to the heart to feel like.

This is your home.

I clamped down on my tongue for a beat to prevent that comment from slipping out. "Stay with me tonight," I told her instead.

Her eyes ballooned for a split second.

"It's too late to disturb your sister's family at this hour." Obviously, I wasn't beyond using guilt to convince her to stay with me. Her home wasn't available, and she'd told me about her plan to stay at her sister's until her tenant's lease ended.

Her lips parted, and I could see the spark of refusal in her eyes.

"And don't even think of trying to find a hotel to stay at," I insisted.

"You're tired." Her hand smoothed against my chest.

My entire body warmed, and I wondered if she even knew the effect her slight touches had on me.

"And?"

"You need to get some rest. If I'm here—"

"I'll sleep better with you next to me," I said before dipping low and hauling her in my arms.

The gasp of surprise she let out had my cock stirring in my pants.

"Let's take a shower," I said as I carried her up the stairs.

* * *

Mia

In a million years I would never get used to Brutus picking me up like I weighed the amount of a loaf of bread. But damn, it felt good, too.

The voice at the back of my mind continued to whisper words of doubt and fear. I wondered if we could really make this work. Brutus' job was obviously very important to him and took priority over everything. As someone who once lived like that, I didn't know if I could commit to playing second fiddle in someone's life.

Ironic?

Hell, yeah.

I was being a hypocrite. Men in my past had asked, some even demanded, that I put my job on the back burner and make our relationship a priority. No, that wasn't completely honest. They wanted me to make *them* the main concern in my life. When I refused, the relationship quickly ended.

"Are you really doing this?" I asked when Brutus lowered me to the floor to stand in the middle of his bathroom. The bathroom in his massive master bedroom. I became too preoccupied with the room around us to listen to his answer to my question.

The bathroom was almost as large as the bedroom. At the center sat a ginormous, chrome, free-standing bathtub. Seriously, the thing looked almost big enough to do a damn lap in. The black marble tile spread throughout the flooring of the bathroom. On the far wall, about six feet beyond the bathtub was a chrome shower system mounted to the wall and overhead.

The flooring transitioned from tile to stone resin that dipped down at the center towards a drain. The design was a doorless shower to minimize water spray but not for privacy.

"Seriously?" I spun around, watching Brutus, who was now shirtless.

He approached with a wrinkle in his brow. "Care to elaborate?" he asked at the same time he reached for the waistband of my shirt.

Mindlessly, I lifted my arms, allowing him to undress me. "You went to Mexico for a vacation when you have a bathroom like this?" I glanced around the glorious room again before my eyes landed on him. "If I owned a bathroom like this, I would never leave."

Brutus went entirely still. He looked as if I'd sucked all the air out of the room. I replayed my words again, trying to figure out what I'd said to garner that reaction. I couldn't figure it out.

"You don't have to leave." His voice was low but there was an earnestness in them that I couldn't shake.

Despite the seriousness in his tone, I laughed like he'd made a joke. Because that's what it had to be.

Brutus' lips pinched, but he went about the task of undressing the both of us. He turned on the shower, and of course, the water pressure was perfect.

Naked, I stepped into the spray of the water. A groan broke free from my lips. The stress of the long travel day melted away underneath the tepid water. A beat later, I felt warmth at my back as Brutus stepped into the shower.

I spun to face him. "I want to wash you," I said. I went to grab the washcloth from Brutus' hand but he held it firm.

His eyes narrowed. "This is my job. Turn around," he commanded with such authority in his voice that my nipples ached.

I folded my arms across my breast. I didn't miss the way his eyes sparked in hunger when they fell to my boobs.

"What if I want to wash you?"

He shook his head, his eyes continuing to remain on my chest. His tongue ran along his bottom lip, and I had to squeeze my legs, making myself ignore the hungry expression on his face.

"You just got home from hours of travel after having to spend an extra night in a foreign city. Let me do this for you," he insisted.

"But you just returned from having to search for a lost child." I tried to pull the washcloth from him, but he wasn't budging. "You were working. You need to relax."

He gave his head a shake. "Washing you is relaxing for me. Turn around," he ordered. That time he didn't wait for me to listen. With his massive hands on my shoulders, he turned my back to face him, and began lathering up my body.

A piece of me wanted to protest, but his hands moving slowly up and down my back, soaking me, was the undoing of my argument.

"You're tight, baby," he murmured in my ear.

My pussy muscles flexed. I peered at him over my shoulder with a side-eye.

"Your back and neck muscles," he added slyly.

"I knew that's what you meant," I lied. My breathing hitched when he pinched one of my cheeks.

"Sure you did," he said firmly in my ear. "But for the record, *that's* tight too," he crooned.

A flush ran through my skin as my body heated. The first night we'd spent together in Mexico flashed through my mind.

I shook my head to rid my mind of those thoughts. Despite him telling me that bathing me was relaxing, I wanted to ensure he was okay. A haunted look had been in his eyes when he returned home.

I leaned back against him while he moved the washcloth over my belly. Reaching up, I ran my fingers through the back of his hair. I had to lift on my tiptoes, and he needed to lean down so that I could press a kiss to the line of his jaw.

"Are you sure you're okay?" I didn't want to pry too much about his job. I knew that was private, but I had to ask.

A muscle in his jaw flexed.

I pulled from his hold and spun to face him. "What is it?"

He'd said the child that was missing was safe. But had he lied? Brutus had a poker face that could fool anyone. And I was pretty damned good at reading people. I'd honed that skill in my sales career.

He shook his head. His fingers trailed down my neck and over my shoulder. He played with the tip of one of my braids, staring at it.

When his eyes met mine again, there was a look of pure vulnerability in them. It almost brought me to my knees to see a man of his size, who exuded power and confidence, wear such a look.

"Children should be protected."

My response to that was to run a hand over his chest. One of his pectoral muscles jumped in response to my touch.

"Wh-What happened?" I had to ask.

"Nothing. The boy's fine." He paused for a beat. "Tonight, but ..." He continued to toy with my braids, his hands easing their way up to my scalp. "Not in his past." He swallowed. "There're so many sick bastards in this world—the type who will take their pathetic feelings out on defenseless children. And women," he added.

"My mother." He swallowed again. "She was terrible at relationships. Some of the guys she dated were okay. Or at least they didn't bother me too much. But some thought it was a good idea to use her as a punching bag."

His hands ran through my braids, but his eyes looked a million miles away.

"Did they—" I stopped, needing to gather my composure to finish my question. "Did they hurt you, too?"

His eyes finally landed on me again. I saw the answer before he spoke.

"Yes. She managed to keep one around for a few years. He was especially terrible. I often got in between their fights." He snorted. "They weren't fights. It was him pounding on her. At nine, when he first came around, there wasn't much I could do except shield her from the blows."

He flinched when I cupped his cheek, but he kept talking.

"But I hit a growth spurt when I turned fourteen." His eyes met mine. There was a brutal look in them. "The benefit of growing six inches over a summer and being on the football team is that it makes it easier to fight back when your mother's five-foot-eight boyfriend thinks it's a good idea to hit her or you."

"I'm sorry," I said, not knowing what else to say. I blinked away the tears in my eyes.

Brutus gave me a small smile, leaning in to brush his lips across mine.

In that instant, I started to understand him a little more. What made him tick. The instinct to protect others was born from his desire to protect his mom.

"That was his last summer with us. I'm pretty sure I cracked one of his ribs. Hard to tell the guys at the bar your old lady's fourteen-year-old kid beat the shit out of you."

I sucked in my bottom lip. "Was your mom upset that he left?" I'd heard stories of women who blamed their children when a man left them. Carlene, my best friend, had one such story.

"Nah." His fingers began massaging my scalp again.

I bit back the moan that tried to claw itself free from my throat.

"Honestly, she was relieved. She'd been trying to figure out a way to get rid of him for a while. She barely dated after Steve left. And five years later…" He didn't finish as his lips clamped together.

He didn't need to finish his thought, though. I knew his mother passed away when he was just nineteen.

"That should've never happened to you." I pressed a kiss to his chest, feeling the tension in his body ease when I did so. Listening to Brutus talk about his childhood made me all the more grateful for my parents and family.

"I like this color in your hair," he said.

I peered down at the blue strands of hair interwoven with my dark brown hair. "I got them redone in Medellín."

"Let me shampoo it."

To my surprise, he stepped out of the shower and returned with a bottle of the exact brand of shampoo I used. I briefly wondered if he'd somehow retrieved the bottle that was in my suitcase, but that didn't make sense. My luggage remained inside of his trunk.

I didn't get the chance to ask before he spun me around and commenced washing my hair. I couldn't help it that time as moans spilled from my lips at the way he massaged my scalp to perfection.

"You're going to make me forget I'm no longer on sabbatical and that I'm back home," I groaned.

Without missing a beat, he leaned over, kissed my shoulder, and said, "That's the plan, baby."

CHAPTER 17

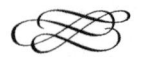

Mia

A week after returning to Williamsport, I strode through the doors of the Italian restaurant with a lightness in my steps I couldn't hide even if I wanted to. I was meeting my sister and best friend for lunch, and after a couple of months of only video calls, I couldn't wait.

Not to mention that after lunch, I was due to head over to the location of my café. I was slated to open my coffee shop in two months and couldn't believe how quickly everything was moving.

"There she is," Sharise said as she stood. Her dark brown, assessing eyes moved over me from head to toe.

I waved and went in to hug my sister first since she was closest. But she pulled back. Again, she looked me over.

"Carlene, are you seeing what I'm seeing?" Sharise asked without taking her eyes off of me.

"Hmhm," Carlene said, moving to stand next to my sister. She, too, gave me the once over. "Looks like someone who has been getting dicked down regularly."

I gasped and covered my mouth like I was the one who said it. "I can't believe you," I whisper-yelled, glancing around at the other patrons. None of them paid us any attention.

It was the middle of the lunchtime rush hour, and everyone else was more concerned with their business lunch or getting their food and heading back to their offices.

"She's not lying, though," Sharise added.

"You two could at least give me a damn hug and say hello before you start in on me."

They both cracked a smile. Sharise was the first to pull me in, followed by Carlene.

"That's better," I said before settling into one of the chairs at the window table my sister always chose because she knew I preferred window seats.

"Sharise already ordered the spinach and onion personal pizza for you," Carlene said.

"You're the best," I told my sister.

"Now, give us all the nasty details," Carlene said, leaning in.

"Excuse you?" I played coy while I unfolded the cloth napkin and laid it across my lap.

"Girl, don't play with us," Sharise added on. "You've been back home for a week, and this is the first time either of us is seeing you."

Our waiter brought over our salads. Carlene hesitated before adding, "And I only have another thirty minutes before I have to get back to my office. I have meetings all afternoon. Spill," she insisted while cutting into her salad.

I rolled my eyes. "Not much to tell. You both already know I met someone while in Mexico." I gave a one shoulder shrug, despite how difficult the words were to get out. Everything in my body rebelled at how I downplayed the relationship between Brutus and me.

But I wasn't ready to confess to anyone the depths of what I felt for him.

"And he just so happens to live here in Williamsport, too," Sharise pointed out. "It has to be fate." She grinned wide.

My sister had earned her PhD in biochemistry and taught for a few years at Williamsport University before giving up her career to become a stay-at-home mom. To say she was somewhat of a hopeless romantic would be an understatement.

"I don't know about all of that," Carlene interjected. She twirled her fork in the air, looking at me contemplatively. "But you do have a new glow about you."

"You don't believe in fate?" Sharise asked. "What about Jason?"

Jason was Carlene's fiancé.

"That wasn't fate. That was me getting him sprung with what's between my thighs."

Sharise gaped at my friend. I burst out into laughter before covering my mouth with the napkin. Carlene tended to say the first thought that came to her mind.

"Is that what happened with you, my dear BFF?" Carlene asked. "Did you get that big ass man sprung on that snatch of yours?"

I playfully tossed a crouton from my salad at her. She caught it and popped it into her mouth.

"You're a mess."

"True." She shrugged.

"We're …" I stopped to try to figure out how I wanted to describe what it was that transpired between Brutus and me. "We connected way before any of our clothes came off," I confessed.

Both of the women at the table frowned.

"You slept with him like what …" Sharise paused, glancing between Carlene and me, "two days after meeting him?"

With a roll of my eyes, I murmured, "More like three. But that's not the point. Yeah, we have excellent physical chemistry."

I stopped talking as our waiter delivered our meals. We ate in silence for a while.

"So, there's more than just the physical between the two of you?" Sharise asked, looking at me with concern in her eyes.

"Yes," I assured her.

Her gaze lingered on me for a few beats longer. "You know it takes more than good sex to make a relationship work."

I made a disgusted sound at the back of my throat. "No, I didn't know that because I'm some kind of idiot." Sarcasm dripped from my tone.

"I didn't mean it like that." She held up her hands. "All I'm trying to say is that you and relationships can get ..."

"Finicky, non-existent," Carlene so kindly added.

I gave her a deadpan expression.

"Don't look at me like that. You know it's true," she defended. "You have a bad habit of hiding behind your work when it comes to relationships."

"I don't have a job anymore," I reminded her.

She snorted. "You're about to open your café, which I can't wait for. And I wouldn't be surprised if you started using your new business as an excuse as to why this relationship won't work."

"Or it's the wrong timing," Sharise added.

With a tilt of my head, I stared at my sister.

"What? Carlene's right."

These two weren't even close friends like that. Yet, here they were ganging up on me.

"All I'm saying, sis," Sharise started as she reached across the table to pat my hand, "is don't let your fear of relationships have you running away from something that could be great."

I shook my head. It was on the tip of my tongue to tell them that out of Brutus and me, I wasn't the one who was the workaholic. But I held back because they were right. I was the one who, for the time being, was out of work. That would change in a few weeks.

Less than a few weeks. Since I came back earlier than I originally planned, I was able to move up the renovation timeline. If things went according to my plan, I could open the café two weeks earlier than anticipated.

While that notion excited me, I heeded my sister and best friend's words.

"Yeah," Carlene said, blowing out a breath. "You know, if you would've asked me three years ago, I would've had a different story. Then Jason came into my life and blew up my whole *men ain't shit* theory."

She rolled her eyes, pretending to be disgusted. But there was that telltale sparkle in her eyes. It was there whenever she talked about him. That gleam only increased in appearance whenever she was in his presence. Carlene might joke about Jason being sprung, but she had it just as bad.

"I was there for all of that," I reminded her.

She nodded, wiping her mouth. "And you were the one who encouraged me to give him a chance. Even when I swore up and down that he wouldn't be shit just like so many men in my past."

My past relationships might not have been perfect or worked out in the long term, but Carlene had encountered some doozies compared to mine. She truly deserved the happiness she'd found.

"I'm so happy for you two," I told her, meaning it.

"I want the same happiness for you." She held up her hands. "Now, I'm not one to believe a woman needs a husband and kids to fulfill them. But you," she pointed at me, "I've known it's what you secretly desired, even if you won't say as much out loud."

"Me too," Sharise added. "You got your heart broken a few times in high school and college, and all of a sudden you became Ms. All About Her Work."

"Really?" I cocked my head to the side. "Is that how you feel?" I looked between the two of them.

"Yeah."

"Absolutely."

"Don't hold back," I grumbled, staring down at the half-eaten pizza on my plate.

"Mia." Sharise's hand slid across the table, retaking mine. "You know we're not saying this to upset you. And we know how much you did enjoy your career, but you used it to hide behind."

Something in my chest shifted, and I squirmed in my chair. I wasn't expecting my sister's words to have such an impact on me.

"If you're as hung up on this new guy as I suspect, don't let your fears get in the way." She squeezed my hand before releasing it.

"Ditto." Carlene stood and placed a few bills on the table. She moved over to me, kissing my cheek. "I love you, Mia. We both do, and we trust you know what's best for you."

"That therapist is working a miracle on you," I joked. But in all seriousness, Carlene of five years ago had a totally different outlook on relationships.

"You ain't never lied," she confirmed. "A good therapist and some good dick will have many women seeing things differently." She cackled, and I tossed my head back and laughed as well. "I have to go. Bye. Good to see you, Sharise."

I watched my friend go, and then turned to my sister.

"How are the kiddos?" I asked, referring to my nephew and two nieces.

"A pain in my butt." She grunted. "Thank God you finally decided to come up for air from that man and come out to have lunch with us. I needed to drop those kids off somewhere to have time to myself."

"Stop it." I laughed. "Don't talk about my babies like that."

"Whatever." She waved a dismissive hand. "You're more than free to come get them whenever you want."

"Maybe I'll pick them up this weekend." I glanced at my watch. "I have an appointment to head over to the café to speak with the foreman for my renovation."

Sharise's eyes lit up. "I'm so happy you're finally opening this café. You've mentioned it for years. I wish I could come but babysitters aren't cheap. And your parents just had to jaunt off on another one of their vacations."

Our parents were on a cruise around the Mediterranean and weren't slated to return until closer to the end of the month. Our mother typically watched Sharise's kids whenever she had to run errands during the day or if she just needed a break for a few hours.

"Love you," I told my sister as we hugged. "Thanks for having lunch with me."

She pointed a finger at me. "Don't think I've forgotten that you still haven't given up much of the details on this man. And I want to meet him soon."

"Slow down, sis. It's only been two months since I've met him," I reminded her.

"Yeah, but when you know, you know. And you have that knowing look in your eyes. Even if your mouth won't say it just yet."

I opened my mouth to respond but I had nothing. I ignored the whispers at the back of my mind that my sister might be right.

Was Brutus the one?

Could I trust myself and this budding relationship to believe in such a thing?

* * *

I SLIPPED on my pair of sunglasses as I exited the restaurant. My shop's location was only a few blocks from the restaurant, and it was a beautiful late summer day, so I chose to walk there.

On the way, I got lost in thinking about the conversation over lunch. Carlene and Sharise had put into words so many things I was feeling. Yes, I was wary of Brutus' job. Both the potential danger and the fact that he had to put in so many hours were worrisome to me. But the truth was, a part of me did have a fear of putting myself out there.

Heartbreak at a young age tended to stick with you. It did for me, at least. And while I was old enough to recognize that not all relationships ended in heartache, and even that the ending of my relationships in the past turned out to be a good thing, it didn't mean that my emotions followed logic.

"Mia?" a voice from my past grabbed my attention.

I looked over my shoulder and had to fight to keep my face neutral when I saw Vincent Davis. My former co-worker.

"I thought that was you," he said, coming up to me with a big grin on his face like we were old friends.

"Vincent, how are you?" I asked just to be friendly. I intentionally kept walking, hoping he would get the hint that I was in a rush.

"I'm great. Work is going well. Ever since you left, I've been able to make some great headway with the team," he sounded cheerful, but I knew a dig when I heard one.

"Wonderful," I murmured and picked up my pace. "I'm on my way to—"

"Speaking of work," he interrupted. "I have been trying to get in contact with you about the Champion account."

My shoulders slumped. I was on the verge of telling Vincent that he couldn't contact me because I'd blocked his number.

"Vince, I don't work for Corsica Pharmaceuticals any longer. I have no information to tell you about any accounts you may or may not have."

His phony smile dropped. He moved to stand in front of me, blocking my ability to keep walking.

"Listen, Mia, I know our last conversation didn't end too well."

"Because I hung up on you for being a pompous ass." I was done biting my tongue. I didn't owe Vincent or my former employer a damn thing. "If you'll excuse me."

I made a move to go around him, and the jerk side-stepped, getting in my way.

"Look," he said through gritted teeth. He even glanced around us as if making sure he wasn't drawing any unwanted attention.

The hairs on the back of my neck stood up.

"I don't know what crawled up your butt, but this is fucking important. My career could be on the line here."

"Am I supposed to give a shit about *your* job?"

He blew out a breath. "Don't let your petty jealousy get in the way of doing the right thing here."

"Jealousy?" My voice went up a couple of octaves.

"Yes, everyone at the job knows the only reason you quit was because I got the managerial job you wanted. Quitting demonstrates a lack of character, in my opinion, but—"

I let out a laugh. "That's fucking hilarious, coming from you. I'm not enduring this conversation anymore. If you have any questions about your job, I suggest you speak to someone on your team. Because as I said, I don't work for Corsica anymore. You and I are no longer co-workers, and we damn sure aren't friends. Therefore, we have nothing to talk about. Move out of my way."

I didn't wait for him to move. Instead, I brushed past him, and that was when he caught me by the elbow. He squeezed.

"What the hell?" I snatched my arm away.

Vincent's eyes widened, and again he looked around at the people who passed us. He quickly stood up straight and ran a hand through his hair as if trying to calm himself down.

"Don't ever touch me again," I told him, clenching my jaw. With that, I turned my back on him to continue to the destination I was going to before he interrupted me.

Flustered, I kept my head held high and glanced over my shoulder a couple of times just to make sure he wasn't following me. I saw Vincent eye me with a scowl on his face before he turned and walked in the opposite direction.

"Asshole," I muttered but did my best to shake off the encounter. I reminded myself that I was on my way to my new place of employment—a locale where I would be more than just another employee. I was to be the owner.

My ambition was to create an environment where everyone who walked through the doors of my café experienced a moment of joy and gratitude. Customers would come for the great tasting coffee and food, but they would remain for the welcoming atmosphere.

I let out a sigh, my shoulders descending from the anxiousness that my encounter with Vincent brought on. Corsica, Vincent, and whatever client account he needed help with were in my rearview mirror. I walked toward my future.

Right as that thought came to me, I smiled when I was about ten feet from the front door of my shop, and I spotted a familiar figure standing out front. A very large, looming figure who scoped out the front of the building.

I stopped to watch Brutus for a few moments. The people bustling about parted for him like the Red Sea. He had an energy all unto himself. I watched as more than a handful of women threw him appreciative looks. Then without warning, his head shifted and he looked my way.

The corners of his eyes creased as his smile was enough to light up the sky.

"Hey, baby."

CHAPTER 18

Brutus

It was as if everything around me had taken on a grayish pallor—one I hadn't even noticed. And then, I glanced over to see Mia standing there. Smiles weren't something I gave out easily or even too willingly, but with her around they come naturally.

The gray tones dissolved, and everything looked clearer.

"Hey, baby," I greeted, pulling her to me when she was less than a foot away. I brushed my lips across hers, reminding myself to not get too carried away. We were in public, and I still had to return to work. Though everything in me wanted to call into the office and tell them I needed the rest of the day off.

That urge had been surfacing more and more lately.

"Hi." Mia's smile beamed as she peered up at me. "What are you doing here?"

"I can't come to see your café?" I faked an affronted look.

She laughed. "Of course you can. I just thought you had to work." She pulled back and squinted. "Wait, how did you know I was even going to be here?"

Mia took a step back and pressed her pointer finger to her chin. I could see the wheels of her mind working but I didn't say anything. I wanted to see what conclusion she would draw.

"You didn't do something creepy like hack into my calendar, did you?"

I barked out a laugh. "Baby, would I do something like that?"

"Yes," she answered quickly.

I shrugged. "You're right. I one hundred percent would." She had no idea the lengths I'd already gone to just to be next to her. Like in Mexico when I had the reservation for her rental deleted from the system.

But this wasn't one of those times.

"You told me last week that today was the day of your appointment with the foreman for the renovation," I reminded her.

Her eyes ballooned, and then her expression collapsed again. "You remembered that?"

"You sound surprised."

Her lips parted but then closed again. It was her turn to shrug. "I mean, it was days ago I mentioned it and you've been so busy with your job, I figured you would've forgotten."

She said it like it wasn't that big a deal, but I frowned. "This is a huge day for you. You're finalizing the specs for your café and setting a date to open." There wasn't any way I couldn't not be here for this. At least for a little while.

Guilt tugged at my gut because I would've preferred spending the entire day with her. I wanted to get a feel for the building and surrounding area, the foreman and crew she'd be working with. Safety was always paramount in my mind.

Luckily, Mia had chosen a building that wasn't just perfect for her store for monetary reasons but also when it came to safety. The corner that her café's building sat on was well lit and highly trafficked. There were plenty of office buildings just a few blocks over, but this particular street housed an array of mom-and-pop stores, a pet groomer business, a used bookstore, and more. It was the perfect location for a coffee shop.

And the area was known for its lower than average crime rate. I looked up the crime statistics in the area the same day Mia told me the exact location of her store.

"Barry," Mia said.

I turned to face the man walking our way. I read it immediately as the foreman for this job. A yellow hardhat rested underneath his left arm while he wore a pair of loose-fitting jeans and a dark khaki colored button-up. The clipboard and pencil behind his ear gave him away instantly. But I didn't need to look at his attire to know who he was.

Yes, I'd also looked him up since Mia gave me his name.

Barry Whitfield of Whitfield Construction & Co. His company had done a lot of work in the area in recent years. It made sense to utilize his services for this job.

"This is—"

"Brutus," I completed Mia's introduction for her, sticking my hand out to Barry. When he took it, I squeezed a little harder than necessary. Our eyes locked, and I narrowed my gaze slightly.

Barry gave me a nod, silently conveying that he understood my protective instincts over this woman and her pursuits.

"Pleasure," Barry said.

"I'm so excited," Mia squealed. I heard the barely contained excitement in her voice. She looked up at me. "Thank you for coming," she said, taking my hand.

I covered her hand and brought it to my lips.

A minute later, the three of us walked through the front part of the building. Barry went over the specs and the layout, mentioning where everything would go. I listened closely while also keeping an eye on Mia. Her excitement was still apparent, but she also asked insightful questions and brought up possible workarounds when Barry told her that something couldn't be done the way she wanted.

Mia had clearly done her research and she wasn't a pushover. Not that I thought she was, but watching someone you care for so immensely having their dream unfold for them before their eyes was like experiencing the removal of an eclipse. Where everything illuminates and suddenly you forgot there was ever any darkness.

"What about the security system?" I asked after about an hour.

Barry blinked, and Mia came to peer at me with a wrinkle in her forehead. "I assumed I could wait until the end to get that installed," she answered.

I shook my head. "No," I replied fervently. "Security needs to be a priority throughout the renovation process." My gaze shifted over to Barry. "Who have you worked with in the past?"

He rattled off a couple of security companies in the city. All of them had decent reputations and their equipment was okay, but I wasn't satisfied.

"What is that look?" Mia questioned.

"You need better security." I didn't give a shit that Barry was standing right there and had highly recommended the companies that he listed. "I've seen the camera shots from some of those companies and you can do better."

Mia shook her head. "But anything better is going to cost a lot more, right?" She turned to Barry, and I gritted my teeth. The sight of her turning to ask another man for something I was an expert on rattled my chest.

I moved in between her and Barry, effectively cutting him out. "Give us a minute," I said over my shoulder told him.

He nodded and then said something about going to check out the pipes in the area that would be the kitchen.

"You don't trust the companies he mentioned?" Mia asked. "I've looked a few of them up and they all have good reviews."

I snorted. "Yeah, those are the reviews they haven't deleted. You need something more efficient and reliable."

"But efficiency and reliability come with a cost."

"One that's worth it if something happens."

She spread her arms. "What could happen?"

I opened my mouth to answer, but she held up her hand.

"No. I'm not an idiot. I know bad things happen and I'm no exception, but what I'm saying is that my shop is only a few blocks away from a police and fire station. This is a very safe neighborhood surrounded by businesses and lots of people around."

"What about those early mornings you have to come to open up?" Mia planned to keep her café open until six p.m. most days, so I didn't have to worry about her closing late. But she planned to be open by seven, which meant she would have to show up by six at the latest to get everything brewed and ready for the morning rush.

It was still dark at that time.

She rolled her eyes. "Aren't criminals still asleep at six in the morning?" She grinned from the joke, but I continued to scowl.

She slumped her shoulders. "You're not going to let this go, are you?"

My frown deepened. "Hell no," I said. "This is your safety we're talking about." The hot anger that rose to just beneath the surface of my skin at the mere idea of someone hurting her had me unbuttoning the collar of my shirt.

"Well." She shrugged and looked around. "I don't know what you want me to do. Between the costs to renovate the space and get the business off the ground, I don't think I have enough of the business loan left over to work with whatever high-end security company you think is good enough."

"I'll do it," I answered quickly.

"I can't use Townsend Security. First of all, I know the price tag is way out of my budget, and second, they—"

"Not Townsend Security, me," I emphasized the last word by pressing my hand to my chest.

"Aren't you Townsend Security, though?"

"Yeah, but I can also do this for you." I glanced around the space that would become her café. "I have some contacts who can get me the equipment that I need to do the installation. I'll have my father come in during the day to work with Barry. He knows all the ins and outs of the security systems I use."

"I can't ask Rick to do that."

"You're not asking. I am. Besides, I'm sure by this point he likes you more than he likes me. He'll do it no questions asked."

She let out a guffaw, and the sound caused my heart to expand. Mia peered around as she ran a hand across her forehead.

"Are you sure about this? It won't put you out?"

"No," I lied easily. It would require me calling in a couple of favors from some associates of mine. Nothing too cumbersome, but I liked to keep any favors I needed on bountiful supply. Mia was worth using them up, though.

Truthfully, I was serious about my father. He often talked about liking Mia. Whenever she wasn't around—which was rare since she'd been staying with me for the better part of the week since she returned home—he made sure to tell me not to fuck this thing up.

Not that I needed advice from him. He was the last person to take any sort of relationship advice from. But it was evident how much he liked her.

"And don't ask again if you're putting Rick out. His ass would knock me over to get here if it meant he was helping you."

Mia burst out laughing, which had been my intention. I loved the melodic sound of it. My phone buzzed, and I cursed.

"You have to go?"

My heart constricted from the question. "Work," I grunted. "I have something for you," I said, pulling up the confirmation tickets on my phone.

"Tickets to the Malcolm Gladwell talk at Williamsport U in two weeks."

Mia gasped. "Those have been sold out for weeks." Her eyes shimmered with delight. "When I found out he was going to be in Williamsport, I looked up ticket prices. There weren't any seats left." She looked from my phone to me. "I was going to try to get two tickets for the both of us."

My smile widened.

"How did you do this?"

"I've got a few connections." I brushed my lips across hers. "And don't forget you need to find a dress for the Townsend gala next month."

Her eyes shone with her grin. "I didn't forget. I found one. I will go in tomorrow to get measured for the alterations."

I'd told Mia about the Townsend gala the night after I came back from finding Cole. She hesitated at first, but when I insisted, she agreed. I'd only ever attended a Townsend function as the head of security. It would be weird playing double duty. But all four of the Townsend wives had asked me questions about Mia, whenever they saw me. Deborah Townsend, the mother of all four brothers, even cornered me one day at the community center and asked to see a picture.

She'd batted her lashes and asked with a smile on her face, but I knew a demand when I heard one. After that, she wouldn't let up until I told her I was bringing Mia to the gala.

"They're all looking forward to meeting you," I said absent-mindedly.

"Really?" There was a surprise in her voice and fear.

"Why does that frighten you?" I asked, alarmed.

"It doesn't …" She paused and, with a shake of her head, amended, "I mean, it's just a little intimidating. I worked with the healthcare side of Townsend Industries at my old job. But I've never met the CEO, let alone the entire family. And this isn't for work."

I hated the uncertainty in her voice. Didn't she know she was the most perfect thing in the world?

"They're just people," I assured, taking her by the waist.

My phone buzzed again, and I growled.

She laughed. "You have to go."

"Tell me you're not intimidated to meet them," I said, ignoring my phone and her insistence that I needed to leave.

"I'm not." When I didn't budge, she added, "Seriously. I know they're just people, a family. A *very* wealthy and powerful family." She grinned. "I'm teasing."

"You make friends wherever you go." It was true. The saying 'never met a stranger' had to have been created with Mia in mind. She'd done it in Mexico. Whenever we went out, she would quickly strike up a conversation with someone in a line or at dinner, on a boat. Wherever.

Her sales career didn't surprise me, given her extroverted tendencies. And when she talked about her reasons for wanting to open a coffee shop, it made total sense. She was a people person. Something entirely different than me. I tolerated most people, but I could do without them.

Except for her.

The thought swept through my mind so seamlessly that I couldn't deny it. Mia was always the exception to my every rule.

"I'll see you later." I reluctantly released her. "I'll try to be home by seven," I said.

It fell so casually from my lips that I only realized what I said when Mia replied, "I get to move back into my place tomorrow."

Due to a new job, Mia's tenant decided to move out of her place a week early.

"You don't have to leave." The words slipped out before I had time to think about them. And when I did pause to think them over, I didn't want to retract them.

She smirked and started to answer, but Barry came up behind us.

"Pipes look good. My guys'll be able to have your kitchen set up in no time," he said.

Before she could respond to him, I took her chin into mine. "We'll talk about this tonight." I kissed her and then turned to Barry. I gave him a short nod before I left, my phone again buzzing in my pocket.

Duty called.

CHAPTER 19

Mia

I twisted this way and that as I checked myself over in the mirror. In the two weeks since renovations began on my shop, things had been hectic. I visited the café almost every day to see the progress. And when I wasn't going over how the renovations were going, I was on the phone with coffee and food distributors and furniture retailers and shoring up a million other details.

I also started my own popup stores at local retailers and farmer's markets to drum up excitement for my new shop. Not to mention, I had a handful of employee applications to go through for barista positions. Life was busy.

But tonight, I was preoccupied with something else entirely. Brutus was taking me out to see one of our favorite authors. After Malcolm Gladwell's talk, we had reservations at a nearby restaurant. It would be our first night out in over a week.

Brutus' job was more than a full-time gig. A few days earlier, he unexpectedly had to hop on a flight with Aaron Townsend to attend some business meetings with him across the country. Additionally, coordinating the security plans for the gala consumed much of his time.

Though he remained very active with work, he still had small ways he let me know that I was a constant on his mind. He'd send me flowers to either my home or the café. When he was away, he mailed a postcard that had a picture of a beach in Tulum on it. He'd written 'thinking of you' on the back of the postcard. We talked almost every evening.

Those talks were when he would try to convince me that I had made the colossal mistake of moving back into my house. As I looked around my bedroom, a room that I typically loved, a sense of emptiness stirred in my chest.

Although my house was my sanctuary, I couldn't ignore the empty feeling that came over me when I lay in bed at night. It was as if my body sensed that Brutus wasn't nearby, nor were we any longer in his space, and it rebelled. I'd had more than one sleepless night in the two weeks I'd moved back in.

My phone rang, pulling me out of those thoughts. It was a video call from Carlene.

"What do you think?" I greeted before turning my head from one side to the other to show her the two different earrings I wore. I couldn't pick which one to wear for the night.

"The studs. Definitely the diamonds." A contemplative expression crossed her face. "The dangly ones are beautiful, but with your hair up like that, the studs show off the column of your neck more."

"Thanks, friend." I set the phone down on my vanity at an angle that she could still see me while I changed the other earring.

"Let me see the total fit," she said when I again picked up the phone.

I moved back to the mirror and turned the phone around. I wore a light brown, high-waist, asymmetrical skirt paired with a cream, puffed sleeve top. I'd removed my braids a few days earlier and decided to wear my naturally kinky coils in a high puff.

"You look good enough to eat," Carlene gushed. "I know Brutus will want to devour you tonight."

"That's the plan," I joked.

Carlene frowned.

"What's wrong?"

She shook her head. "Nothing. I don't want to bring you down right before your date."

"Talk to me," I insisted before plopping onto my bed. I still had another fifteen minutes before Brutus would arrive.

"Jason and I went over invitations to the wedding last week."

"Right." I nodded. Carlene and Jason's wedding was about six months out, and they were starting to step up their planning.

"He brought up whether or not I was going to invite my mother."

"Ohh." I blew out a breath. Carlene's mother was a sore spot for her.

"Yeah." She tutted. "Girl, I thought I'd done all of this work in therapy. I had healed or whatever they say you need to do, right? Hell, you know that even agreeing to marry Jason is a huge leap of faith for me."

I nodded in agreement but kept silent to let her talk it out as needed.

"So, I discussed the issue with my therapist. Then I went to Jason and told him that I would invite her. He was supportive." She paused before launching in. "I had to reach out to my uncle to track down my mother's address. I didn't think the right thing to do would be to send her an invite in the mail, not after three years of no contact. Instead, I called her up and asked if she was free. She was a little nasty, but I figured it was to be expected after so many years without speaking."

A sinking feeling for my friend started to form in my belly. "What happened?"

"The same thing that always happens with that woman. First, almost as soon as I got to her house, she launched into a big ordeal about how ungrateful I was after all she'd done for me. And you know, I kind of snapped. I asked what the hell she had done for me. Don't you know that bi—" She cut herself off. "That woman, and I'm using the term very generously, had the nerve to tell me that giving birth to me was what she'd done. That I needed to show her some damn respect because she sacrificed her body for nine months to bring me into this world."

"That's terrible," I said because I knew the abuse Carlene had suffered at the hands and mouth of her mother and her mother's boyfriends over the years.

Carlene huffed. "Like giving birth to me was some damn favor she did for me."

I could see my friend pacing back and forth.

"What did you say? How did you respond?"

She stopped pacing. "You know, I started to tell her exactly what was on my mind. To let her know what a horrible mother she was and why I hadn't spoken to her in years. But I didn't. When I was about to lay into her, a calm came over me. My therapist's voice popped into my head and reminded me that my mother was an imperfect human who probably couldn't comprehend how she hurt me. Then I remembered how old she was when she had me. She was only fourteen."

I blinked because I never knew her mother was that young.

"Yeah," Carlene said, noting my surprise. "Young as hell."

"She was practically a baby."

"A baby having a baby. In some ways, she's probably still that same fourteen-year-old girl. I didn't need to get down to her level, curse her out, and ruin the rest of my day or week. I left."

"That's it? You just walked out?"

"Pretty much." She nodded. "Then I called Jason, and he left work early to let me cry on his shoulder for the next hour." A small smile creased her mouth. "He's downstairs making dinner because he knows how much I love his lobster mac n' cheese."

"And because you can't cook worth a damn," I joked.

Carlene cracked up, falling back against the couch in her den. "True that. Why do you think I'm marrying the top chef at a Michelin star restaurant?"

We both laughed.

Carlene sobered up first. "For a long time, I didn't think I was worthy of this type of love. It's hard to believe in something like that when you grow up in the kind of environment I did."

I nodded.

"But I'm glad I didn't let my past dictate my future," she added.

I pinched my brows together. "Why do I feel this is turning into a lecture for me?"

"Because it is, now hush while I drop some knowledge on you."

I sucked my teeth.

"Hush," Carlene insisted again.

I clamped my mouth shut.

"I love you, Mia. You've been my best friend for almost twenty years now. And I doubt I would've had enough faith to take the leap with Jason if you didn't push me a little. So, I'm here to do the same for you."

"I'm listening," I said.

"Then stop interrupting me," she retorted. "As I was saying, let that man love you. You and I don't come from the same background. Your parents are the poster children for happily ever after. But I think when that didn't happen for you in your first few relationships, you started to doubt that it could happen. You hid behind work, and yes, I know," she said, holding up her hand to stop what I was about to say.

"You don't work at that job anymore. And yes, you are busy opening up your new shop. A dream you've wanted for years. But don't use it as an excuse."

"I'm not," I insisted.

"Are you sure?"

"What are you implying?"

"Didn't he ask you to continue staying with him? But you decided to move back into your home anyway?"

"What's wrong with moving back to my house? A house I pay the mortgage on," I reminded her.

"Nothing's wrong with it. If you did it for the right reasons."

"We've only known one another for three months."

"Jason and I said I love you after the first two weeks," she explained as if I didn't know this story already. "We moved in after three months. Yes, it took more time for us to fall into our groove, but I'm saying that when you let yourself open up to the possibility, it gets easier to trust your gut."

I smirked, unbelieving that Carlene was on the phone telling me all of this. A few years earlier, I could easily see Sharise saying these words. My sister, much like my parents, found the love of her life early on and hadn't looked back. Carlene was a different story.

However, as I listened to her and thought back on the conversation the three of us had at lunch a few weeks earlier, it started to resonate. There were some ways in which I was holding myself back from Brutus. I didn't want to risk another heartbreak, but that was just silly because my heart was already deeply invested.

He made it impossible for my heart not to be.

"I hear what you're saying," I told my friend.

"Good. Hang on." She pulled the phone away, and I heard her yell something down to Jason, I presumed. "Jason wants me to go taste test something for him. Look, just know I'm not saying you should marry the man tomorrow. Heck, I haven't even met him yet. I'm suggesting that you let whatever fear you have go and allow yourself to show up. The same way you used to show up for that raggedy ass job that didn't appreciate you."

I chuckled. "Go taste test your man's food before he gets restless."

"Bye."

After disconnecting the call, I thought over her words and wondered again if Brutus and I could make this thing work, for real.

Not a minute later, a text came through on my phone.

Brutus: **Business meeting ran late. Will have to meet you at Williamsport U. Already sent a car to pick you up.**

I swallowed as doubt formed in the pit of my stomach. I'd had to send a similar text canceling or postponing a date due to my former job. I pushed past the feelings that told me Brutus was brushing me aside.

He's sending a car and said he'll meet you there, I reminded myself.

A second later, I stood from the bed and heard a car pulling into my driveway. With my head lifted, I chose to meet the driver.

CHAPTER 20

Mia

The energy in the lecture hall at Williamsport University was enough to replace the slight feeling of rejection that'd hung over me before leaving my house. Brutus had texted me right before I arrived, ensuring that the town car he'd sent had picked me up without any issues.

While I wished he was with me to see our favorite author, I still felt his presence. And that obliterated some of the negative feelings from earlier. Remembering I was there to see Malcolm Gladwell speak in person had me bouncing on my toes a little bit. For a moment, this felt like destiny of some sort.

Once I finally decided and turned in my resignation at Corsica, life started to fall into place. The loan, documentation, and everything I needed to start my coffee shop had come together so well that I was able to plan my three-month sabbatical.

A sabbatical that turned out to be only two months.

A smile split my lips. My trip away was only cut a month short because I met and fell in love with Brutus.

I stopped short.

Fell in love.

Those three words pierced through my thoughts. Their impact landed right in the center of my chest. I was in love with Brutus. Deeply in love.

Right when my mind began reeling, wondering if it was too soon to make such a declaration, I heard someone call my name.

"Mia? It's so good to see you again."

I turned to look over to the right. Among the people piling into the lecture hall, I spotted Maureen Pettiford. Maureen worked part-time as part of the administrative staff at Corsica.

"Maureen, how are you?" I asked genuinely. While I didn't care for a few people at my old job or the management, Maureen wasn't one of them. Though, she sometimes could be more talkative than I liked. I just knew not to tell her any of my business if I didn't want it spread around the office.

Maureen's smile widened, and she snapped a finger before pointing at me. "That's right, you love Malcolm Gladwell," she remembered.

I nodded. "I do."

"I should've expected to see you here." She wrapped her arm around the man at her side.

I recognized Jarrett, her husband.

"Hi, Jarrett," I said with a wave.

"Mia. Good to see you." He cleared his throat, and then held up his finger. He pulled his phone out of his breast pocket. "Excuse me."

I watched him stride a few steps away, checking his phone.

Maureen rolled her eyes. "He's always working." Her lips twisted as she looked over at her husband. "You're the one who wanted to be here," she reminded him.

Suddenly, I felt like I was witnessing what should've been a private conversation.

"He's the one who loves Malcolm Gladwell," she told me. "That book about what makes someone successful and what's it called?" She snapped her fingers.

"*Outliers?*" I provided.

"That's it. Jarrett all but raved about it for weeks after reading it.

Now, look at him." She gestured toward Jarrett, who was now on an actual call in lieu of just texting. "That's what I get for marrying a workaholic."

My stomach muscles tightened.

"All he does is work," Maureen continued. "You know what it's like." She looked at me expectedly.

"Excuse me?" I asked.

She snorted and waved a hand. "He's like you. Working all crazy hours of the day and night. I tell him all the time corporate law cannot be that damn exciting. He promised me that we'd have the entire night to ourselves." Maureen moved in closer. "Our oldest was sick a few weeks ago. Something he brought home from school. He, of course, passed it to his sisters. Then I got sick. Had to take a week off from work to care for all of us because he," she gestured toward her husband, "was on a business trip that he just couldn't cancel."

She made a disgusted sound at the back of her throat while folding her arms.

"I'm sorry," I said, unable to think of anything better to say.

"It's not your fault," she quickly replied. "It's his. I don't know how you do it." She thought for a moment. "But I guess that's how. You don't have a husband or kids," she stated bluntly.

I gave her a side-eye. One she didn't pick up on because Maureen always had a problem recognizing when it was time for her to stop talking.

"So, where are you working now? I know a workaholic like you found a job in no time."

I hadn't told many people at my former job about my plans to take a three month break before opening my coffee shop. I was glad for that decision right then.

"Oh," Maureen started before I could respond to her question. She grabbed my arm like women who were friends, sharing the latest gossip, did.

The woman didn't even notice when I eased my arm out of her hold.

"Well, if you want to know, that managerial role you were eyeing right before you left might be vacant again soon."

That made me perk up. Though I didn't truly want to know, a small piece of me was interested in what Maureen had to say.

"The position that Vincent took?"

Maureen eagerly nodded.

"He quit?"

Maureen let out a laugh. She shook her head. "No, but he's this close," she pinched her thumb and forefinger together for me to see, "from losing his job. Three accounts under his supervision have decided to sever ties with Corsica."

My eyes widened. "Which ones?"

"Champion, Lutheran Hospital, and Walker Medical." She ticked off each name on her fingers.

"Those were three of our most loyal accounts." I wondered what would make them part ways with Corsica.

"Yeah." She huffed. "They *were*."

A part of me felt territorial. I had worked hard to earn all three of those accounts more than five years earlier. Then, I remembered that the happenings at Corsica were no longer my concern.

"That's too bad."

"Tell me about it. Vincent is losing his mind. Turns out, no one wants to work with him, and with Meera Pharmaceuticals infringing on our market…" She trailed off and shrugged.

"Well, that's not my business anymore," I said flatly, tired of talking about the company I used to work for. They made their bed. They could lay in it.

"Are you here with anyone?" Maureen glanced around as if searching for someone to magically appear at my side.

My shoulders sagged ever so slightly underneath the weight of her question. I did my best to hide it, but I couldn't help but feel a little bereft. As much as I felt cared for by Brutus' kindness in sending the car, I wanted him by my side.

But I told myself I couldn't be selfish. I'd canceled plenty of dates before due to work. When one worked for one of the most wealthy and influential families in the city, it was expected, at least some of the time. I could give him the benefit of the doubt.

I lifted my chin and started to tell Maureen I was alone, but a deep voice behind me interrupted.

"There you are," Brutus said while his hand slipped around my waist. Pulling me into his hold, he leaned down to place a kiss on my cheek.

Everything inside of me felt like the sun had decided to shine on us. A hum broke free from my throat. I blinked my eyes open and smiled up at him.

"Hi."

He greeted that with a brilliant smile. Those three words I'd felt earlier came back to mind. I did not doubt that I was in love with Brutus. But I bit my tongue, holding them in.

Brutus looked past my shoulder, reminding me that we weren't alone.

I turned back to Maureen. Her mouth hung open, but when she looked over at me, she clamped her lips shut. Still, as she peered up and up at Brutus, I noticed the interest in her eyes.

"I'm Brutus," he introduced. "And you are?"

"Babe," I started, "this is Maureen. We used to work together."

Brutus nodded, looking over her assessingly. His expression remained pleasant yet impassive.

"Pleasure." He turned back to me. "Did you save us a seat?"

Just that fast, he'd dismissed Maureen from the conversation. It bordered on this side of rude, but honestly, I didn't care too much. The last thing I wanted was to hear anything else about Corsica.

"I was entering when I ran into Maureen."

Brutus took my hand. "Good. Let's take a seat in the front." He peered at Maureen. "Have a good night."

I barely managed to toss Maureen a wave over my shoulder before letting Brutus lead me to the front of the lecture hall. I would've told him that it was unlikely we could find seats in the front row, considering the number of people in attendance. Yet, like they had been waiting for us and us alone, two chairs sat empty, side-by-side.

When he sat, I leaned over and pressed my lips to Brutus' cheek. "Thank you."

* * *

Brutus

I felt like an ass.

Work had me busy as hell all day.

Both Aaron and Joshua had outside meetings that they needed security detail for. Typically, that wasn't an issue, and we could coordinate the security for their travel without a problem. But I recently had to implement extra security measures because a few more threats had made their way onto my desk.

Add to that the fact that we continued to be short-staffed. When I let Taggert go, I knew it had to be done, but the fucker was a good damn security specialist. The problem was that he became more of a liability than an asset. Yet, it had been difficult to replace him with someone as highly skilled.

"Did you enjoy the talk?" Mia asked as held her chair out for her in the Asian fusion restaurant.

The sound of her voice pulled me out of the musings about work. My stomach sank with guilt as I took my seat. She peered across the table with those beautiful, expressive eyes, and I wanted nothing more than to make her happy.

"Gladwell is always a good talk."

It felt like the lighting in the room went up a few notches with the widening of her smile.

"I can't wait to read his latest book. I think it's going to be on the level of *Talking With Strangers*," she said.

"And you better not start it without me," I warned.

"What's to stop me?" she asked, her voice dipping to a sultry tone.

"I have something that'll—" My phone buzzed with an incoming text. Anger roiled in my belly. This was happening more and more—my annoyance at the interruptions from my work phone. But when I was with Mia that was the only place that I wanted to be. The only place that mattered.

I gave her an apologetic look across the table. She smiled but it didn't quite reach her eyes.

"It's okay."

With a sigh, I checked my phone. It was a text from Joseph. He alerted me that the extra staffing we inquired about hiring for next week's gala was a go.

"Everything all right?" Mia asked while unfolding the cloth napkin across her lap.

"Minor work thing." I reached across the table for her hand. I intertwined my fingers with hers, grinning at how small her hand looked in my massive one. But there was not a damn thing tiny about Mia's presence. Not as she sat across from me and not in my heart.

"Were you able to hire more staff?"

I paused as our waitress brought out glasses of wine and appetizers of pork and vegetable dumplings along with edamame.

"For the gala, yes," I answered once our waitress left. "But …" I pushed out a breath, wondering what the hell I was going to do about the few weeks after the gala. Three out of the four Townsend brothers had travel plans. Some were for business and while others were for family downtime.

I didn't like the increased threats that targeted the family. With a family like the Townsends, often there were former or current business rivals who were bound to talk shit. My office received a handful of threats every month, but something stood out to me about the most recent ones.

"Do you want to talk about it?" Mia asked with a lifted eyebrow.

I squeezed her hand in mine. I rarely talked about work with anyone. On occasion, with Jameson or another one of my friends in the same line of work. But it was an unwritten rule between us that we didn't share specifics of our jobs. Though, we might ask for another's input if they had experience with a particular situation.

Hell, I rarely talked to my father about the job, and I'd taken over the position from him.

Blowing out a breath, I leaned into the table. "Staffing issues."

Mia frowned contemplatively. She looked fucking delectable when she wore that expression. As if she was trying to solve the world's problems.

"We're spread a little thin," I told her. "Nothing to worry about. Or that I can't handle."

She squeezed my hand back. "I bet Rick wouldn't mind helping out for a short while."

I blinked. "My dad?"

She laughed, and the sound shot straight to my dick.

"He's the only Rick I know."

I narrowed my eyes. "What do you know that I don't?"

She shrugged. "Not much. But when he and I were talking the other night—"

"What other night?"

"Three nights ago, when you had to work late. We talked on the phone."

I blinked again. "You had a conversation with my father?"

She nodded. "We talk sometimes." She said it like it was no big deal. "The first time, he called me because he thought you were with me. He wanted to make one of those peanut butter and banana sandwiches and wanted directions."

I let out a curse, which only made Mia laugh.

"He's adorable." Only she would call my sixty-something year old, behemoth, and crotchety father *adorable*. "Anyway, you were sleeping, and I didn't want to wake you. So, I walked him through the process of preparing the sandwich, and I recommended he add some honey."

I leaned farther into the table. "That's why he puts honey on his sandwiches now."

"Probably. Anyway, that night we talked on the phone for about thirty minutes. Since then, he calls me every now and again. Just checking in. He loves hearing about my coffee shop."

Mia leaned closer. "I think he's a little lonely. He'll probably never admit it."

I snorted. My father wouldn't admit that.

"Maybe you should ask him to help you for a little while. It'll make him feel like he's useful."

I sat back in my chair right as our waitress brought out our appetizers. I'd never even considered asking my father for help while we were short-staffed. He was retired and, as far as I knew, enjoying his retirement.

If what Mia said was true, I bet he wouldn't mind traveling for a short business trip or family vacation. Looking at her across the table, I knew it was the truth. She was good at reading people. And somehow, people just opened up to her. Hell, I did, and I was terrible at opening up to anyone.

"What do you and my father talk about?" I asked, wanting to know.

She paused mid-chew, peering at me. "You," she replied after swallowing a piece of her tuna roll.

"Care to elaborate?" I leaned on my elbows, not giving a fuck about etiquette.

Grinning, she shook her head. "Nope." She popped the "P" which caused the memory of her making that same sound a few days earlier when my cock popped out between her lips.

Before I even entirely pulled up the image in my mind's eye, my dick stood at half mast. Mia smiled and told me she knew what was on my mind.

"Maybe it's time to take this dinner to go," I said, already holding up my hand.

"No," Mia insisted. "You promised we'd go dancing tonight after dinner. And since it looks like I'm going to need all of my energy, I'm finishing my dinner."

"Fuck," I gritted out between my teeth. She was right about needing her energy. I might have been tired from a long day at work, but never was I too exhausted to fuck my woman well into the night.

CHAPTER 21

Mia

"You didn't let me finish that last dance," I fake complained as Brutus barged through the doors of his bedroom with me in his arms.

"You're going to finish tonight, baby. I promise you that." As soon as the words were out of his mouth, his lips landed on mine. He pulled a moan from me. The moisture that already pooled in my panties from me rubbing against him while we salsa danced increased.

When he pulled away, I was left breathless. There was a fire in his eyes that yanked at my core. Within seconds both of our hands were everywhere. We tore and ripped at one another's clothing. Briefly, I wondered if this incredible passion would ever fizzle out.

Brutus put his lips directly on my favorite spot on my neck, and I had my answer.

No.

No other man could bring this type of passion to my surface.

"Oh, God. I need you," I whimpered.

"You have me. Every single ounce of me is yours," he said before sinking to his knees.

I inhaled sharply as his hands made their way up my thighs,

reaching my panties. With one smooth yank, he tore the lace material away from me. I didn't even bother admonishing him for destroying a pair of my panties. I was too hot and flustered to care.

"Mine," he growled before pulling me closer and using his massive hands to spread my legs apart. From his angle on his knees, he was in the perfect position to reach my cat with his mouth. And he devoured me like he'd been waiting all day to feast on his favorite meal.

"Shit." Throwing my head back, I palmed the back of his head. I thrust my hips into his mouth, giving him more of what he wanted. Brutus groaned against my pussy. The sound reverberated up my spine.

When his tongue slowly grazed across my clit, my knees became weak. I would've fallen if not for his firm, capable hands holding me upright. Brutus adjusted and easily swung one of my legs over his shoulder, locking me in a position that kept my pussy right where he wanted it.

The orgasm ripped through me, blinding me for an instant. I bit my lip so hard that I nearly broke the skin. But before I could fully come back down, Brutus bulldozed his big body between my thighs. He placed me on the bed after removing my dress overhead.

When he went to remove my bra, I smacked his hand away. Sitting up on my knees, I decided to take matters into my own hands for a little while ... as long as he would let me.

I slowly undid the clasp of my bra and peeled the material away. His eyes fell to my breasts as they spilled out. His gaze zoomed in on me, and a glint shone in those orbs. For a moment, he reminded me of a predator, contemplating the best way to consume his prey. That thought alone had my belly quivering.

"Baby, if you don't hurry up and get your ass over here, I'm going to—"

"What?" I asked. "I had to wait for you tonight," I told him, but there was no heat in my voice. "You can wait on me for just a—" That was the last syllable I got out before his long arms reached for me.

In the blink of an eye, I was on all fours on the side of his bed.

Brutus hovered over me from behind. I heard the distinct sound of a condom wrapper opening only moments before he slid into me.

We both let out something between a sigh of relief, a groan, and a growl. This man always had a way of pulling all types of animalistic sounds from me when he was deep inside of me. And deep he was.

He hit one of my walls so good and my back arched so profoundly that I thought my spine might crack in two. Even if it did, I would beg him to keep going.

"Do you like that?" he asked, his lips grazing over the skin of my ear.

I shivered.

"Do you like when I fuck you this deep, Mia?" He thrust in again, and I saw stars.

My arms began to shake, and I didn't know how much longer I could hold myself up.

And right before I gave up my second orgasm of the night, his movements stopped.

"Wh-What are you doing?" I gasped, outraged.

"You didn't answer my question."

What was his question again? I didn't really care.

"Brutus, please?" I begged, shameless and uncaring about it.

"You want me to please you?" he questioned with a small jut of his hips. It wasn't nearly enough to make me come. Just enough to make my pussy yearn for more.

My moan turned into a growl of frustration. "If you don't fuck me right this instant, I'm never sucking your dick again."

A deep, insidious rumble emerged from his lips.

"You love how my dick tastes too much to stop doing that, baby," he taunted. His hand moved around to my clit. He eased his fingers through my pussy lips and started massaging circles into my button. "Just like I love your pussy too much to never eat you out." His other hand tightened on my waist and pulled me aggressively into his body.

A woosh of air escaped my lungs from the move.

"It'll be my cock in your mouth and *only* my cock for the rest of our lives, Mia." His voice was hard and unyielding. "Say it," he demanded.

I blinked as tears gathered in my eyes. I had no idea what the hell he wanted me to say. At that point, I'd give him my left kidney just for him to provide me with some release from this fire he ignited in my belly.

"Please," I guessed.

His hand on my waist tightened. "Say it."

I'd heard lions in the Animal Planet documentaries I sometimes watched growl with less ferociousness.

"Yours," I finally said. "I'm yours."

"Always," he added.

I nodded. "Always."

That must've been the right words because he began thrusting again. And in no time, my body responded to his ministrations. We came together. I felt Brutus stiffen behind me and then shudder as he released his seed into the condom he wore.

* * *

Brutus

"Move in with me," I said while Mia rested in my arms. We had both caught our breaths after round two.

She didn't respond for a little too long, and I had to look down at her to make sure her ass hadn't fallen asleep. I had plans for at least one more round before I let her close her eyes for the night —that and convincing her to move in with me where she belonged.

I was a blatantly selfish bastard when it came to her. Somewhere along the line, I'd learned to accept that.

Her head popped up from my chest, and she stared at me. "I'm waiting for the punchline."

I wrinkled my forehead. "That wasn't a damn joke. I want to live with you. It's time we move in together."

Laughter spilled from her lips. But I wasn't in the mood to hear that melodic, hypnotizing laughter of hers. Not if she thought I wasn't serious as shit about this.

I sat up against the headboard. Mia also rose, sitting on her knees, facing me. When she went to use the sheets to cover her breasts, I pulled them from her hands.

"Don't get shy on me now, baby."

She pursed her lips. "This is probably a conversation we should do with our clothes on."

"Why?"

Her mouth gaped open. "Don't you think this," she gestured up and down the lengths of our naked bodies, "could distort our thinking?"

I shook my head and clasped my hands across my body. "Absolutely not." My gaze dropped to her chocolate tipped nipples, and my mouth watered.

"See? Exactly." She jutted her hand in my direction. "That's what I'm talking about."

I grinned. "Baby, I've got bad news for you. You could be wearing one of those fucking mumu thingies, and I'd still be looking at you like this. I'd fuck you wearing one of those, too," I added.

She twisted her lips in an attempt not to laugh, but it broke free. Mia sobered quickly. "I haven't even opened my shop yet."

"What does that have to do with us living together?"

She ran a hand through her hair, which was in total disarray from the bun she'd had it in earlier.

"It's a lot of change for me in the past few months. From leaving the career I had for over a decade, living abroad, falling in—" Her words broke off. She cleared her throat. "And now trying to start my own business."

"You're not trying," I corrected. "You're doing it."

Her eyes shone with gratitude. I took one of her hands into mine and pressed a kiss to the outside of her palm.

"Still," she started again, "a lot is happening, and moving in with you would ... I just need a little time."

As much as I hated it, I heard the pleading in her voice. She wasn't ready to make this move. I loathed it, but I understood it. Truth be told, I never would've thought of myself as the type who fell so fucking fast and as hard as I have. But there I was. A lovesick fool who knew he'd found the one to spend the rest of his life with.

And while I wouldn't pressure Mia into saying yes to moving in with me that night, I knew it was only a matter of time. She was mine, and I always claimed what belonged to me.

CHAPTER 22

Mia

"Can you get the back zipper for me?" I asked Brutus as I spun my back to face him. It was the evening of the fundraiser gala hosted by Townsend Industries. I'd chosen a burgundy, A-line gown for the event. The chiffon material of the dress made it billow out at the bottom when I walked, while the sequined corset top showed off my lush figure.

My favorite part of the dress, however, was the sheer lace cape that draped over my arms.

I glanced over my shoulder as Brutus approached, hovering over me. He looked good as hell in his tuxedo. He had it tailored to his exact dimensions. He'd added a burgundy bow tie and handkerchief to match my dress.

I gasped as I stared at his reflection in the mirror before me. Instead of zipping the dress up, he'd lowered the damn thing.

"Why don't we stay in tonight?" His hand flared out over my back, easing its way down. Right before he made it to my ass, his phone rang.

I laughed as he cursed. "That's why we can't stay in tonight," I reminded him. "You have a job to do."

A muscle in his jaw ticked as he answered the phone. "What?" he answered tersely. "I'm on the way."

"Something happen?"

"Joseph was just calling with an update." He ran his hand over his shortly cropped hair. "Everyone's in position, and the family should start arriving shortly after we do." He looked down at his watch.

"You never mentioned what this gala was for," I reminded him.

With a nod, Brutus answered, "It's to raise money for the community center the women started a few years back. All of the money raised tonight will pay for things like community college classes, to subsidize childcare for mothers at the community center, and to help with first and last months' deposits on apartments for women who're getting back on their feet."

"That's amazing," I told him. "Next year, I'll have to donate in the name of my coffee shop. Tonight, I'll write a check in my name," I thought out loud. "We should get going."

He bent down and pressed a quick kiss to my lips. "Keep those ready for me at the end of the night."

"I will." I grinned.

Twenty minutes after leaving my house, Brutus and I strolled, arm in arm, into the fundraiser held at a historic building in downtown Williamsport. The inside of the colonial-style building was transformed into a whimsical wonderland. Overhead hung wisteria flower vines with candlelight intertwined around the vines.

The candlelight and low overhead lighting created a peaceful and somewhat otherworldly ambiance. It was inviting and very beautifully done without being pretentious.

"Excellent, you're here," a man said, approaching us. He was older, with a gray streak running through his dark hair. He turned blue eyes on me and smiled. "You must be Mia."

I stuck out my hand. "And you must be Joseph," I greeted.

When he took my hand and pressed a kiss to it, a rumbling sound next to me caught my attention. Brutus glared at his second in command.

"The family will be arriving in five minutes," Brutus said. "You should go check to make sure everything is in order." There was an edge in his tone that hadn't been there a moment ago.

Joseph's grin widened. "Why don't I go do that?" He nodded at me before looking over at Brutus again. "Just remember, you're off tonight."

Brutus grunted, and I chuckled. Tugging his tuxedo jacket a little, I said, "He's right. You're off tonight. Enjoy yourself."

His lips tightened as he bent lower, bringing his lips only a few inches from mine. "You enjoy yourself. My *job* is to make sure you and the people around me are safe while you do so." His voice held that sexy edge to it.

My gaze fell to his mouth, and unconsciously, I ran my tongue across my bottom lip. I'd completely forgotten about the fact that we were in public. For a moment, I suspected Brutus did as well. He drew his arm around my waist and pulled me to him. The warmth from his body filled my chest and spread throughout the rest of my body.

"You might've been right," I purred, my eyes still on his mouth.

"About what?"

I grinned, finally meeting his hazel eyes. "Maybe it was a better idea to stay in tonight."

A low rumble emerged from his throat. It would've almost frightened me if it didn't turn me on.

"But then we wouldn't have had the chance to meet you finally."

I jumped, startled by the new intrusion. Behind us stood Tyler Townsend, who was practically NFL royalty at this point. Tyler's hazel-green eyes sparkled in interest as he tossed me a half smile.

"Tyler, can't you see you interrupted a private moment between them?" a petite, Black woman next to Tyler said. She was gorgeous and easily identifiable. Everyone knew how crazy Tyler was about his wife, Destiny.

Destiny's baby bump wasn't hard to miss as she rested her hand on her belly.

Not only that, but I'd been a long-time fan of her personal finance podcast, *Fashion and Finances*. She co-hosted it with her best friend and cousin, Resha.

"Oh my goodness," I rasped out. "I'm a big fan."

"See?" Tyler said, looking at his wife. "She's a fan of mine. It's no interruption."

"No," I corrected, causing three pairs of eyes to pin me. "I'm sorry, um, Tyler ... Mr. Townsend. You're great. But I meant your wife. I've listened to your podcast for years. If it weren't for you and Resha, I would've never had my finances together enough to leave my job and start my business. Your advice was the reason I started saving and investing my annual bonuses and why I bought a house much smaller than what I could afford."

I turned to Brutus with wide eyes. "Remember I told you how much I loved the book she wrote a few years ago? I have both the hardcover and audio versions," I told Destiny.

I stopped talking and pressed my lips together, realizing I was gushing a little.

Clearing his throat, Brutus pulled me into his side protectively.

For her part, Destiny busted out into a laugh. "Sorry, big guy." She slapped the back of her hand against her husband's chest. "It's not always about you."

Good-naturedly, Tyler shrugged. "It hasn't been about me since the day I met you."

A sigh fell from my lips. Brutus' hold on my hip tightened. He leaned in. "Don't let his pretty words influence you. He's full of shit," he quipped.

I turned to Brutus and ran my fingers through his beard. "He's not the only one who talks a good game."

I thought I said it loud enough for only him to hear, but when I turned back to the couple before us, they both stared between us. A mischievous smile played on Tyler's lips.

"I'll be damned," he said just above a whisper.

"Tyler, Destiny, this is Mia," Brutus introduced.

I stuck out my hand. "I'm so sorry. I tend to jump right in the deep end on the conversation part. Just ask Brutus. I practically talked his ear off during the plane ride when we first met. He saw my book ..." I trailed off. "See? I'm doing it again."

Chuckling, Tyler shook my hand. "No worries."

"Nice to meet you," Destiny said, shaking my hand. "To finally meet you. We've heard a lot about you."

My eyes bulged. "Really?" I peered up at Brutus.

He gave me a casual look but didn't say anything. Before I could interrogate him on that, another couple approached. Joshua and Kayla Townsend.

"She's a hugger," Destiny said a split second before Kayla engulfed me in an embrace.

"You're so beautiful," she complimented. "This burgundy is gorgeous."

I felt at ease with the women instantly. Sure, part of it was my extroverted personality, but they were kind and sweet.

"Thank you."

"I hear you're opening a coffee shop?" Kayla asked after a few minutes of conversation.

As usual, excitement sparked when I started talking about my shop. "A few more weeks until it opens."

"It's going to be phenomenal," Brutus said, an assuredness in his voice that settled the little sparks of fear and doubt that came up whenever I thought about my new venture.

"This guy loves his cup of coffee in the morning." Kayla thrust her thumb at her husband.

"With three kids, it's more like two and a half cups these days," Joshua said, chuckling.

That started a long conversation about my time on a Colombian coffee farm and the popup shops I'd done to build a customer base for my shop.

I became wrapped up in the conversation talking about my favorite topic as of late. But now and again, I would catch sight of Brutus. While most of the time, his gaze lingered on me, I would often see him surveying the room. He was doing that scanning thing of his where he was assessing everyone he saw. Try as he might take a night off, he was in his protector mode.

But not once did I feel like he paid more attention to security issues than to me.

"Brutus, can we talk to you for a minute?" Joseph asked about thirty minutes after we arrived.

I didn't need to know Joseph well to hear in his voice that this was a private matter. He was asking to speak to Brutus alone.

My man's eyes dropped to me. I felt his reluctance to leave me. Indecision warred in his eyes.

"It's okay," I said to him in a low voice. "You're needed."

With a pinch in his lips, he lowered and pressed a kiss to my cheek. "I'll be back ASAP."

CHAPTER 23

Mia

Brutus' ASAP turned out to be longer than expected. More than twenty minutes had passed since Joseph called him away. Yet, I didn't feel out of place among the invitees who attended the gala.

"Wait, what's the name of your shop?" Kayla asked after I'd spent almost all of that time describing how to make the perfect cup of coffee.

"Cup of Joy," I answered proudly.

"Perfect," Destiny said.

"What's perfect?" a deep voice said out of nowhere.

The two couples in front of me parted to reveal Aaron Townsend and his wife, Patience. I'd seen pictures of the couple in a few business articles. While the Townsends kept their personal lives as private as possible, there were pictures of the couples at fundraiser events.

"This is Mia," Tyler introduced.

"Brutus' Mia?" Patience asked, excited. Her brown eyes widened. "It's nice to meet you finally." She went to shake my hand, but a grunt from her side stopped her

My eyes landed on Aaron as he remained scowling. There wasn't a hint of a smile to be found on his face. This man was almost as intimidating as Brutus … no, maybe more so, though he didn't hold Brutus' height or physicality.

Patience made a tutting sound and waved a dismissive hand in her husband's direction. "Pay him no mind. He's still angry that our oldest son beat him in a basketball game this week."

"He cheated," Aaron nearly snarled.

Patience rolled her eyes again, looking exasperated, as she stuck her hand out for me. "Nice to meet you."

"So," Tyler said, slapping Aaron on the shoulder, "your old ass is finally getting schooled by the kid, huh?"

Almost everyone laughed, apparently unbothered or used to Aaron's demeanor.

"Wait until those triplets are running circles around you on the football field," Aaron shot back.

That caused Tyler's smile to drop.

But Destiny cackled. "I tell him every day."

Tyler pulled his wife into his arms and whispered something in her ear. While I couldn't hear what he said, I could imagine since Destiny's eyes glossed over. I was sure that if she were a few shades lighter, I would've been able to spot her cheeks turn crimson from whatever he'd whispered.

Also, I didn't miss the possessive way Aaron wrapped his arm around his wife's body as soon as she was back by his side. He continued to look on at me in an assessing manner. I would've grown uneasy if it wasn't for the rest of the family.

"Let me introduce you to Donnell. He loves coffee," Kayla offered, taking me by the arm as we made our way around the large room.

"Donnell," Kayla called.

A tall, dark-skinned man turned to us with a smile.

"This is Mia. She's starting a new coffee shop over on Grant Avenue."

His smile grew. "I was just telling Mike about wanting to find a new shop." He turned and tapped a man on his shoulder. "This is my husband, Mike," Donnell continued. The two men asked me multiple questions about the shop.

This went on repeatedly as Kayla or Destiny introduced me to one and then another gala attendant.

"Mia?" a familiar voice said while I was in the middle of a conversation with yet another attendee.

I spun to find Vincent Davis. I fought to keep my smile in place.

"Do you two know each other?" Kayla asked, looking between us.

"We work together," Vincent answered.

"*Used to*," I corrected, sharper than I intended. "We used to work together."

"Yes, Mia trained me when I started as a sales rep at Corsica Pharmaceutical," Vincent said. "Then I got promoted to a managerial position, and Mia quit."

I didn't mistake the scathing tone in his voice, but I chose to ignore it.

"Resigned," I told Kayla. "To start my coffee shop."

"Yes, well, some of us had the grit and fortitude to persevere through trying times," Vincent added.

He didn't give me a chance to say anything before he pivoted to Kayla.

"Which is exactly why I, and Corsica Pharmaceuticals, would be a match made in heaven with Townsend Industries' healthcare sector."

I gaped as Vincent pulled out a business card and thrust it in Kayla's direction.

She openly stared at the card and then at Vincent. "I don't work for Townsend Industries," she said calmly. She glanced over her shoulder. "But the CEO of Townsend Industries is right over there." Kayla pointed over her shoulder in the direction of Aaron Townsend.

"I'm certain he would *love* for you to interrupt him while he's with his wife at a charity event to talk business." Sarcasm dripped from every word. "Give it a try."

With that, Kayla wrapped her arm around mine, and we strolled away from Vincent. Laughter spilled from my lips.

"I bet he's still standing there looking like Boo Boo the Fool."

From over my shoulder I saw that, sure enough, Vincent stood there at the center of the room, looking like couldn't decide on his next move.

"If he had done any research, he would know that I'm a naturopathic doctor. I'm the last one who would advocate for a pharmaceutical company in a business deal." She waved a hand in the air. "Nothing against conventional medicine or drugs when necessary."

I held up my hands. "I get it. The products I sold often saved thousands of lives but some of the side-effects can be brutal."

She nodded. "And that's when they're used correctly. You don't want to know about the cases I've seen when those drugs are put in the wrong hands."

I shook my head. "I bet I don't."

We talked for a while longer, meeting more attendees. After a few more minutes, I started to look around for Brutus. It didn't take too long for our eyes to lock.

He strolled toward me, a determined gleam in his eyes. "Sorry. An issue I needed to help work out."

"It's fine." I pressed my palm to his chest. "I'm having a great time."

He frowned.

"A lot better now that you're back by my side."

That changed his frown into a smile. I was caught by surprise when he leaned in and brushed his lips against mine. The kiss was too brief for my liking, but it held a promise of what was to come later in the night.

"Aw," Kayla sighed, reminding us she was still present. "I'm so happy you finally went on vacation, Brutus." She gave us a wistful look before heading toward Joshua, who stood across the room, waving her over.

"I'm pretty happy about it, too," I said, tugging at his tuxedo jacket a little.

He palmed my arms and stroked them up and down. "I'm fucking ecstatic about it."

"Does that mean you'll vacation more often?" The question popped into my mind, and I blurted it without thinking.

"As often as you want me to," he replied. There was no hesitation in his response.

"Do you mean that?"

"Brutus?" Aaron called from behind him.

A brief look of aggravation crossed his face.

"You know what?" I pointed behind me. "The restroom is up this stairwell, right?"

Brutus nodded at the same time Aaron reached us.

"I'm going to use it. You two talk."

Brutus squeezed my hand. I observed Aaron with that ever-present scowl was in place.

I made a beeline for the stairs toward the bathroom—a sigh released from my lips. Though Aaron had barely said two words to me, I felt like he was watching me. Suspicion laced his stare. While it didn't make me exactly uncomfortable, I could tell he was suspicious of me.

I gazed upon the artwork as I made my way up the stairs. The early founders of Williamsport had busts and portraits painted of them that filled this building for visitors to observe.

The bathroom was just around the hallway from the stairwell. I breathed a sigh of relief to find that there wasn't a line. I did my business before checking the mirror to touch up my makeup and then headed out.

I started for the stairwell that was opposite the one I'd come up to be able to observe more of the artwork. However, before I could even exit the hallway, I was confronted by a tall male figure.

"Aaron ... Mr. Townsend," I corrected for some reason.

His lips thinned, and for the first few seconds he didn't say anything. His presence filled up the space in the hallway, and while he made an intimidating figure, I didn't feel threatened.

"Are you here for him?" he asked bluntly.

The implication in that question was apparent to me. Someone in his position, both in his family and the role in his family's company, I imagined it had become second nature to be wary of people. To question their motives.

I didn't need to think of my answer. "I'm *only* here for him," I said with all of the confidence in my body.

His gaze shifted over his shoulder, then back to me. "Why?"

That question threw me for a moment, and I felt my hackles rise. Not because I was personally offended, but because why wouldn't I be with Brutus?

"Because he's amazing," I said, thinking about the man who waited for me downstairs. "He's brilliant and loves learning. The attention he pays to detail is mind-boggling but so attractive. He's protective and, at times, scary, but his heart is so damn big that sometimes I get scared that it'll consume me whole."

I shut my mouth just before I told him that I probably wouldn't mind if Brutus' big heart did consume me.

Aaron studied me for a few more beats. "You love him."

Not a question, a realization.

A conclusion I'd come to weeks earlier but still hadn't said out loud.

I nodded. "Yes, I do." It felt like a relief telling someone. I hadn't even admitted it to Carlene or Sharise, the two closest people to me in the world. "I love him," I repeated because it felt so good to say again.

Aaron took a step back. He nodded and then turned for the stairs again.

"Do you?" I asked to his back.

He stopped in his tracks.

"Because he loves your family. And he puts his life on the line for you. He'd never tell me the details, of course. But I know he does." It had to be love that gave me the courage to say all of this to a man I didn't know. And one, I imagined, didn't just look intimidating but very well could be when he needed to.

Aaron turned back to me. "He's guarded my family for years. He spends almost as much time with my children as I do. He holds my wife's life in his hand when she's not in my sight. Of course I do. He's part of my family."

I swallowed the lump in my throat. I didn't have to ask to know that Aaron wasn't the type of man to say what he didn't mean.

"You should tell him."

His eyes widened in surprise. I got the impression he wasn't a man who was easily surprised either.

But I was on a roll, so I kept going.

"He believes he doesn't have any family beyond his father. If you love him, too, you should tell him."

He threw another look of contemplation my way. He didn't say a word, but he didn't need to. We just said everything that needed to be said between us. We'd come to an understanding.

I watched Aaron head back down the stairs. I continued in the other direction, taking in our conversation. It warmed my heart to know that the Townsends didn't think of Brutus as just their head of security. But I also meant what I said. He needed to know it. They needed to tell him.

I thought of the young boy who only had his mom to rely on. And he'd watched as men abused her. I realized the night he told me that those experiences he'd had as a child were what created his desire to protect others. To the extent that he'd put his very body in the line of fire to keep them safe.

I peered up at the artwork but didn't notice it. I was already planning how I wanted to tell Brutus that I was in love with him. Lost in my thoughts made me unaware of my surroundings.

Which was why when Vincent came up behind me, I didn't hear him.

"I've been looking for you."

I jolted and spun around. "I was on my way downstairs." I tried to move around him, but he side-stepped, getting in my way. My stomach dropped. I felt this encounter would be even uglier than the one we'd had on the street over a month ago. The strange gleam in his eyes told me so.

"Vincent, I don't know what your issue is, but you need to get out of my way," I said sternly.

"My fucking issue is you." He thrust his finger in my face.

"Number one," I said, fists balling at my sides, "I have nothing to do with you. Number two, it's no one else's fault that you can't do your job." I threw the words in his face, uncaring. I remembered back to the previous week what Maureen had told me about Vincent losing multiple accounts.

"Instead of being here in my face, it would serve you to worry about how to keep your job."

I started to push past him when he lunged at me. On instinct, I spun, knocking his arm away, then grabbing his wrist and twisting it. He folded over like a lawn chair.

"I told you the first time about putting your fucking hands on me," I gritted out.

"Get the hell off of me, bitch. Ah!" He screeched when I twisted his arm farther and braced his elbow with my other hand. I was in the perfect position to break his arm if he pushed me too damn far.

"You're obviously hard of hearing. So I'll tell your stupid ass again. Keep your hands to yourself, and the next time you see me, cross the street. Stay the hell away from me and out of my way."

With that, I pushed him away from me, letting him go.

"You stupid cu—" He had been starting to charge me again, but a giant hand wrapped around his throat and slammed his back into the wall. His head crashed into the glass that housed a fire alarm, cracking it.

I gasped at the sight of Brutus with his hand firmly around Vincent's neck.

"You don't like your life very much?" Brutus asked. His voice was eerily calm despite the furious expression on his face.

"Brutus?" I called tentatively. He was like a vast, barreling bear. It was best not to startle them lest they rip whatever was in their sight to shreds.

In this case, that would be Vincent.

While I didn't like Vincent and wouldn't mind seeing him get his ass beat, I didn't even want to think of the consequences Brutus would face if he seriously injured the man.

"You couldn't possibly," Brutus continued, not answering me. "Because putting your hands on my woman like that is the shit death wishes are made of."

I inhaled sharply when Brutus thrust Vincent's head against the fire alarm once more. The glass shattered.

"Shit," I cursed. If he did that again, he'd set the alarm off and clear out this place. I couldn't let that happen. He'd be in real trouble. "Brutus, please." I took the chance to reach out for his arm. "He didn't hurt me."

Yes, he'd tried. But I wasn't harmed.

Finally, Brutus looked at me out of the corner of his eyes.

"Um, maybe, let him go." A foul odor caught my nose, and I sniffed at the air. My eyes widened. "Is that…" I trailed off as I stared down at Vincent's crotch.

I slapped my hand across my face and squeezed my eyes shut. "Please let him go. I'm sure he's embarrassed enough."

I gestured at Vincent's soiled pants.

A muscle in Brutus' jaw ticked, but he loosened his grip on Vincent's neck and stepped back. He released him, and Vincent doubled over, coughing and holding his now red neck. I did not pity him. He needed to learn to keep his hands to himself.

"You have two seconds to get the fuck out of my sight," Brutus warned, sounding exactly like the bear I thought of a moment ago.

"Brutus, we—" Joseph said as he came up the stairs. He paused, assessing the situation before him.

"Security," Vincent called out, sounding strained. He hadn't learned how to keep his mouth closed. "Help!" he pleaded while stumbling in Joseph's direction. "This man just attacked me. I want him arrested," he demanded in between coughs.

Joseph looked over Vincent's shoulder to Brutus, who didn't bother saying anything. Brutus motioned with his head for Joseph to take Vincent out.

"Let's go," Joseph said, pulling Vincent toward the stairs.

"Did you hear me?" Vincent continued. "He tried to kill me."

"If I tried to kill you, you'd be dead, motherfucker," Brutus replied, his voice as matter of fact as possible.

"See?" Vincent gestured toward Brutus, but I didn't miss how he moved behind Joseph. "That should count as a threat. You're security. It's your job to arrest him."

Joseph snorted. "I didn't see or hear shit." He turned toward Vincent. "And he's my boss, so you're shit out of luck." He paused and sniffed. "Did you?"

A sheepish look passed over Vincent's face for once.

"You pissed yourself?" Joseph sounded outraged. "You definitely can't stay here."

He took Vincent by the arm but held him as far from him as possible as he dragged Vincent down the stairs.

"You could get in trouble for that," I said, rounding on Brutus.

He shrugged like it was no big deal.

"What if you hurt him? He is the type who would sue you."

"Let him." In one move, he swept me into his embrace, tipping my chin to look up at him. He searched my face as if examining me for injuries. "Where'd you learn that move?"

I blinked. "What move?" Then I remembered. "Oh, that arm lock?" I grinned in pride.

He nodded.

"I've taken more self-defense classes than I can count. Once I got into sales and started to have to travel for work, my dad insisted that I start taking classes with one of his former partners."

My father was a retired Williamsport police officer.

I glanced over my shoulder. "Who knew I'd have to use them on a freaking co-worker?" I snorted.

"Former co-worker," Brutus corrected, his face taking on a grim expression.

I didn't like that look. He stared over my head as if searching for Vincent. Like he regretted letting the other man walk away.

"Hey."

His eyes dropped to me.

"I had it handled. Vincent wouldn't have hurt me."

That didn't seem like it pleased Brutus.

He lowered and kissed my forehead. My knees went a little weak, but I was able to hold onto my balance.

"If you say so. But I've seen bastards like him before." He cupped my face. "And because you weren't injured, I'll let you decide how I handle him."

I blinked. "What?"

"Two options," he continued. "His job or his life?"

A lump formed in my throat, and for a few seconds it was impossible to push coherent words past it.

"That, um. You're not for real."

The smile he gave me bordered on feral. "He can lose his job or his life for putting his hands on you."

I shook my head to make sure I was hearing him correctly. I made myself push out of his embrace. "Brutus, you know normal men do not go around asking questions like that, don't you?"

"I'm not normal."

I had no response to that because it was a fact.

"His job or his li—"

"Job. His job," I blurted out, recognizing I needed to give this evidently crazy ass man some sort of answer before he took matters into his own hands. "He's on the way out, anyway. From what I heard."

Brutus nodded like he had made a decision.

Who the hell had I fallen in love with?

CHAPTER 24

Brutus

"I'm hungry enough to take a bite out of your arm," Mia groaned as we pulled into a spot overlooking the city of Williamsport. I had one of my staff pick up my car and deliver it to me at the gala, so that I could drive Mia and me once it was over.

A pang of guilt tugged at my stomach. "You shouldn't have waited for me," I told her for the third time. Even though I was supposed to have the evening off, I couldn't help doing a final walk-around once the gala ended. That led to me ensuring that all of the family got home safely and conferring with my guys to ensure everything was well.

It was well after midnight before I left. I'd told Mia that I would drop her off at my place and then return to finish work, but she insisted that she wanted to stay with me. And sucker that I was for her, I liked the idea of keeping her close. Even if it was late.

"Let's go," Mia said, ignoring my comment. "I'm hungry."

She snatched up the bags of food we'd just picked up, leaving me to carry our drinks. We got out of my SUV, rounding it to sit in the opened back compartment. Once Mia placed the food down, I lifted her to sit comfortably, facing the city below us.

"Do you always eat so late after one of these events?" she questioned while handing me a napkin.

I nodded. "I need to stay sharp while working. Food tends to fall low on the list of priorities." There were many moving parts of a significant event like the one we just left. Food was the last thing I concerned myself with. That was until I got my ass home and would almost pass out from hunger.

"You need to eat." Mia held a French fry to my lips. "Eat," she insisted.

Chuckling, I let her feed me the fry. My stomach growled, demanding more.

"See? Here." She handed me the double cheeseburger I'd ordered before unwrapping her crispy chicken sandwich.

"This looks amazing," she said, staring at her food. "Do you order from this place often?"

I nodded. "Mac's stays open until two in the morning. They're used to seeing my face on late nights. Their burgers are the best. The chicken sandwiches, too." I jutted my chin toward her sandwich. "They use a special sauce only they know the ingredients to."

I watched as she took a healthy bite.

Mia chewed for a few seconds and then let out a sound that went straight to my cock.

"That's so good," she moaned before taking another bite.

"You like it, I presume." I stuck another fry in my mouth.

"I love this sandwich almost as much as I love you." She went in for another bite.

The air around us felt like it had stopped moving. The sounds of the bugs in the trees surrounding us went quiet. All I heard were those three words coming from her mouth.

"Say it again." My voice sounded ragged.

She blinked and then wrinkled her forehead. "I love this sandwich almost as much as I love …"

Our eyes connected. Mia lowered her hands, still holding her food, to her lap.

"Repeat it."

"I love you." She quickly added, "I didn't mean to blurt it out just like that. I wanted to find the right time to tell you. And certainly, I didn't want to do it over fast food burgers, but honestly, this is kind of the perfect time to tell you because it's beautiful out here," she said in a rush.

"Yeah, I love you." The smile she gave me was brilliant, beaming.

All of the sounds surrounding us ceased to exist. There weren't any cars on the road below us, no animals or birds in the trees, and even the way the wind rustled the leaves silenced. The only thing I could hear was my heartbeat in my chest. It pounded loudly, echoing those three words she'd just given me. Wrapped up in that beautiful mouth of hers and presented as the gift they were.

I hadn't been the type to look for love. Somewhere I concluded that I wasn't the type who was destined to find "the one." Not once had I ever sought it out. I was content in my life, and then I went on vacation.

"Move in with me," I said without a second thought.

Mia frowned. My heart felt like it shriveled up in my chest.

I tossed my burger and fries down on the bag Mia had turned into a makeshift plate between us. Brushing my hands of crumbs and grease before I took her wrists into them, I said, "I want us to live together. Why don't you want that?"

I hated the desperation that crept into my voice. For a man like me, showing vulnerability didn't come easy.

"I do," she said in a rush.

I pushed out the breath I held.

"But we ... we haven't even known each other that long," she confessed.

"So?"

A nervous laugh spilled from her lips. Instead of making me feel lighter like it usually did, that sound tightened the vice that started to wrap around my heart.

"I'm opening a business." She blinked up at me. "I just quit my job a few months ago. I'm starting a new business and fell in love. All of this happened in the past five months. I'm a little ... verklempt." She pushed out a breath.

I tightened my hold on her wrists. Not painfully so, but like she was my anchor. Because, yes, in such a short amount of time, she had become just that.

"I love the hell out of you," I told her. "I want to wake up to you every morning, go to bed with you every night. I want to reach over in the middle of the night and pull you close to me just because I can. It's your coffee I want to come down to the kitchen when I wake up. You're the woman I want to argue with about whether the toilet paper roll goes up or down."

She grunted. "It's up," she insisted. "For the life of me, I don't know why it's such a hard concept for you." She sighed, sounding exasperated.

A chuckle slipped from my lips because I love fucking with her about it. "See? As much time as you spend at my house or I at yours, we practically live together already."

Her lips parted to give a rebuttal, but she stopped. Obviously, there wasn't a comeback because she knew I was right.

"You haven't even met my parents yet."

With a lift and fall of my shoulders, I brushed the concern away. "I'll meet them. Do you want me to give them a call right now?" I released one of her wrists to retrieve my cell out of my pocket.

"Don't you dare." She paused and gave me a look. "How do you even have their number?"

I swallowed. Would it behoove me to tell her I could easily access the phone numbers of everyone close to her, including her parents, her best friend, and her sister? Hell, I also had her brother-in-law's cell and knew the office where he worked.

But no.

I kept that information close to my chest.

"You probably gave it to me at some point," I said. "We'll have dinner with them the week after your shop opens. They'll love me. All parents love me."

The space between her eyebrows narrowed. "The parents of your past girlfriends loved you?"

A bark of laughter burst through my mouth. "Hell no. Only because I haven't had any past girlfriends," I confessed with a shrug. "Not in the last decade or more." Girlfriend implied a relationship, and I wasn't one for those in the past few years. But with Mia things changed.

Besides ...

"And you're not my *girlfriend*," I said the last word like it singed the back of my throat to say it because it did. "You're my fucking woman. My everything. I love you more than I thought was possible. I want you to be ..." I paused to keep from expressing my actual thoughts.

Mia was meant to be more than just a *girlfriend*. Like we were in fucking high school.

"I want you to live with me. Us. Together." That was the only acceptable outcome of this conversation.

She gave me a contemplative look. I could see the wheels turning in her mind. "I want the bigger closet."

I grunted but said, "Done." It'd hurt a little to relocate my suits to the second closet in my bedroom.

"And the left side of the bed," she insisted.

I shook my head before she finished. "No." There was no bend or give in my voice.

"Why not?" She pulled her wrists from my hands.

"The left side is my side because it's the closest to the door."

"So?"

"If there's an intruder—highly unlikely because of my security system—but on the off chance that something like that happened, me sleeping on the left side puts me in between them and you."

Her face softened. "Oh." Her voice sounded slightly breathless. "In that case ..." Her eyes dropped to her hands. "I'll move in with you." Mia's eyes locked with mine. "After the grand opening of Cup of Joy."

That was only a few weeks away. Too many days for my impatient ass, but I would make do.

"And you have to meet my parents soon. My dad can be intimidating," she warned.

I cupped her face. "So can I." I took her bottom lip in between my teeth before slowly pulling away.

"Hurry up and finish your food so I can spend the rest of the night devouring you."

* * *

Mia

"Ahh," I gasped, words sticking in my throat.

I'd agreed to move in with Brutus, and he was making it his business to show me why that was a good decision. With my legs spread eagle on his bed, his head in between my thighs, his promise to devour me was more than kept.

Lifted on my elbows, I could make out the dark strands of his hair. I reached down, threading my fingers between those silky strands, right before he rimmed my clit with his tongue. My hand instantly tightened, yanking on his hair as my back arched into his mouth.

If I were in my right mind, I would've realized how painful my tugging must've been on his scalp. But Brutus made no move to deflect my hand. Instead, he went even harder, tonguing my pussy like he was searching for the secret sauce.

"Shit, Brutus." Those two words came out more of a plea than anything else. I wanted him to keep going but also wanted to beg for him to stop. The rush of emotions was too overwhelming. "Wait," I managed to pant out while trying to scoot away from his relentless mouth.

Brutus followed me, securing his arms around my thighs even tighter. "Mine," he growled like a man possessed.

When he put his mouth back on me again, the explosion was instantaneous. A rush of liquid came released as I orgasmed ... more than I'd ever experienced before. Upon opening my eyes—not even realizing that I'd squeezed them shut—I peered down to see Brutus, beard soaking. A drop of my fluid dripped from his beard.

I stared wide-eyed, wondering what the hell had just happened.

A slow, arrogant grin spread over his lips. "You squirted, baby."

I blinked. "Wh-What do you mean?" I knew what squirting meant. I wasn't dumb or a virgin, but ...

"Have you ever done that before?"

I shook my head. "Not with anyone."

A few times while pleasuring myself, it'd happened. But not with another lover.

"Now you have," he said as he crawled with panther-like precision up my body. He kissed his way up my legs and across my waist, biting and licking at the stretch marks on my belly. Months ago, in Mexico, I'd been slightly self-conscious about how he relished so much affection on my stomach. What society deemed imperfections.

But Brutus treasured it, never minding the swell of my belly or the way my hips jiggled. If anything, he adored every inch of it.

"Oh God," I groaned when he dipped his tongue into my belly button. That was a particularly erogenous zone for me. And he'd taken note the first time he discovered that fact. He let his tongue play in the hole in my stomach, and my pussy grew wetter.

"Please," I begged, long ago shoving away any pride I had when it came to him.

"What do you want, baby?" he asked in that horrifically taunting way of his. The kind of tone that let me know he had every intention of dragging this out. I wanted to plead and beg him not to torture me just as much as I wanted to smack the hell out of him for even thinking of it.

"You," I said, sounding all types of wanton. "I want you."

His face hardened into a mask of pure need. A vein in his neck popped. "I want to fuck your face."

He didn't give me time to respond before he stood at the side of the bed and positioned me so that my head hung over the side of the bed.

Fuck.

I groaned as I watched, upside down, as he stroked his dick. My mouth watered, and I opened wide while at the same time reaching down between my legs.

"No," he said in a harsh tone. He snatched my hand away from my aching pussy. "Don't touch what's mine. But you can take what's yours," he said, bringing his cock to my mouth.

I licked the drops of precum that spilled out, savoring their semi-sweet taste, before taking him fully into my mouth. When Brutus released my hand, I made good use of it by playing with his scrotum. He cursed and pushed himself deeper into my mouth. I took him to the back of my throat.

I gagged a little from how deep he went, but that only made me wetter. Brutus liked to push me to the edge without going all the way over. And because he pleased me in ways I couldn't have even dreamed of, I didn't mind.

"Fuck, that mouth is killing me," he groaned. The sound did something to me, and I sucked harder, determined to make him spill down my throat. I kept playing with his balls while using my mouth to get him off.

"You're so fucking beautiful with my dick in your mouth."

In the recesses of my mind, I knew I probably looked crazy. I laid upside down, my mouth as wide as possible while tears streamed out of my eyes from how deep he was. Regardless, Brutus' words drowned all of that out. He meant it.

"You're fucking mine, Mia," he continued as if reciting a prayer. "Fucking mine."

It all became too much for me, hearing the groans and heaviness in the way he panted. I attempted to reach between my legs with my free hand to get some relief.

Brutus spotted the movement and swatted my hand away. I almost pulled away from him in frustration, but then he bent over my body. He slid his hand down my center to my core and began relieving the pressure building there.

"Come with me," he commanded while circling his fingers over my clitoris. At the same time, he bumped his hips, forcing his cock down my throat while holding onto my other hand, keeping it secure to his body.

The man's balance was incredible.

But that wasn't what I focused on at that moment. My eyes squeezed shut, and I felt his body go tight. The telltale tingling in the soles of my feet started and shot up my legs, straight to my pussy.

We both came in a rush. Brutus spilled so much damn cum into my mouth that it leaked out of the corners, down my cheeks. I did my best to slurp all of it up. And when he pulled his cock from my mouth, I chased it like the greedy skank I was. Only for him, though.

Brutus actually chuckled, watching me seek out his dick for more.

"I'm not done with you yet." A dark promise filled his statement. "Turn over onto your knees."

Did he wait for me to follow his instructions?

No.

His big hands moved me into position, until I found myself kneeling face down, ass up.

"Spread your cheeks for me, baby," he said in that deep, smoky voice.

Out of the corner of my eye, I watched as he moved to the nightstand to pull something out. My next inhale caught in my throat when I saw that it was a brand new bottle of lube.

He moved behind me, stepping in between my feet that hung off the side of the bed. "Hands," he demanded, moving my hands to my cheeks. "Spread."

Tiny little explosions went off in the pit of my stomach and pussy at the command in his voice. I did as he asked, willingly, opening my puckered hole for him. We'd discussed this act. He'd played with my hole before during sex. But this was the first time I would take his massive length inside of it.

"Brutus," I whispered, uncertain.

"Shshsh." He leaned over and kissed my temple. The move so fucking tender and reassuring that I almost came again. "I'll take care of you."

In that moment, I didn't have a doubt in the world that he would do just that. So, when I felt his fingers begin massaging the lube into my hole, I opened up for him. My breathing hitched and the heat that had only started to recede from my last orgasm began to rebuild on itself.

My stomach rumbled in anticipation when he lined his cock up at my back entrance. He started to push his way in, and I tightened up.

"Let me in." That time, his voice wasn't insistent or demanding, but patient. As if he'd wait eternity for me.

I spread wider, inhaling and exhaling to calm myself. Brutus pulled back slightly before pushing in again. A groan from the depths of my soul escaped its way up my throat and out of my mouth. The room around me blurred.

"Fuck, look how your ass takes me so perfectly," he croaked out. He must've been half out of his mind, too, because how was I supposed to watch what he was doing to me? But I felt it all. Every ridge as he pushed into my forbidden entrance.

The pressure eventually faded into that warm bliss of having him inside of me.

"Every hole on your body belongs to me," Brutus leaned over to say in my ear. "Say it."

"Yours. It's all yours." He didn't need to ask me twice. The last time I hesitated he stopped what he was doing, and I almost blacked out from the orgasm deprivation. I refused to go through that again.

"Damn straight," he said while thrusting his hips. He took my hips into his hands and thrust as deeply as he could go before slowly dragging his dick out and doing it all over again. Repeatedly, he brought me right to the edge only to retreat.

"Please," I begged.

"I could never deny you," he said before reaching around to stroke my clit. At the same time, he pumped into me, and I came for the third time that night while seeing stars behind my eyelids.

The last word I heard before drifting off on a bed of clouds was, "Mine."

CHAPTER 25

Mia

I stood at the center of my café with butterflies in my stomach. It was two weeks after the gala and the night I agreed to move in with Brutus. The following morning would be the official opening of Cup of Joy.

I surveyed the space, counting wooden tables with black chairs. My stomach rumbled. What if black was the wrong color? This place was supposed to spark joy in my customers, not bleakness. A tiny hint of panic rose in my throat. It was entirely too late to call the furniture store I'd worked with to pick out a new color.

"I can feel your anxiousness, baby."

I jumped as Brutus came up behind me. For as big as he was, he had a way of blending into his surroundings and moving so quietly you could forget that he was even there. Not that I'd forgotten. The way my body tingled was my alarm system that he was near. It was just that my mind raced in about thirteen different directions.

"I can't believe in just a few short hours this place will be open for business," I confessed.

I looked around the space with the tables lining the wall on one side and sat facing the windows on the opposite side of the room. The area at the center remained open, showing off the wooden tiling and giving the café an open air feeling. At least, I hoped that's what it did.

At the front of the shop, all the way across from the door stood the ordering counter. Specialty bags of coffee from the farm I worked and bought from in Colombia sat on the counter. I'd carefully written in calligraphy the opening day menu. We offered various types of coffees, espressos, chais, and smoothies made to order.

The glass case next to the counter stood empty. The following morning, I would fill it with the beautiful and delicious pastries provided by a local baker who worked from home. Mentally, I went through everything that was stocked in the back refrigerators. We had enough milk, cream, syrup, coffee beans, and more to last us for quite some time.

"Oh my God, what if no one shows up?" I blurted, my eyes going wide as I looked around the room. "I put so much of my life savings into all of this. And that's not including the business loan for this place."

Brutus moved in front of me, his bulky body filling my vision. He took my hands into his, squeezing them. "It's going to be amazing."

"How do you know?" Even the assurance in his voice wasn't quite enough to overcome the sudden fear that gripped me. This had been a dream of mine for so long that it was becoming a reality was almost too much to take in. "I know it's silly. It's just a coffee shop. Those pop up every day, right?"

Then the statistics on how many businesses fail each year ran through my head.

"Breathe," Brutus ordered.

I exhaled, my shoulders deflating slightly.

"Cut all of that negative shit out of your head right now. Remember all of the reasons you wanted to open in the first place. Hold on to them. That's all you need." He kissed each of the knuckles on my right hand.

The tension in my muscles relaxed. "You're right."

I shifted from one foot to the other as I looked around. Still, something felt off. Everything was in its rightful place. The syrups were lined up against the coffee bar right next to the shiny, barely used espresso machine. Coffee beans rested in the coffee grinder, waiting to be ground first thing in the morning.

In the far corner of the café, closer to the door sat three plush chairs with the coffee table at the center. The space was the perfect coffee corner for small gatherings of study groups. I envisioned friends wanting to catch up, retirees finding a space to consume their morning beverage while people watching in that spot.

"Something's missing," I said. But I couldn't put my finger on it.

Brutus kissed my hand again before stepping away. "You're right."

A sharp inhale split the air around us. The panic began to clog my throat again.

"There is something you missed." He said it but there was a grin on his face. How could he smile like this was a joke?

I spun around, following the direction he walked. With his back to me, he picked up something on the table. When he turned to me, he had a large, black box. He moved closer and pulled back the cover of the box, revealing what was inside.

"Oh my …"

"Back in Mexico," he started, "you said you had to have a chess set for your coffee shop."

I smacked my forehead. That was it. That's what had been missing.

"You remembered?" I don't know why I formed it as a question. Right in front of my eyes was the proof that he remembered my off-hand comment. I'd only mentioned it once when we went into one of the coffee shops in Tulum.

In the run up to open Cup of Joy, with all of the necessary renovations, hiring decisions, coordinating deliveries with distributors and most important, marketing, I forgot all about the chess set.

But Brutus hadn't.

I ran my finger over the hard yet smooth stone of the board.

"It's hand-crafted onyx and stone."

The cream and brown squares of the board almost shone, and the beautifully handcrafted off-white stone pieces sat on one side while cream and brown pieces sat on the opposite. It was stunning and the colors blended in so well with the color scheme of my shop.

"How much was this?" I asked, knowing it had to be in the four figure range, at least.

Brutus' lips twisted into a frown. He held up one of the kings between his thumb and forefinger. "I figured you might be a little leery of one of these getting lost. So, I have a matching set made out of plastic. You can use those during the day, if you'd like," he continued, evidently not planning to answer my question. "But this one," he held up the chess set, "is for us."

He waved his head, directing us toward the chairs around the coffee table. "Let's play."

I had to blink away the tears for a few moments before I could follow him. Growing up, my father had often told me and Sharise to believe only about a quarter of what a man said. But to watch what they did.

Anyone can use those three words to try to convince you he's legitimate. However, are his actions in alignment with those words? Does he show up for you? Can you rely on him when you need him the most?

"I love you," I told him as I moved to sit in his lap.

I ran my hand down the side of his face as he smiled. He turned his head to kiss the inside of my palm. "I love you."

The warmest, coziest, most comforting feeling spread from my chest throughout the rest of my body. It swept away the final remnants of doubt and fear I had about my shop. Whether the business succeeded or failed, I'd taken the leap of faith to change my life, and in the process ended up meeting and falling in love with the most wonderful man on Earth.

What more could a woman ask for?

CHAPTER 26

Mia

"Gloria, can you grab a couple more of the fruit pastries from the back for the display case?" I asked my part-time employee.

When Gloria entered the kitchen area, I let out the breath I held. Glancing at the clock on the wall, I saw that it read seven-thirty. We'd only had two customers so far on this first day of opening.

"It's early," I reminded myself. The morning rush should be starting as soon as people made their way into their offices. My shop was intentionally located in a part of the city that was close enough to high rises that we'd attract workers as they went into business for the day. But it was also a few blocks from Williamsport University to attract the student population.

When the fear that crept in last night tried to rear its ugly head again, I looked over at the corner of the shop where the chairs and coffee table sat. On top of the table sat the beautiful chess set that my man purchased for me. The only difference was that the plastic pieces sat on the board instead of the handcrafted originals. Those were behind the counter, reserved for me to take out when I wanted.

A smile made its way to my lips when I recalled how late we'd been in this place the night before playing against one another. Brutus won, of course. He was so damn keen and aware of the board. But it took my mind off of the worry, same as the memory did right then.

The opening of the front door grabbed my attention. A familiar, smiling face met me.

"Kayla, hi," I greeted Joshua Townsend's wife.

"Good morning." She eyed the shop. "This place is delightful. I couldn't wait to get in this morning. I just dropped the kids off at school for an early morning tutoring session, and I missed my cup of coffee."

"We can't have that, can we?" I moved behind the counter, my fingers eager to start to prepare whatever she ordered.

Kayla sniffed at the air. "I'll have whatever's brewing in the air."

I laughed. "I just grounded up our famous arabica beans."

"Let's do a latte," Kayla added. "Oh, and one of those fruit pastries. I missed breakfast this morning." She pointed at the glass case at the pastries Gloria had just brought out.

"This is to go, I assume?" I knew Kayla had a day job. It was probably nearby and she needed to hurry to get into the office soon.

"To stay, actually," she said in a delighted tone. "I have some extra time this morning."

"Coming right up." I got busy preparing her latte. I hummed along with the sound of the espresso machine as it prepared her shot, followed by the steamed coffee. It was a relatively simple order but how much it delighted me to fulfill it.

This is your dream, my mind continued to tell me. Unfortunately, that doubt was quickly followed up by the realization that one customer alone couldn't keep the doors of this place open.

"Mm," Kayla moaned after taking a sip of her drink. "So smooth and creamy." She blushed slightly. "Don't tell my husband I said that out loud for anyone but him."

I covered my mouth as I laughed along with her. "I heard nothing." I covered my ears, causing her to laugh a little more.

The front door opened again, and Destiny Townsend walked in.

"Perfect, you're open. I couldn't wait to get here," she said as she wobbled over to us.

"Good morning," I greeted as she came to stop in front of us, her hand resting on her belly.

"Morning, Mia. Hey, Kayla. Resha and I are recording early this morning and we're interviewing a couple of people, so we need coffee for the whole team."

"Oh." I moved around to the counter to start to take Destiny's order.

"This is probably going to be a big one. And you have muffins, right?"

I pointed to the glass case. "We have what's there plus more in the back."

"Perfect. Resha loves her a good muffin. This kid, too." She rubbed her belly.

"Would you like to sit?" I offered, extending my hand toward the closest free chair. "I can come over and write your order down."

She waved me off. "No, I'm fine. Okay, let's see …" She rattled off orders for ten drinks in total, three muffins, a couple of scones, and a few more pastries.

I grew concerned over how she was going to carry this all to her car, but before I completed her order, the door opened again and in walked Tyler.

He approached the counter wearing a frown. He glared down at his wife. "You were supposed to wait for me."

"Hey, Ty," Kayla called with a wave from her seat.

"Kayla." He acknowledged before scowling at his wife again.

"You were taking too long to get ready. I knew you'd meet me here," Destiny said.

"You're lucky I had the morning off."

The two bickered in a way that was extremely cute, Tyler obviously upset that his wife would even attempt to lift a finger in her condition. And Destiny having to remind him for what seemed like the thousandth time that she was pregnant, not incapable.

I giggled at how adorable they were. And for a moment, I

wondered if Brutus would be that protective over me if I ever got pregnant with his baby. I remembered our time in Mexico when we'd gotten a little carried away and failed to use protection. He hadn't even seemed frightened once we realized what we'd done.

Then I brushed the thought aside, because of course he would be as protective. Hell, I would venture to say that he might even be worse. He was already protective. The measures he went through to ensure that I had a security system that met his standards in my shop were incredible. All of the system hadn't been completely installed yet, a fact which led him to try to get me to delay the opening, until it was finished.

My thoughts about his protectiveness scattered when the door opened again, and in walked Patience with their mother-in-law, Deborah Townsend. A twinge of awareness scattered up my spine, and I started to suspect something was going on.

"Deb, you have to try the fruit pastries," Kayla insisted to her mother-in-law. "But the latte is even better."

Deborah's blue eyes gleamed in delight. Before I knew it, Gloria and I were making a dozen beverages between the two of us for their staff at the community center. Patience also ordered a few of the scones and a couple of smoothies for the volunteers at the center who didn't drink coffee.

I had just completed their order when a handful of more customers began filing in. My heart smiled as the café filled with people eager to try a new coffee shop, or having already sampled our coffee at one of the pop up stands I'd done in the weeks running up to our opening.

Before I knew it, the clock read close to nine-thirty. Yet, the shop felt as if it were just getting started as more patrons poured in. I glanced over at Gloria and worried if I had enough staff for this morning rush. Biting my lower lip, I looked around the shop and my stomach filled with butterflies. As much as I enjoyed the experience of preparing the different beverages we sold, I itched to get from behind the counter and interact with the people who stopped by.

"I hope you enjoy it," I said to my latest customer while I stood at the register. "Please come back and tell your friends." I handed the man in a business suit his green smoothie and watched as he exited through the door closet to the counter.

I didn't have time to watch for too long before I was serving another customer. Don't get me wrong, these were great problems to have, but I felt slightly stifled behind the register. I wanted to learn the stories of the customers who chose to take a seat while they enjoyed their drink or breakfast sandwich.

In my peripheral, I was delighted to see a couple of younger guys had taken up residence in the chairs in the corner. They were engaged in a chess game—just as I'd envisioned.

I heard the kitchen door behind me open and assumed it was my employee bringing new supplies from the back.

"Gloria, can you—" I broke off and covered my mouth as I laughed.

Standing in front of me was Brutus wearing a Cup of Joy apron. The apron in and of itself wasn't so funny, as it was the exact black and brown apron with the shop's logo of a coffee cup pouring into a smile onto a woman's face. The hilarity was that the apron was about three sizes too small for my man's colossal frame.

Yet, Brutus wore it with pride. "This was the only available one you had in the back." He frowned. "I should've gotten one specialty made for me."

I swallowed. "What are you doing here?" I asked as he came to stand at the register next to me. I looked over him again. Underneath the apron he wore a light gray button-up and black suit pants. Apparently, he'd removed his suit jacket to put on the apron.

He'd rolled the sleeves to the elbow, showing off his solid and veiny forearms. I had to look away because why did even his forearms turn me on?

"I came to work," he answered, casually.

"Work? Here?"

He grinned at me sideways. "Where else?"

"Your job," I replied like it should've been obvious.

He leaned in and kissed my temple. "Today, this is my job. It's the first day of your dream. You didn't think I'd miss it, did you?"

"Yes," I blurted out honestly. "You went to work this morning."

He gave me a slight shake of his head. "I had to do a couple of things at the office this morning. Went in early to make sure the staff was on top of it all." He paused and faced me, turning up the wattage on his smile. "But from here on out, I'm all yours."

Brutus spread his arms wide as if to say *use me however you want*. My body heated at the images my mind started to conjure up. When I met Brutus' eyes again, I could see my exact thoughts mirrored in his scorching gaze.

Someone cleared their throat, making me jump. I turned to a man standing in front of the register.

"I'd like to order a latte."

I opened my mouth to greet him and take his order, but Brutus cut me off. "I'll help you out."

With the proficiency of a seasoned barista, Brutus took the man's order. I stood there, watching him, slightly dumbfounded. This man never ceased to amaze me. How could I have ever doubted how important I was to him?

"Show rather than tell."

My dad's words echoed in my head. Brutus wasn't much of a talker outside of people he didn't feel comfortable around. But he showed his feelings in his actions.

"You can go talk to your customers," Brutus said, once he completed the man's order. He gestured toward the broader part of the shop, where a handful of customers lingered. "I know you want to speak to them. Go," he insisted. "Gloria and I can handle the orders. Right, Gloria?"

"Right," she answered without hesitation.

I popped up on my tiptoes and pressed a kiss to Brutus' cheek, unable to stop myself. I started to move around the counter, but stopped. "Did you tell all of the Townsend wives to show up this morning?"

Truthfully, I knew the answer, but had to ask.

He wrinkled his forehead. "Tell?" He shook his head. "I have no idea what you're talking about. Besides, didn't you mention opening the shop at the gala?"

I had, but I don't think I mentioned the exact date of my grand opening. I didn't want to come across as if I were using Brutus or his connections to drum up customers. I was a saleswoman, yes, but I also understood the importance of relationships over business.

"Thank you," I said anyway. There was no doubt in my mind that Brutus had at least mentioned that today was the opening day of Cup of Joy to the family.

With a lump in my throat, I moved from behind the counter into the main area of the shop. I spent the next hour or so talking with customers, getting to know them, and even playing a few rounds of chess with some patrons.

By the end of the day, my heart felt like it would explode from how full it felt. And as I closed up the shop for the first time, with Brutus right beside me, I wondered what, if anything, could stand in the way of this happiness.

CHAPTER 27

Brutus

"If you're nervous, you can tell me," Mia said as I backed out of my driveway. It was two weeks after the opening of Cup of Joy, and we were on the way to her parents' home to have dinner. Mia's sister and brother-in-law would also be there.

I reached over and brought her hand to my lips. "Are you nervous?" I could hear it in her voice, so I didn't need to ask but still chose to.

With her free hand, she stroked her thigh as if trying to relieve some tension. "Yes, a little." Sucking her teeth, she shook her head. "I'm a grown woman."

"Don't I know it," I said, giving her a glance and smirk before looking back at the road.

"Shut up." She pulled her hand free from my hold to swat at my shoulder. "What I mean is even though I'm fully grown, my parents' opinion still matters to me." She pinched her lips. "For years, my mother wanted me to settle down, get married, have babies, and become a stay-at-home mom like she was. Like Sharise. She blamed my job and working too much for never finding a good man."

Mia sat up straighter.

"And my dad ... well, he was less vocal than my mom about wanting me to marry and have a family, but he would tell me to make sure I found someone who was worthy of me. I could tell he barely approved of the few guys I introduced him to over the years."

She shrugged. "But then again, he didn't like Boris when he first met him, either." Boris was Sharise's husband.

I raised an eyebrow and looked over at her. "Why?"

Mia snorted. "Because he thought Boris worked too much. The first few times they tried to have him over, he had to cancel for school or work. Boris worked three jobs while in college. My dad told Sharise she deserved better than someone who couldn't put her first."

She laughed.

"What?" I asked.

"It's just ironic. My dad was a workaholic himself. Many nights he stayed late at work or would pick up a second shift. It worked out since all that extra work helped him retire early at fifty-five, but I think he didn't want to see either one of his daughters go through what he put my mom through."

I didn't say anything to that. A slew of memories of the times in which I'd been called away from a dinner or out of my sleep in the middle of the night because of my job came to mind.

What I'd told Mia the night of the gala about not being nervous about meeting her family was true. However, her words hit me in my chest. She did deserve someone who would put her first. Always.

My job made that impossible.

And her family was important to her. It was one of the many things I loved about her. In the months that I'd known Mia, I started to realize how much I craved a family. That was part of what drew me to my job and why I loved it as much as I did. The Townsends were as close-knit as they come. I'd seen how wealthy, powerful families played the part for the public, but behind closed doors, they were either at each other's throats or barely speaking to one another.

Not the Townsends. You could feel the warmth between all of them.

Family.

I wanted that. Always had. I came to realize it was why I sought Rick out after my mother died and why I kept him close despite the fact that he was able to live on his own and had plenty of money to do so.

As I looked over at Mia in the passenger seat, I recalled that time in Mexico when I went in her raw. I hadn't said it out loud, but I wouldn't have minded if she ended up pregnant. I grew disappointed when she told me she'd gotten her period the following month.

Even back then, I knew. I wanted a family and I wanted it with her.

So, while I wouldn't exactly describe myself as nervous about meeting Mia's parents, I recognized it for the big deal it was. This would bring us one step closer to my end game.

* * *

"Mama, it smells good," Mia said as we entered her parents' home, behind her mother. "What did you make?"

"Biscuits and gravy with fried green tomatoes on the side," Mrs. Raymond said casually.

"Aw, man," Mia exclaimed, pressing her hand to her stomach. "My mouth is watering. Where's Daddy?"

I followed the two women through the entryway and into the living room.

"You know your father likes to make an entrance," she said dismissively. Her mother turned her gaze on me. Mia had gotten her height and shape from her mother, who appeared to be barely above five-four. But that was all Mia got from her mother in the looks department. Mrs. Raymond was a few shades darker than her daughter, with a pair of deep-set dark brown eyes to match.

"Brutus, we're glad to have you over finally," Mrs. Raymond started.

"It's my pleasure to meet you." I handed her the salad that I'd prepared for dinner. "This is our contribution to dinner."

Her eyes shifted to her daughter after looking at the clear lid of the salad bowl. "Mia, you made salad?"

Mia shook her head. "That's all him." She beamed up at me.

"I hope you're not allergic to anything. There are some pine nuts in the salad."

Her mom's smile widened, and for a beat I did see the resemblance to Mia's smile. Mia had inherited her brilliant smile from her mother.

"No allergies over here. And I tell Ray all the time we need to eat more vegetables. He'll get a kick out of this." Mrs. Raymond laughed.

When she left us to put the salad in the kitchen, I turned to Mia. She ran her teeth over her bottom lip. I lifted my hand to her chin, taking it between my thumb and forefinger to pull it free.

I was about to tell her I was the only one allowed to suck on that plump lip when footsteps against the wooden floor drew my attention. Standing in the center of the living room entrance stood Ray Raymond, Mia's father. Yes, that was his real name.

His nickname was Ray-Ray. Not something that Mia shared with me but the information I'd found through my own means. He stood at just under six feet, and his lighter complexion and slightly angular features would've given him away as Mia's father if I hadn't already known. She was the perfect combination of her parents.

"Daddy." She went over to hug her father.

Something inside of me clenched up at seeing her in another man's arms. Even if it was her father. Stupid emotion. I knew it was, but shit, I couldn't help it.

"Baby girl," he greeted before his eyes moved to me. He didn't say anything at first, but I didn't need to wait for him to speak.

"Mr. Raymond." I approached with my hand outstretched.

"Daddy, this is Brutus," Mia said, looking between us.

He didn't smile, but he did shake my hand. "The young man she met in Mexico."

"On the plane to Mexico," I corrected.

No break in his somewhat icy demeanor as he continued to look me over. And despite the cold reception, I kind of liked this man. I liked men who were protective of their families and the people they loved. Mr. Raymond cared for his daughter. His affection was evident in his eyes when he looked at her.

"How's that coffee shop, daughter?"

"You were just there yesterday," she commented with a laugh.

"Had one of those scones and a caramel mojito?" He pinched his brows together as if knowing that wasn't the right word but not quite certain. "Janice!" he called to his wife.

A beat later, Mia's mother came from around the corner, out of the kitchen. "Why are you yelling in my house like that?"

"What's the name of the drink I had at Mia's shop yesterday?"

"Caramel macchiato," Mia and her mother said simultaneously.

"That's it." He snapped his fingers. "It was good too. I wanted to get another one but your mama ..." He patted his rounded belly.

"The doctor told you about all of that sugar," Mrs. Raymond scolded. "Sharise and Boris—" She broke off when the doorbell rang. "That should be them."

A few beats later Mia's sister, Sharise, and her husband, Boris, walked through the door, greeting her mother. I was introduced to the couple, who opted to leave their kids home with the sitter for the night.

Not long after, we ended up in the dining area where Mia's mother served a delicious meal of biscuits and gravy with a side of chorizo sausage, along with the salad I'd brought. Sharise had made a fruit salad to have a lighter dessert.

All the while, the family talked over dinner, catching up. I was included and asked questions here and there. One point of interest for Sharise was how Mia and I met. She asked lots of questions about our time in Mexico, but I got the impression she knew most of the answers. Either she wanted to see how honest I would be or how outright I would be in front of her parents.

Boris was quiet and somewhat reserved but not in an 'I don't want to be here' kind of way. More so, he was the type to let his wife do the talking while he was comfortable sitting back and observing. I could relate to that. Mia, her sister, and their mother were the extroverts of the group. But I enjoyed watching them interact with one another.

They were so in sync, even when a minor disagreement would break out. It was quickly settled, or one would declare the other was wrong, and they'd roll their eyes and move on with the conversation.

Mr. Raymond didn't speak much, only interjecting a "yeah" or something of the sort every so often. But I could feel his eyes on me when he thought I wasn't looking.

He quietly assessed me while I did the same. I aimed to figure out how to approach the conversation I intended to have with him before the night was over.

Unfortunately, I wasn't the one who got to broach the subject first. Mrs. Raymond suggested that we all move to the living room to have our dessert. I caught a brief look between Mr. and Mrs. Raymond after she said it. That was when he approached me and asked to speak with me privately.

I started to follow Mia's father in the opposite direction of the rest of the group, but Mia caught my hand. I kissed her forehead.

"We'll be right back," I promised.

She nodded and then went to help her mother in the kitchen. I followed Mr. Raymond until we came to a door that led to a back porch.

"Take a seat with me, Brutus," he said.

I eyed the wicker furniture on the patio before sitting in a chair directly across from him. Between us was one of those small, glass patio tables. The kind a strong gust of wind could blow over.

Mr. Raymond sat forward in his chair and tapped the table with his forefinger. He gave me one of those appraising looks again before he asked, "What do you do for a living?"

"Head of security for a well-established family and their business, based here in Williamsport."

His expression didn't change. "The Townsends?"

"Sir," I started, also moving forward in my chair, "the family I work for entrusts me with their livelihoods, their lives, and the safety of their children. I do not give the name of my employer willingly. I'm sure you already know by now, but out of respect for my—" I stopped short of calling the Townsends my family.

That thought hadn't ever occurred to me, but I came a hair's breadth away from making that declaration out loud. I tucked that knowledge away to unpack at a different time and place.

"Out of respect, I don't talk about who I work for." It was also out of necessity.

"I understand that," he noted. "What are your intentions with my daughter?" he asked bluntly. I wondered how many other guys Mia had introduced to her parents over the years. Mr. Raymond was asking questions like he would of a high school boy. Was he *that* out of practice with intimidating his daughter's men? Honestly, I should be happy about that.

It meant Mia hadn't introduced him to a lot of men in the past. *Good*. I'd also be the last new man to meet her parents.

"To marry her."

His eyes bulged and he expelled a huff of air. "Excuse me?"

I was sure he heard me well enough the first time, but I repeated myself. "Mia is who I want ... will spend the rest of my life with. Of that I'm sure. She's brought a light to my life I didn't know was missing. I'll spend the rest of my life doing everything in my power to do the same for her."

"Are you asking for my permission to marry my daughter?"

I just barely bit back the laugh that threatened to escape my throat. Mr. Raymond was Mia's father, and I would grant him the respect he deserved, but ask for permission?

I supposed it would've been the correct thing to do. But how does one ask for permission for what already belongs to you?

With a shake of my head, I said, "Sir, your daughter has become my world. I have every intention of making her my wife. I'm asking you to accept that your daughter has found a man who will cherish her in every way she deserves for the rest of her life. Who will protect her with everything in him. Because I'm that man. I knew it from the very moment I met her."

His lips twitched, but he held on to the blank expression he wore. I appreciated his stubbornness.

"Do you have a ring?"

Shit.

I cursed myself for my failure. In the weeks since Mia's shop opened and a few trips for work, I hadn't had time to even look at engagement rings. Then I had to decide whether or not to surprise Mia or let her pick out one she loved. Though I liked my suits tailored and my shoes shined, I wasn't much of a jewelry man. And this was something that she would wear for the rest of her life.

I hated to admit it, but I needed help making that one decision.

"Not yet," I admitted.

"That's a problem, don't you think?" He didn't wait for me to answer. "Unless you plan to propose to my daughter without a ring." He hiked up an eyebrow.

"Not in my life. I just need time to find the right one."

His facial features eased as he relaxed. "Well, given the time you two have known each other, I can tell you're a man who doesn't waste it." He nodded. "Good. My Mia deserves a man who knows what he has in her."

"I do," I assured.

He stood, and I did the same.

"Well then, you have my acceptance." He stuck out his hand for me to shake. "I had you looked in to," he said as he released my hand.

I gave him a curious expression.

He glanced over his shoulder as if making sure we were alone. "Had some of my buddies still on the force do a background check and all of that. I knew who you were before you walked through my door."

At that, a genuine smile crossed my lips.

He grinned as well. "And I already know you did the same."

I neither confirmed nor denied, but evidently didn't need to. Mia's father was a police officer for almost twenty-five years. He'd have certain connections.

"My daughter is a good judge of character. You find her the right ring," he said.

"Yes, sir." I nodded because that was my intention to get as soon as possible.

Now, I just needed to figure out what the hell type of ring would be perfect for my woman. And who the fuck would help me pick it out.

CHAPTER 28

Brutus

"Did you speak with Rick this morning?" Joseph asked, standing in front of my desk.

I nodded. "Robert and Deb are enjoying the final hours of their vacation. Even took Rick's ass horseback riding."

Joseph let out a bark of laughter. "I bet he loved that."

I grinned. "He cursed up a storm about it." I grinned at the reminder of my father's pissed off rant about being forced to ride a damn horse while taking on security for the elder Townsend's vacation in the Bahamas. The truth was, I heard the affection in his voice, and Deb and Robert would've never forced my father to do anything he wasn't comfortable with.

He was just a blowhard. But Mia's advice from a few weeks earlier worked. I hadn't realized that my father might be lonely. It did him good to take on a job every now and again.

"I handled that other issue for you as well," Joseph said, the volume of his voice dipping. It wasn't necessary since there wasn't anyone else around, and my office was secure. But his tone let me know exactly what situation he was talking about.

Vincent Davis.

Mia's former co-worker. The stupid bastard who had the damn nerve to put his hands on her the night of the gala. Just thinking about him caused a surge of fury to push through my body. I paused and made myself inhale.

I'd promised Mia that I'd spare his life, but the fucker didn't know how close he came to meeting his maker that night. Or in the weeks since.

He'd merely walked away with the loss of his job. I personally met with the head of his department at Corsica to let him know that his employee had left a foul taste in my employers' mouths that night.

Vincent had already had one foot out of the door, according to his manager. That was the straw that broke the bastard's back.

"Last we checked on him, he was packing up his shit," Joseph continued.

"To where?"

He shrugged.

"Find out," I ordered.

The phone on my desk rang. I nodded at Joseph as he left before answering.

"Brutus," Aaron snapped, "I need you in my office."

"On my way."

I checked the time, seeing that it was a little after five. I had planned to remain in the office until five-thirty or so, and then swing over to Cup of Joy. Before Mia, I wasn't a guy who hung around in coffee shops. Not like I had time for that type of shit anyway.

But lately, the best part of my days was entering her café. Mia infused the café with her liveliness and, more often than not, her laughter. Most of the time, it would hit my ears as I entered while she talked with one customer or another. The patron base of the shop was steadily growing. People came back not only for the drinks but for the atmosphere.

Mia drew people to her. At times, I was slightly jealous of how much other people got her time and attention when we were out in public. I wanted to wrap her up and keep her just for myself.

But that would be selfish as fuck of me.

She thrived on interaction with others. That and her love of coffee and attention to detail made her new shop the success it was growing into.

Instead of keeping her all to myself, though, I'd go hang out at her shop whenever I could just to watch her. Sometimes, I'd help out behind the counter.

A smile was on my face the entire elevator ride up to Aaron's office. When I stepped off and headed down the long hallway toward his corner office, I wondered what he wanted. A piece of me hated to admit it, but I hoped it wasn't something that would require a lot of time or for me to stay too late.

Aaron's schedule often fluctuated and changed when things came up. Though it was my job to keep up with the changes in all of the family's schedules and be at the ready when they needed me, my heart pulled me toward Cup of Joy.

"Brutus," he said as I entered.

I was surprised to find Joshua seated on the couch in his office as well.

"I thought you weren't going to get back until after six," I told Joshua. He had a meeting across town.

"Plans changed. I canceled the meeting," Joshua answered. There was a glint of something in his green eyes. Like he was withholding some critical information.

"Deal didn't work out?" I asked, knowing he was working on a potentially lucrative real estate deal.

"Not this time." But he smiled like he still somehow won the lottery.

I wondered what was going on, and before I could ask Carter and Tyler entered Aaron's office. Carter closed the door behind him. He wore his captain's uniform from the Williamsport Fire Department.

"Shit," Carter cursed. "We're still dealing with that four-alarm from last night. I thought I was gonna miss this." He clapped me on the shoulder as he passed, throwing a huge grin my way.

"Your ass better had been here," Tyler told him. "This is important."

"I'm here, aren't I?" Carter shot back.

"Would someone like to tell me what's going on?" I asked, glancing between the four brothers.

My gaze landed on Aaron since it was his office. I assumed him to be the ringleader of all of this. Whatever *this* was.

"We're waiting on one more person," Aaron replied, folding his arms across his chest. He looked over at Joshua. "He's late." Aaron bared his teeth in obvious irritation. But what else was new?

I looked at my watch. It was five-fifteen. "There weren't any other meetings on your schedule for the day," I told Aaron.

"No, there weren't," he said pointedly. "Not on your calendar." His answer was cryptic. Aaron wasn't the type to give information away until he was good and ready.

A muscle in my jaw ticked in frustration. When it came to my job, I had to be the type of guy who was able to adjust and rearrange my schedule when necessary. However, the pull to leave work and go see my woman was a fucking leash around my heart. With each beat, I could feel a vice around it growing slightly tighter.

Before I could get too annoyed a knock sounded on the door.

"That's him," Aaron said, his gaze never leaving me.

"Who?" I asked but had already moved toward the door to open it. My instinct to always be the first to open the door, in case there was a problem on the other side, was ever present.

"Jeremiah?" Jeremiah Guilia was the family's jeweler. He had a prominent store not too far from Townsend Industries, but he made house calls for the family. Jeremiah often paid a visit when anniversaries or holidays would come up or just when one of the Townsends wanted to buy a new piece of jewelry for his wife, which wasn't an uncommon occurrence.

"Brutus." His smile was affable as his eyes wrinkled at the edges. His tan seemed to become even more pronounced when he smiled. The man had no doubt just returned from some sort of vacation. With as much as the Townsends tended to splurge with him, he could retire on a private island somewhere.

"Gentleman," Jeremiah greeted as he entered the office.

I shut the door again and watched as Jeremiah rolled a small suitcase over to the long table in Aaron's office.

Tyler strolled over and peeked over Jeremiah's shoulder as he set up the display of jewelry he brought with him. Tyler whistled. "You pulled out the big guns for this one." He slapped Jeremiah's shoulder.

"That was what I was instructed to do," Jeremiah returned.

"That you were," Carter interjected.

I cleared my throat. "Would someone like to tell me what this is all about?" There was a tension in my voice that I tried to suppress. Yes, this was part of my job sometimes, but I felt slightly uncomfortable watching one of the brothers pick out a necklace or whatever for his wife, while I still craved to get home to mine.

Not my wife, the reminder in my head growled.

Not yet.

A situation I planned to change soon enough.

"It's for you," Joshua said, bringing my attention back to the men in the room.

I creased my brows and waited for further explanation.

"Come on, big guy," Tyler urged, moving closer and pulling me by the arm toward Jeremiah's setup.

When Jeremiah stepped aside, I spotted the array of engagement rings that he'd brought with him.

"What the hell is this?" I asked, still eyeing all of the differently cut diamond and other precious jewels.

"It's our gift to you," Aaron said as he moved to stand beside me.

Joshua flanked my other side while Tyler and Carter moved to the other side of the table, standing across from me.

"I knew you were a goner the minute you extended your trip in Mexico," Tyler said. He chuckled. "I told Aaron Brutus would only ask for more time off because he found the woman he's going to marry."

Aaron grunted, which for him meant he was cosigning what his brother said.

"That day in the office when you asked Aaron about being a father was when I knew," Joshua said.

"And then we met her at the gala," Carter added.

All four of them looked between one another and then their gazes landed on me.

"She's legitimate," Aaron surprised me by saying. "She loves you." He cleared his throat and looked as if he wanted to say something else.

"What Aaron is trying to get at is that we love you, too," Joshua started. "We haven't done the best job of letting you know that you're more than just our bodyguard."

"Personal protection specialist," I corrected.

They all chuckled.

"You're as much a part of our family as any one of us is. We'd be lost without you. So …" Tyler outstretched his hand over the rings. "We also know you're shit at picking out jewelry."

Carter guffawed. "Yeah, like when he said Michelle would love that huge, gaudy necklace." He laughed, making me frown.

"You said she liked green. It was an emerald."

"That was twice the size of her neck. The thing was hideous." He peered over to the corner. "No offense, Jeremiah."

I'd half forgotten the man was still there.

"None taken."

"Don't even get me started on his input when I went to pick out Destiny's last birthday gift," Tyler chimed in, shaking his head.

"Fuck," Carter groaned. "I don't even want to think about it."

I glared at the table across from Carter. "Fuck you."

That made all four of them laugh even harder. Yeah, I was shit at picking out jewelry, which was part of the reason I procrastinated on choosing a ring for Mia. However, impatience started to get the better of me, and I'd stopped by a jewelry shop the week before, but walked away with nothing.

I examined the rings in front of me. There were princess cut diamonds, pear shaped, oval, and even heart shaped rings. They all glinted at me as if beckoning me to choose them. And those were just the diamonds. Jeremiah had brought a stock of other rings with varying types of precious gems on them.

"It's on us," Joshua said, clapping me on the back.

I looked over at him with a wrinkle in my forehead. He nodded toward the rings. "We'll help you choose. Any ring. And if there's one here that's not right, Jeremiah will bring in more. Either way, we're footing the bill."

He looked toward his brothers, who all nodded as if it was a done deal. Even Aaron.

"Fuck," I whispered. These bastards caused a lump to form in my throat. One I had to work to be able to swallow.

There was silence in the room for a minute. They all gave me the time to compose myself. This feeling of being alone had overtaken me for so long that I started to not even notice it. It got shoved into a black box, placed into the back of my mind, never to think about or acknowledge.

It was my responsibility to ensure the Townsends were safe. What started as just a job became more along the way. But I denied that because becoming friends with the people you're protecting can pose a danger to the job. It becomes more difficult to say no to a friend or family member than just a client.

I glanced up from the table. "This doesn't mean I'm letting any of you go on vacation without additional security," I said, glaring at them in warning.

"Wouldn't think of it," Tyler said.

"Just so we're clear," I muttered, looking back down at the rings, "no." I shook my head.

Their faces darkened, which made me chuckle. "I need your help picking out the right ring for my woman. But I can't let you buy it."

"It's our gift to you," Carter protested.

I nodded. "And I appreciate it." I looked them all in the eyes so they would see my sincerity. "But any ring on my wife's finger will be one that I paid for."

Aaron clapped me on the back. "Damn straight."

Tyler hummed. "We'll pay for the bachelor party then."

They all agreed, sending them all into a fit of cheers and hell yeahs.

"I'll let you numbskulls pay for that."

"Great. Now that that's decided …" Joshua started, and then turned to Jeremiah, who'd remained silent throughout our talk. He waved him over. "Let's help this man pick out a ring."

CHAPTER 29

Mia

"Mmm, that feels amazing," I hummed and laid my head back against the arm of the couch. Brutus and I had just finished eating dinner and sat down to watch that new movie *Prey*. As soon as we sat, he pulled my feet onto his lap and began massaging them.

I loved owning and working in my coffee shop, but my body was still adjusting to standing on my feet all day.

"If I knew I'd get foot massages every night, I would've moved in sooner," I joked. It'd been three weeks since we had dinner with my parents and two weeks since I moved into Brutus' home. Though I had been nervous, the transition into his house felt natural. He had no problem clearing space for me and exchanging pieces of my furniture with his to blend our styles.

"See what you've been missing?" he replied before swatting my thigh. "Next time say yes the first time and you won't miss out."

"Hush, you." I playfully poked his side with my foot.

Instead of responding, he stuck his thumb in a particularly sensitive part of the sole of my foot. I groaned deeply, my eyes falling closed. "Damn."

"I hope that sound doesn't mean you're in here doing something you have no business doing in public," Rick said, coming to a stop in the entryway of the living room. He covered his eyes with his hand as if needing to hide from whatever we were up to.

"We were," Brutus said in a flat tone. "Get out."

I chuckled and sat up. "We were not. Join us to watch the movie," I told his father, loving his company. "How was lunch with my father?"

The day I moved in, my parents showed up. Rick, my father, and Brutus refused to let my mother or I lift a finger. Between the three of them and the movers Brutus hired, I was left twiddling my thumbs. My father and Rick struck up a conversation, and before the end of the day, the two of them were chumming it up like old friends.

Since then, they'd gone out to lunch a few different times. I loved to see it because I felt like Rick needed more friends in his life and so did my dad.

"Just fine," Rick said, which meant he really enjoyed it. "That daddy of yours knows his shit when it comes to chess. Next week he's taking me to that historical site he told me about."

"Why doesn't he take you now?" Brutus offered, glaring at his father.

With a laugh, I swatted his arm. "Don't be rude."

He frowned, and I could see the remorse in his eyes. "Sorry, Dad."

Rick waved a dismissive hand. "I'm just fooling with you, son. I have no intention of interrupting your evening."

"You're never an interruption, Rick," I said genuinely.

"You're not," Brutus said.

I knew he meant it, but I also knew he wanted some alone time. He'd only gotten back from a five-day business trip with Joshua and Aaron Townsend earlier that afternoon. I'd missed the hell out of him, too, so I could understand his frustration.

"No. You two need your alone time. I wanted to thank Mia for the dinner she prepared. This lasagna is to die for."

"Please don't die for it. I promise I'll make it again soon, and there's plenty of leftovers," I quipped.

"I'll leave the two of you—" The rest of his comment was cut off by a simultaneous buzzing of Brutus' and my phones.

Brutus' back went straight as soon as he heard the sound. "That's the notification that's connected to the alarm at your shop."

A pit in my stomach instantly formed, but I immediately thought of a reasonable explanation. "Maybe a stray cat or something set it off?" The excuse sounded hollow even to me.

Brutus was already on his feet, texting something or someone on his phone.

"That alarm doesn't go off over a thing like that," Rick said in his stead.

I could feel the tension coming off of Brutus in waves. I had no idea who he was contacting, but I imagined it was the police.

"Dad, stay here with Mia while I go find out what—"

"Absolutely not," I demanded, rising to my feet. "That's my shop and I want to know what's happening with it." There was no way in hell I was about to sit at home twiddling my thumbs while Brutus went to figure out what happened to my shop.

"I'm not about to let you walk into a dangerous situation."

"Let me?" I let out a humorless laugh. "You're not letting me do anything because that is my shop." I pressed my hand to my chest for emphasis. "If anyone is going to go down there, it's me. If someone broke into my shop, I want to know about it. Besides, that alarm you had installed also alerted the police right away, too. They'll want to speak with me, and I'll have to file a police report as the owner."

I didn't wait for Brutus to respond before I marched over to the door and slipped into the sneakers I always left sitting there.

"Stubborn woman," he grumbled as he did the same.

Within a few minutes, we were on the way to my shop. Though I'd insisted on going, I was glad that Brutus drove because I was shaky the entire way there. Barely two months into my dream opening, and someone was already trying to sabotage it?

*　*　*

Brutus

"This was probably just some neighborhood kids or something targeting a new business," one of the uniform officers behind me said.

I didn't pay him any attention as I examined the broken window of Mia's shop. Someone had tossed a fucking brick at the window. Their stupid asses didn't realize that it was reinforced glass. The window cracked, but it didn't shatter. However, that didn't fix the fact that the display window to Mia's shop would need to be replaced.

But that wasn't my immediate concern. What had me seeing fucking red was the spray painted 'Bitch' across the glass. Whoever did this was trying to send a message. This felt personal. I kept my thoughts and observations to myself.

"Yeah, we had this problem a couple months ago a few blocks from here," the officer continued.

"Did you ever catch the guys who did it?" Mia asked, coming from the side entrance of the shop. My father flanked her closely. I'd only let her out of my sight because I knew he wouldn't let anything happen to her. That and the handful of officers who were present allowed me to relax with Mia on the scene.

Plus, I suspected whoever was behind this was long gone. In all likelihood, the shrill alarm that'd gone off as soon as the brick hit the window scared the person away. What pissed me off the most was that I had failed to finish the installation of Mia's security system. The parts that allowed the cameras to function were on backorder for months. I'd hoped I had time to have it completely installed before anything like this happened.

Fucking fool. I cursed myself for not being on top of my shit.

"Yeah," the officer answered Mia's question. "Was a group of teens who had worked at the fast food place not far from here."

"Where are they now?" My voice came out as dark as my mood. I only realized it when the officer shrank back a little from my question.

"Uh, last I heard, they were in juvie."

"Then this wasn't them." I turned back to the window, clenching and unclenching my hands into fists.

Mia came up to me, wrapping her arms around mine. Her touch calmed the growing anger in my body.

"Maybe it was a similar group of kids," she suggested, looking up at me with concern in her eyes.

"Probably," I agreed but didn't believe it. I only wanted to calm the fear I saw in her eyes. However, the reality was my gut was telling me this wasn't a group of teens.

We spent the next hour answering questions from the police, filling out the police report, and checking around the shop to take in all of the damage. Whoever had done this only vandalized the outside of Mia's shop. The security system had done its job, preventing them from getting inside. And whoever it was had tried.

I pointed out to the police that the shop's back door had been messed with. When Mia pulled up the alarm's information, we found that someone had attempted to disarm it, but was unsuccessful.

While Mia spoke with two officers, completing the report, I moved closer to my father. Keeping my voice low, I told him, "This feels a little more high level than some kids being assholes."

He turned keen eyes on me and nodded. "I've already reached out to Robert, and he's assured me that we have all of the resources at the Townsend disposal to figure out what the fuck is happening."

I nodded, reassured that my father was already two steps ahead of me.

"Those boys wanted to come down here when Robert told them what happened." My father leveled me a look. "Expect them to give you shit for not being the first to tell them."

I shook my head almost in disbelief. I was the one they called when shit went down, not the other way around. But, thinking about the week before, it started to make sense.

"You're a part of our family."

And as if to put an exclamation point onto that memory, my phone rang in my pocket.

"Aaron," I said.

"What's going on?" he asked, his voice bordering on threatening.

"Father said Mia's shop was vandalized," Joshua said, sounding as if

Aaron placed his phone on speaker. "Is she all right?"

"I'm fine," Mia said, overhearing the conversation since I'd also put mine on speaker. "Thank you for your concern."

"You're Brutus' wif—" Joshua broke off. "Woman. And therefore, family. You don't ever have to thank us for being concerned about our family."

Mia's eyes watered as she peered up at me. "I-I still haven't even told my family yet."

"Come with me, Mia," my father said. "We'll call your daddy and let him know everything's under control."

I watched my father as he guided Mia a few steps away.

"Brutus," Aaron said in a tone that let me know it was time to take them off of speaker mode.

"The cops think this was done by some teens with nothing better to do."

"You don't," Josh said, a statement, not a question.

"I took some pictures that I'm going to review and I want to get my hands on the prints they took from the scene. But no," I answered. "My instincts tell me this is something else."

The very thought had my free hand flexing again.

"Whatever you need." Aaron's voice took on a grim, deadly tone.

Glancing over in the direction my father had taken Mia, I made sure she wasn't close enough to overhear. "I might need one of those houses you keep empty before all of this is over."

I looked back at the cracked window in front of me. Something about this read personal. And there was one person I could think of that might've had a vendetta against Mia.

"Say it, and it's done," Josh commented.

"I'll get back to you." I hung up the phone before cracking my knuckles. I would do my own investigation into this vandalization. The police were fine for what they could legally do, but I wanted answers faster than they could provide, given all of the red tape they had to go through.

Before the night was over, I was already planning to have a face to face with Vincent Davis.

CHAPTER 30

Brutus

It took a damn week to get that one on one with Vincent Davis. The son of a bitch, who'd been unemployed since the week after the gala, had moved out of his luxury apartment in downtown Williamsport. It took a little effort to discover that he had to move in with his girlfriend on the other side of the city.

I stood in the underground office of Townsend Industries, which very few people knew about. Most of those who did get to discover this part of the building weren't too happy when they left.

The monitor on the wall, next to the large, metal door, alerted me that Joseph was on his way in with Vincent beside him. A few beats later, the two bells chimed once Joseph disengaged the lock. The door opened slowly.

"What the hell is this?" Vincent demanded, looking behind him at Joseph.

"Don't worry about him," I said, standing at the center of the room with concrete floors and walls. I jutted my head toward the wooden table and chair off to the side of the room. "Have a seat."

"Fuck this. I don't need anymore of this bullshit," Vincent barked, his face starting to turn red.

I glowered at him. "You're talking awfully spicy for a motherfucker who pissed himself the last time he was in my presence."

His eyes bulged, and cheeks puffed out in embarrassment.

"Sit the fuck down," I demanded. I followed him with my gaze as he cautiously ambled over to the chair and took a seat. I turned back to Joseph. "Make sure you remind Erik to be on time to get Cole, Victoria, and Diego for their three-thirty pickup," I told him.

He grinned before peering at his watch. "On my way."

"This shouldn't take too long," I told Joseph. "Be back in about fifteen minutes."

The door closed behind him with a soft *click*.

"You know, I can sue you for what you did to me the night of that gala. I had to get three stitches in the back of my head from the glass that cut my scalp."

I gave him a pitying look. "I'll give you my address so you can send me the ER bill." I threw him a smile that probably read more deadly than friendly. If the fear that clouded Vincent's face was any indication.

I sauntered over to the table and picked up a copy of the Corsica Pharmaceuticals Employee Handbook. I started flipping pages of the book.

"If you're trying to intimidate me, it's not working," Vincent said after a long moment of silence. He sat up straighter in the chair as if regaining some confidence.

I flipped another page.

"And what the hell are you doing with that?" He thrust his thumb toward the book. "I don't work for that fucking company anymore."

"No shit?" I said as if I didn't already know.

He snorted. "Like you didn't have anything to do with me getting fired. You and that—"

"That what?" I barked, my anger finally sparking as I got in his face.

He shrank back. "Mia," he answered in a voice just about a whisper.

"What about my wife?"

His eyes bulged, mouth falling open.

No, legally she wasn't my wife yet, and I still hadn't proposed, but he didn't need to know those details.

"What? It wasn't bad enough that you two got me fired?" Vincent asked, obviously not knowing when to keep his trap shut. "From a job that I was very good at, by the way."

"If you were so fucking good at it, it never would've been so easy to get them to toss you out on your ass."

His face reddened even more. "Listen, I was damn good at my job. It's not my fucking fault Mia didn't know how to work the system. Instead of getting jealous of me and quitting, she should've taken notes. Hell, I would've left that managerial position and gotten promoted within a year, eighteen months tops. It would've been open for her to take on if only she waited."

"Waited for you to leave her scraps behind?" I said through gritted teeth. "After she fucking trained you and taught you everything you needed to know about the job?"

"She taught me some stuff, yeah, but so what? That doesn't mean I should've put my ambition aside for the job I wanted. If she was the better candidate, she would've gotten it. I got that job fair and square," he said while pounding his chest.

"Yeah, by screwing the hiring manager, right?"

His mouth fell open. "How did you— I don't know what you're talking about."

I grunted. "I bet you don't. It's the same woman you're living with now because you lost that nice apartment in the skyrise, not too far from here. Shame." I shook my head, looking down at him.

"Fuck you. My life is none of your damn business." He abruptly stood up and pushed the chair away, giving himself space to move away from me.

"You made your life my business when you fucked with my wife. You were pissed at her for not being at your beck and call when she quit, right? And when she finally put her foot down and stopped answering your calls, that pissed you off, didn't it?"

I got in his face, towering over him by half a foot.

"Get out of my face," he demanded but he was the one to take a step back. "This is why you brought me here? To threaten me? I'll fucking sue you and all of those Townsends for harassment and kidnapping or whatever this is."

I took a step in his direction, and he moved back.

"And if you put your hands on me, you're going to jail," he threatened, holding up his cell phone.

I straightened and smoothed down the sides of my suit jacket.

"No hands. Got it," I replied. "You seem like the type of fucker to get the police involved. But would you place that call before or after you admitted to vandalizing Mia's shop?"

I wanted to pat myself on the back for how calm my question came out, though I was seething just beneath the surface.

The memory of Mia crying the night we returned home from surveying the damage done to her shop pissed me off. Hearing her express concerns over having to pay for a new window this early in her business when cash flow was tight. Thankfully, that concern wasn't founded because her insurance company immediately worked with her to restore the damage.

Still, the hurt and anguish on her face that night rattled around in my mind. And if this motherfucker were responsible for that look, he would meet my wrath before day's end.

"What are you talking about?" Vincent questioned with quirked eyebrows. "Hey," he said, holding his hands up, "if that bitch is trying to pin— Oof!" He grunted when I smacked his stupid ass across the face with the employee manual still in my hands.

"Watch your fucking mouth," I said calmly, ignoring his groans of pain as he held his nose. I saw blood spill out between his fingers. "You're going to want to get that checked out once you leave here ... *if* you leave here," I amended.

"This is a crime!" he bellowed. "You just assaulted me," he screeched, still holding his nose.

"You tripped and fell." I shrugged. "I happened upon you in the hallway and brought you into our office to make sure you were all right."

That would be the made-up version I'd tell anyone who asked.

I stepped closer, and when he tried to move away, I stomped down on his foot with my much larger one. "Vincent, listen to me."

I got dangerously close.

"Now, I've already spared you once. Well, not me." I pressed my hand to my chest. "Mia did. After the gala, I asked her how she wanted me to handle that situation. You could've lost one of two things. Your life or your job."

His eyes bulged as my comment settled in.

He squirmed to free his foot, but I pressed harder, making him wince.

"It's by the kindness of my woman that you're still breathing. She chose your job." I sent another grim smile his way. "So, it pains me to know that you would squander her act of altruism by then going and breaking into her shop. Truly." I made a pained expression for emphasis before releasing his foot.

"Did you vandalize her shop?" I asked. Though I had my suspicions, I couldn't be sure. Vincent was the first person I thought of who might hold a grudge against Mia. Naturally, he was the first one I sought out to question about the break-in.

But there was something not quite right about it.

Whoever had done the break-in also tried to utilize the backdoor's alarm code to get inside. They'd failed, but something about that to me screamed that this wasn't some group of teens who just happened by a coffee shop and wanted to mess with it. Nor did it seem like Vincent, not exactly. Nothing in his background indicated that he had experience with B&Es.

Yet, he was a vindictive SOB. I recognized that the moment I met him for the first time. And someone who wanted vengeance was capable of just about anything if pushed far enough.

"I never touched her fucking shop," he said, that false bravado returning to his voice, even though he continued to hold on to his nose. "And you can add slander to the list of reasons I'm going to sue your ass."

"Really? What lawyer will you get to take on the case?" I glared at him. "Look around you. Do you know where you are? Do you think the people who own this building don't know you're down here? Do you honestly fucking believe I'm that fucking stupid not to cover all of my bases?"

He glanced around. "I'll sue the Townsends, too." His voice had much less bravado than time around.

The laugh that spilled out of my mouth was genuine.

"Good luck finding a lawyer in this city, this state who isn't already in their back pocket. And what will you use to hire them? The two hundred dollars that's in your bank account?"

That got his attention. He blinked.

I again crowded his space. "You're fucking with some shit you have no idea about. I let you walk away with your life once. I don't give second chances. Did you vandalize her shop?"

I asked, but I knew he wouldn't come out and say it if he had. I just needed to look him in the eyes as he answered to find out the truth.

"No," he screamed. "Fuck no. I don't even know what you're talking about."

I stared into his eyes, looking for any hint of deception. A new tension coiled in my belly when I didn't see any. As much as I wanted to crush his skull for that bullshit he'd pulled at the gala, I held back.

"Where were you last Thursday night?"

His forehead wrinkled, and he suddenly snapped his fingers. "I wasn't even in town last Thursday night."

I gave him a doubtful glare.

"Honestly." He held his hands in front of his body, the proper amount of fear finally emanating from him. "I-I stayed overnight in Easton because I had a job interview. For a job I didn't get," he grumbled that last part. Easton was a city about ninety minutes from Williamsport.

"I don't give a shit about your job prospects," I snapped.

"Th-The interview went longer than I expected, so I decided to stay at a hotel that night. I didn't get back into town until Friday morning."

He lowered his eyes to the floor and dropped his chin to his chest.

I knew a look of shame when I saw it, no matter how quickly Vincent tried to cover it.

"There weren't any hotel charges on your credit cards," I said.

His head snapped back up. "How did you—"

"Not the question you should be asking. Where the fuck were you last Thursday?" I demanded, slamming my fist into the wall right beside his head.

He flinched.

"I-I didn't lie." His voice quaked. "I was at a hotel, but I had to use my girlfriend's credit card because all of mine are maxed out."

That last part I knew was genuine. The quiver in his voice revealed his guilt.

"I assume she doesn't know you used her credit card?"

He swallowed, his head falling again.

Useless.

I hated it, but I believed him. He was douchebag enough to either steal or open a credit card in his girlfriend's name and use it behind her back. He was a user, a leech. He'd done as much with Mia at Corsica, used her for his own gain and tried to continue doing it even after she left.

But if he wasn't in Williamsport last week at the time of the break-in then he wasn't the one responsible. He could've hired someone to do it for him, but two things: he was broke as fuck and the break-in felt personal. Someone who had a stake in the game.

"Give me the name of the hotel," I demanded. I'd have to verify that he was there that night before I completely took his word for any fucking thing. "And if it turns out that you're lying, there isn't a place on this Earth that you can hide from me," I warned.

His eyes bulged, but he didn't say anything.

Good.

I removed the pen I always kept on me from my breast pocket and handed it to him along with the employee manual. "Write down the name of the hotel, phone number, and name of the person who checked you in."

"I don't remember all of that."

"Write what the fuck you remember," I barked.

I gave him some space because I couldn't stand being so close. I straightened the wrinkles out of my suit, my mind already going through the list of other suspects for the break-in.

A rival competitor, perhaps.

Another former co-worker.

I would have to ask Mia again if she knew anyone who might have a grudge against her. She continued to hold out hope that it was just a stranger who happened across her shop and wanted to cause trouble.

My gut said otherwise.

"I should've known that when I saw Mia on the street she'd cause me all types of problems," Vincent muttered as he handed me the pen and the employee manual.

"What the fuck did you say?"

His eyes fluttered and he sputtered, like he knew he'd just put his foot in his mouth.

"Repeat that shit," I ordered.

"She told me to leave her alone after I was just trying to ask her a couple of questions about the accounts she used to manage."

"And she had to fucking tell you to leave her alone." My voice dipped deathly low as I decreased the space between our bodies. "Which means you were fucking harassing her. Did you touch her?"

His mouth flapped open and closed.

"Did you fucking touch her?" I bellowed.

He jumped and held up his hands, cowering away from me. "I was just trying to talk to her. She's the one who made— Ahh!" he screamed when I slammed the employee handbook across his face.

His head snapped right and upward from the impact of the five-hundred-page manual. But I wasn't done. I held the manual in front of me and slammed it into his stomach. The force of the hit made him curl over, and a second later, whatever he'd had to eat that morning spilled out of his mouth and onto the floor.

I frowned in disgust. "I should make you lick that up," I said, standing over him as he remained on all fours. "You're lucky I didn't know about that shit earlier."

I moved to the door, but right before opening it, I said, "It would be in your best interest to leave this city. Because if I ever run across your fucking face again, our next conversation won't end so nicely."

With that, I opened the door to find Joseph standing there. "Make sure Vincent gets home okay," I said before exiting the room.

"He looks worse for the wear," Joseph said with humor in his voice.

I looked from him to Vincent, who struggled to lift himself to his feet. "I did as he asked. Never laid a hand on him." I held out the manual.

There were more ways than one to hurt someone without ever touching them.

CHAPTER 31

Brutus

"Oh, and I forgot to tell you this," Mia said, excited as she sat in the passenger seat of my SUV. She pressed her palm into my forearm. I glanced over at her and smiled because she was so damn beautiful. The ring in my left pocket felt like it weighed a fucking ton.

I wanted nothing more than to have it on her finger already. It'd been a month since the break-in. Three weeks since I questioned Vincent, who turned out to be telling the truth. I verified with the hotel and their security staff that he was there that night. He forgot he'd been there with a woman he hired to spend the night with him.

But that wasn't my business.

Since he left Townsend Industries, the fool had the right sense to pack up and move out of the city. It probably helped that I had the security footage from the hotel sent to his girlfriend along with the bill paid for by a credit card in her name.

Satisfied that the break-in wasn't by Vincent still left me on edge. Who the fuck else could it have been?

"We're starting a book club," Mia exclaimed, pulling my attention back to the conversation. "A few of my customers asked me about it. And then last week when Patience stopped by, I told her about it, and you know how much she loves to read." Mia clapped because she was so excited.

"I think she's going to try to join. It'll be like two nights a month." She threw me a pointed look. "And before you ask, no. We are not reading *The 48 Laws of Power*."

I chuckled.

"What day and time are you having the book club?" I asked after sobering up.

"I think Thursday nights at like seven-thirty to eight-thirty or something like that. After the shop closes for the night."

"No." The one word reply tore from my throat.

She pressed her hand against the base of her neck. "No, what?"

"Having an after-hours club," I replied as my hands tightened on the steering wheel. "If the book club ends at eight-thirty, you probably won't get out of the shop until nine. It'll be dark." I knew how Mia liked to talk. Especially when it came to books. I loved it about her, but this was about safety.

"It won't be that late," she insisted. "Besides, there will be a group of us. It's been a month since the break-in, and we have the cameras now. I'm sure no one will try anything."

I shook my head before she could even finish her statement. "It's not safe. I already have Rick going in with you or closing with you on the days I can't be there."

"Something that is completely unnecessary by the way." She turned her body to face me in her seat. A frown tugged at the corners of her mouth.

Despite the frown, I found it hard to take my eyes off of her to concentrate on the road. She wore a cream, off-the-shoulder top with a pleated leather skirt that stopped a few inches above the knees.

She matched the outfit with a pair of over the knee black boots. The outfit gave a glimpse of her plush thighs, and every time I looked at her I found my mouth watering.

"It won't be changing," I said firmly. We'd had this argument many times over the past month. She hated that I had my father accompany her to work in the early morning when I was away or had an early morning myself. Neither my father nor I budged on the issue, though. Her father showed up a few times to pull a shift with Rick.

"You're all ridiculous. The kids who vandalized my shop are probably long gone or got it out of their system." She brushed invisible lint off her skirt.

"Good for them if they have. If they haven't …" I peered at her out of the corner of my eyes.

"Anyway, we're doing the book club." She held up her hand when I started to reply. "We can work around the time. Maybe make it a little earlier. Or have it on Sundays right after we close at five. That way it won't be dark out once we end."

I bit my tongue because it was a reasonable compromise.

"And get this, another customer brought up the idea of hosting a monthly game night. I've talked to a few customers, and some of them seem to like the idea. And you know the bookstore a few blocks over?"

I nodded.

"They're having some author signing events and have asked that Cup of Joy cater it."

She sighed in contentment. "Three months into my dream, and it still feels surreal." She reached across the threshold, taking my hand.

I squeezed it before bringing it to my lips to kiss.

"You're the best part of it all, though."

My heart stuttered in my chest.

"For so long I put off my dream to build what I thought was supposed to be the right path. Breaking the glass ceiling and moving up in the company I worked for was my lot in life. I enjoyed it for a while, but it left me drained and a little bitter, to be honest," she admitted.

"I would never call you bitter," I told her with a wrinkle between my brows.

She chuckled. "I hid it well." She shrugged and kept going. "But I don't think I even realized it until I quit. And then I went off on what I thought would be some time to rest and regroup before coming back to open my shop. I did that, but most importantly, I met you."

I looked over to see her eyes watering.

"You've been the best gift of all. Thank you for taking your first vacation in five years." We both laughed at that. "Without it, we probably would've never met, and now, I can't imagine my life without you."

"Stop talking," I said, abruptly.

"What?"

I hated the confusion in her voice, but she was making it too damn difficult to keep my head on straight. Thankfully, we arrived at the Mexican restaurant I'd bought out for the night.

"Baby, tonight is about you. So, you can't say all of this sweet stuff to me right now because it's making me lose my shit. I need to focus on delivering you the best night of your life. And I can't do that with you making me want to yank you onto my lap, spread your legs, and make you scream until your voice is hoarse and your pussy is throbbing from all of the times I made you come."

"Brutus…"

I caught sight of her squeezing those ample thighs together. I had to tell my dick to calm the fuck down.

"We're here." Tonight would be the night I'd ask Mia to be my wife.

* * *

Mia

Was Brutus actually … nervous?

I eyed him skeptically as he helped me out of the car, taking my hand. His odd reaction to what I'd just told him left me puzzled. We'd said I love you more times than I could count over the past two months since I'd moved in with him. He was the sweetest, most caring relationship I'd ever had. Of course I would say all of those things to him. Ordinarily, he took it in and responded with some sweet sentiment of his own.

Tonight was different.

He seemed stiff and yes, nervous, which was totally out of character for him.

"Is everything okay?" I asked as he guided us to the door of the restaurant. I didn't even notice that Brutus' car was the only one in the parking lot.

However, I did take note when he pulled the door open, and we were greeted by the beautiful hostess, welcoming us in perfect Spanish. Gazing around the dining space, I squinted in confusion.

"Why are we the only ones here?" I asked.

"Because I rented out the place." He sounded so casual about it all. Brutus placed a hand on my lower back and steered me to follow the hostess.

I gasped as we came to our seats in the middle of the dining area. The other tables and chairs had been pushed aside or removed. At the center was a lone green picnic bench. I looked around and noticed the paintings on the wall of different locations in Mexico, one portrait of Frida Kahlo and a few images of vibrantly painted sugar skulls.

It all was reminiscent of Mexico, which made sense. But it looked almost familiar ...

"I requested they make up the place to come as close to our first date as possible."

My eyebrows nearly touched my hairline. I looked around the dining space again and saw it. It closely mimicked the restaurant's decor where we stopped the first night in Tulum and had the most fantastic pork belly tacos.

"What are you up to?" I asked Brutus, eyeing him.

"I couldn't fly us to Tulum for one night," he said, regret lacing his tone. He helped me sit before he moved to the opposite side of the bench and took a seat across from me.

He stretched out his arms, opening his hands for me to take, which I did.

"You have to work in the morning, and I know you wouldn't want to be away from the coffee shop so soon after opening."

"Plus, you have to work, too," I added.

He kissed the inside of one of my wrists. "I would've taken off."

I scoffed. "Babe, *you* take a day off? The same man who went half a decade in between taking vacations."

He shrugged. "That was BM."

"BM?"

"Before Mia."

I tossed my head back and laughed when he winked. "We've discussed how ridiculous you look when you wink."

Brutus was the only man I'd ever known who couldn't wink. He looked so funny trying to do it. It wasn't sexy at all, but it was endearing whenever he attempted to because I knew he did it to make me laugh.

"Made you laugh. That's all that matters." He grinned.

"Thank you for recreating our first date." I hadn't thought of it as a date that first night. We had just been traveling all day and were hungry. He'd given me a ride to Tulum, so it felt natural for us to stop and eat. But, thinking back on it, yeah, it was our first date, I guessed.

"Your drinks," our hostess said.

We hadn't even ordered anything. Our hands pulled apart to give the hostess room to place the drinks in front of us. I looked down and recognized the mojito which was the same drink I had that first night. Brutus had the exact type of Mexican beer that he'd ordered.

"To memories," he said, holding up his beer.

I clinked his bottle with my glass. "To memories."

"New and old."

I nodded and took a sip of my drink. "Wow, that's good." It wasn't too sweet like some bartenders tended to make mojitos. It was very reminiscent of the drink I had back in Mexico.

"Buenas tardes," a male waiter appeared at the side of the table. He placed a basket of tortilla chips with a bowl of guacamole on one side and salsa on the other. "On the menu tonight, we have three types of tacos; pork belly tacos, cauliflower tacos, and beef tacos. The chef is preparing your order, and it will be out shortly. My name is Armando, please let me know if you need anything else in the meantime."

I turned to Brutus. "That's the same menu we had in Tulum."

He nodded, the smile on his lips creeping up to meet his eyes. There was a twinkle in those hazel orbs.

"What are you up to?" I asked again.

"Big things, baby. And memories," he answered cryptically.

It was pointless to ask him what he had planned for the rest of the night. He would never play his hand before he was ready. He had uncanny patience when it came to matters that needed it. It made him great at his job, but sometimes it could drive me to insanity. Like when he took his time, on purpose, bringing me to orgasm just to drag it out.

And like tonight.

I knew something important was happening. It made sense. The nervousness I'd picked up on earlier, the gleam in his eyes. There was always an intensity in his eyes when he looked at me. But that night, it was even more apparent. He wouldn't stop staring at me. Like if he even blinked for too long, I would disappear.

"Did you bring me here because you have to go away for a month with Aaron Townsend or something?" I guessed. "Is that why you want to make tonight memorable?"

"No," he answered seriously, shaking his head. "Contrarily, I've done some negotiating on my work schedule."

This was news. I snagged a tortilla chip and dipped it into the guacamole. "Oh, yeah?" I hedged, before taking a bite of the chip. Though I tried to come across as casual, inside I was holding my breath.

I'd come to terms with Brutus' work schedule, especially since he never, not once, made me feel like I came second to his job. Yes, he worked a lot, sometimes twelve or more hours a day. But he never made me feel like I came second to his career. He always made sure to let me know that he was thinking of me and that he loved me.

Thus, I had no room to complain about the hours he put in at work. Especially since I knew what it was like to work a demanding job. And now, opening my own business, I worked long hours there, too. However, there was always room for our relationship. I had my priorities in order now.

"I've come to an agreement that we'll keep my schedule as close to eight to five as possible, during the work week. One weekend a month, and travel only when required. That should take me down to traveling only every other month or so," he explained. "And I'm having Rick hire a handful of more guys to take on the hours I'm giving up."

"What brought about this change?" I hadn't asked or put any pressure on him to adjust his work schedule.

"You."

"Me?"

He nodded. "You're my future, Mia. My present and my future, and I want to make sure you know that you're the priority in my life."

My vision blurred from the tears that crowded my gaze. Blinking, I reached across the table. "I love you. Every day you make me feel wanted, loved, and cherished. I know I'm your priority, not because you say it but because you show me."

I hesitated, clamping my lips shut.

"But what?" he asked.

"But I know how much you love the Townsends. They're your family, too. You've made promises to protect them, not just as part of your job but because you care for all of them so deeply. Are you sure you're okay with decreasing your hours?"

He pulled my hand to his lips. I loved it when he kissed my fingers.

Before he could reply, Armando brought our plates of food out. Everything smelled divine and looked even better. A comfortable silence fell between us as I lifted a pork taco to my mouth and took my first bite.

The smokey BBQ flavor from the grill filled my mouth and mixed with the lime juice I'd squeezed on top. The flavors danced across my tongue, and I savored it all.

"These taste just like the tacos from that restaurant," I said, surprised. They were identical to the pork tacos we had that first night. I remembered that taste because we'd eaten at the place many nights after that first one. I'd had many plates of tacos in my time in Mexico, but that restaurant was the best.

These tacos were identical.

"It should," Brutus said after he swallowed his first bite.

I squinted, silently asking him to explain. Instead, his eyes went over my head. I followed his line of sight as a man in a black apron and a white chef's hat approached us with a massive grin.

"Cortés?" I screeched. He was the head chef and owner of the place we dined at that first night. "What are you doing here?" I asked while standing to hug him. We'd spent so many nights at his place that I'd gotten to know him.

Cortés dipped his head in Brutus' direction. I released him to see Brutus on his feet, glaring at Cortés.

He took a step back but chuckled good-naturedly. "Your boyfriend flew me out for the special occasion. Said that you would want our tacos to remember this evening."

I turned to Brutus. "An occasion he still hasn't clued me in on."

"I was trying to wait until after dinner."

"I want to know now."

He chuckled but came around the table, holding his hand for me to take.

"Impatient woman."

I smiled. "Glad you know it."

"Come here." He took me by the hand, bringing me toward the empty space.

The lights lowered, shining a spotlight on us. I peered around to see how the dimmed lighting made the bright colors on the sugar skulls and paintings stand out.

It was almost as if Brutus and I were transported back to the first night in Mexico. The feeling that something really big was happening penetrated my belly. It was the same feeling I had that night as well. Except, standing in the middle of that restaurant, with only the two of us, I felt it tenfold.

"What are you doing?" I asked dumbly as he sank to one knee.

"Mia," he said, pausing to pull something out of his left pants' pocket.

I inhaled deeply when I saw that it was a black, velvet box. A ring box. I had no doubt what he was about to say, but still, I held my breath.

"I'm not the type of guy who talks to random strangers on

airplanes."

I covered my mouth with my hand, laughing. He pulled my hand from my mouth and held onto it.

"But you just refused to stop talking."

"It takes two to hold a conversation." I glared at him.

His deep, smoky chuckle reverberated throughout my body. "True. I couldn't not talk to you, even when you judged my choice in books."

"If you're talking about *The 48 Laws of Power*—"

"Can I finish, please?"

I smirked. "Sorry."

"Anyway, I'm pretty sure I fell in love with you on that plane ride. And I've never looked back or regretted it. These months with you have shown me that I was surrounded by family the whole time, but it's also made me see how anxious I am to start my own family. With you. Mia Renee Raymond, will you be my wife?"

He opened the ring box with his free hand and held it up for me to see.

"Oh my goodness," I gasped, covering my mouth.

"I had help picking it out."

"Thank God." I braced my hands against my chest. "Babe, I love you but we both know your taste in jewelry ... leaves something to be desired," I explained diplomatically.

He growled, curling his top lip.

A guffaw spilled from my lips. Looking at the ring again, my lips spread into a huge grin. In the box sat a two karat yellow diamond set in what I suspected was a white gold setting with Swarovski crystals lining the ring's rim.

"This is breathtaking," I said.

"You haven't answered me," Brutus reminded me.

Blinking, I laughed. "Yes, of course yes! I'll marry you."

He rose to his feet faster than a man his size should be able to and scooped me into his arms. Laughter bubbled up my throat when he spun us around in a circle after putting the ring on my finger.

Who would've thought that quitting my job and finally following my dreams would also lead me to the man I couldn't live without?

CHAPTER 32

Mia

"You look stunning," Carlene gushed as we sashayed toward the nightclub we'd decided to go to for the night. It was only three weeks since Brutus proposed. However, Carlene, Sharise, Michelle, Kayla, Patience Townsend, and I had all met up for dinner and were then headed toward the club to dance the night away.

"She's right," Sharise agreed.

I shimmied my hips a little in the tight, formfitting black jeans I wore with a sheer black top, with a leopard-print jacket that was in the style of a cape. It left plenty of room for my sheer top to display the beautiful way my titties were sitting in the black silk bra I wore underneath the shirt.

Brutus' head almost exploded when he saw me come out of the room, dressed to go out.

"I have to agree," Patience said as we approached her, Kayla, and Michelle. Destiny, who was on the verge of delivering at any moment, remained at home. Even though she'd wanted to come, Tyler put his foot down on the matter.

All three women had agreed to accompany Sharise, me, and

Carlene for my supposed bachelorette party. I say supposed because no matter how many times I told Carlene that it was too early for a bachelorette party, she insisted. She was getting married in a month, so I'd told Brutus that once my best friend was married, we could sit down and discuss the details for our wedding.

The man typically had the patience of an owl, but he hadn't liked the idea of putting off setting a wedding date, even if it was only a month.

"I'm surprised Brutus let you out of the house in that," Kayla said.

"Tuh," Carlene tutted. "You should've seen him. If Sharise and I weren't there, I doubt he would've let her come out."

I waved her off, laughing because she was right. He had almost blown a gasket.

"Well, we're here. That's what's important," I said. "Ready to celebrate, ladies?" I asked, throwing my hands up.

A round of cheers rent the air, and I became renewed with energy for the night. In the months since meeting and falling in love with Brutus, it felt like I'd also gained the women he worked with as new friends. They were all so sweet and welcoming. But from what I'd seen of their husbands, I was surprised they could make it out of the house in some of their outfits. Brutus had some of the same jealous and possessive streaks I'd seen in their husbands.

"Reservation for Raymond," I told the security working the door at the upscale nightclub.

He nodded and stepped aside, easily letting us in. "Guess it pays to have connections," Carlene said in my ear.

"Guess so."

"Who wants a drink?" I asked.

Everyone shot up a hand.

"With five kids, I think you deserve one first," Sharise said to Patience, who laughed.

"First round's on me," Patience offered.

"Absolutely not," I countered. "All of you ladies came out to celebrate with me, and I truly appreciate it. Let me buy the first round." I'd never wanted to have a traditional bachelorette party, and the fact that my best friend was getting married in less than a month made me less inclined for one of those.

But the women around me had insisted on some sort of celebration. The least I could do was buy them all a drink.

"No," Kayla said. "This is your night. Besides, we've already reserved our spot in the upstairs section." She pointed over her shoulder.

I peered up to see the cordoned off area that Kayla pointed to.

I smiled. "That's perfect, but I'm still getting us all drinks," I insisted.

"Then let me help you."

I ordered a round of everyone's drinks, and Kayla and I waited while Patience, Sharise, Carlene, and Michelle headed up to the VIP area.

"Are there seriously security guards standing watch over the VIP?"

Kayla let out a laugh. "How do you think we got our guys to agree to not bothering all of us for the night?"

I raised an eyebrow. "They didn't." I shook my head.

"They did." She laughed harder. "Don't give me that look, either. Brutus was the main one insisting on how dangerous it could be."

"It's just a nightclub," I said while taking my dirty martini from the bartender.

We paid, and I followed Kayla up to the VIP.

"Yeah," she agreed. "But try explaining that to any of them. Also, Brutus is the type that sees danger everywhere."

"Especially since someone vandalized my coffee shop a couple of months ago," I stated.

Kayla turned to me once we reached the lounge area of the VIP section. There were low sitting chairs and loveseats, perfect for sitting and talking, but also provided enough space to dance to the dancehall music that blared throughout the club.

"How's that going, by the way? Did they find whoever did that?" Kayla asked.

"Did what?" Michelle inquired as I handed her my drink.

"The attempted break-in," I explained. "The police think it was some teens or something." I shrugged. "There haven't been any issues since. Well, a few hang-up calls, but ..." I shrugged because what business didn't receive hang-ups now and again?

I tossed my hand in the air with my drink in the other. "Let's not talk about that now. We're here to have fun."

Carlene threw her hand up. "Amen to that."

We laughed, and all drank and danced to the music. After a couple of drinks, the second and third, which our waitress brought us, I'd forgotten all about the talk of the break-in. I was sure it was just some kids with nothing better to do.

I doubted there'd be a repeat since Brutus finally got the special security camera equipment he wanted for my shop. He barely got it out of the package before he was down at Cup of Joy hooking it all up.

"Let's go down and dance," I suggested once I finished my fourth or fifth drink of the night. I'd lost count by then and decided it was probably time to cut myself off.

"Are you sure you want to do that?" Carlene asked.

"Yeah," Sharise agreed. "You know how protective that fiancé of yours is."

My grin felt wobbly, and I knew my eyes were glossy. Both from the alcohol and the emotion that welled up in me.

"My fiancé." I drew out that word, liking how it tasted coming out of my mouth. My body warmed, and my hips started moving on their own. I either needed to dance or take my butt home to my man.

"Come on," I whined and grabbed my sister and BFF's hands while gesturing for the other women to follow.

"We'll be right behind," Patience said for her and Michelle as she held up her half-finished drinks.

"I'm down," Kayla said, leading the way down the stairs to the main dance floor.

It was pretty crowded, but we made room. And when Beyoncé's "Church Girl" came on, we all screamed in excitement.

I threw a hand over my head and started winding my hips to the music. I tossed my head back and forth, and when Queen Bey told us to twirl our hips, I followed instructions to the T. Carlene took my hands, and we danced while singing along to the lyrics.

When one song melted into another, Carlene and I switched so that Kayla and I danced while my sister and friend danced with one another. A couple of men tried to intervene, but Kayla politely dismissed them. I didn't pay them any attention because they were harmless.

"I'm going to get another drink," Carlene said in my ear. "Do you want something?"

I shook my head. "I'm feeling good." She and Kayla headed in the direction of the bar.

"My feet hurt," Sharise complained. "I'm not used to wearing heels on the dance floor anymore. I'm going back upstairs. Come with me?"

I shook my head. "Oh, I love this song!" I shouted as a Doja Cat song came on. "I'll be up once this one's over."

"Maybe I should wait until—"

"Go," I insisted. I could tell Sharise was starting to feel uncomfortable. She winced in pain, and I felt terrible. "I'm fine. Kayla and Carlene will be right back."

"Okay."

I watched as she went in the direction of the stairs. When she disappeared behind a crowd of people, I briefly closed my eyes and let the music penetrate my body. I snapped and swayed to the beat, throwing my back in a circle, feeling myself.

When I opened my eyes, a man grinned down at me. He said something, but the music was too loud. Either that or mouthed the words. When I shook my head, instead of taking the hint, he started to lean in, possibly to repeat himself.

But right before he could even reach my ear, he paused. His eyebrows raised, and a cautious expression appeared on his face. A warmth moved behind my back, and goosebumps sprouted on my arms.

Before I even turned around, I knew what or who had spooked the guy.

"She's got a dance partner," Brutus said from behind me, his hands moving around my waist, tugging my back against his hard chest...

The man held up his hands in a surrendering fashion and backed away. My lips twitched, but I fought to keep the laughter at bay.

I spun and wrapped my arms around his neck. Lifting on my tiptoes, I said, "That was rude," in his ear.

His arm around me tightened. "He wanted to dance with you."

I glanced around. "I do need a dance partner. I wonder if—" I broke off on a laugh when he growled.

"I'm the only motherfucker you need to dance with for the rest of our lives."

"Yeah?" I teased. "Then let's see how well you keep up."

"That's not even up for debate," he said, taking my hand and spinning me in a circle that landed me right back in his arms. A fast-paced salsa song came on, which felt perfect.

We moved like liquid, all smooth and fluid, our bodies matching the rhythm of the beat. We'd danced together so many times in the past few months, but it always left me in awe of how well he moved. And how well we moved together. Every time we danced, it was as if my body was telling me we were destined for one another.

"I love you," I slurred.

He chuckled. "Sounds like you had a little too much to drink."

I planted my hands on my hips at the same time the song ended. "Are you calling me drunk?"

"Yes." He kissed my forehead. "Let's go upstairs."

"I'm not drunk," I protested but let him lead the way, my hand in his, up to the VIP section. I probably shouldn't have been, but I was shocked to see Carter, Joshua, and Aaron beside their wives in the VIP section.

"We've got company," Michelle said, grinning. "I knew they wouldn't stay away for too long."

"Damn, straight," Joshua replied.

"Brutus, I didn't know you could dance like that," Patience called over the music.

"He's a phenomenal dancer," I said before kissing his cheek.

He tightened his hold on my waist.

"Babe, maybe you should take some lessons from him," Patience turned to Aaron to say.

His brothers broke out into laughter, as did Brutus.

"He's beyond my help," Brutus quipped.

Carter and Joshua laughed louder.

"That's a fact," Carter yelled.

"He moves like shit," Joshua said, his arm wrapped around Kayla.

"Leave him alone," Kayla protested, swatting at Joshua's chest.

"Fuck all three of you," Aaron snarled. He wrapped an arm around his wife and leaned in to say something none of us could hear. But by the way Patience's eyes bolded, I could take a few guesses as to what it was.

I spun around to face Brutus. "I'm not done dancing with you yet," I said, pulling him away from the others and to a clearing where we could dance.

"Thanks for coming," I said sometime later.

"You're not pissed we intruded on your night?" he asked, grinning.

I shrugged. "I was starting to miss you." That was the truth. I was missing my dance partner on the floor before he showed up.

"That's what the fuck I like to hear." He leaned in and kissed me.

"Ugh, you two need a room," Carlene interrupted us. She held up her cell phone. "My man's calling me, asking when I'm coming home. You know he likes to wait for me."

I grinned. "It's early."

Her eyes bulged. "Girl, it's almost one in the morning."

My mouth fell open. I'd lost track of time between dancing with them and Brutus and the other men showing up.

"I've already ordered an Uber. Sharise and I are going together," Carlene said.

"Wait, I'll walk you both down."

"We'll walk you down," Brutus added.

I didn't even argue because I knew he wasn't about to let me out of his sight. I would have told him it wasn't necessary, but yeah right.

Minutes later, I hugged my sister and best friend before they exited the club, their Uber waiting outside for them. Brutus made sure to take the name and number of the Uber driver "just in case," as he put it.

I appreciated that he was protective over the two closest women in my life, though.

"I have to go to the bathroom," I told him.

"I'll wait for you."

"Go upstairs," I insisted. "It's right around the corner. I'll be quick, and then we can say goodnight to everyone."

He hesitated. I knew he was cautious, but he was going a little overboard. He'd been the same way since the night of the attempted break-in. At the time, I had to remind him that my shop was harmed, not me.

"I'll wait here," he said.

"Suit yourself." I headed in the direction of the ladies' room and was delighted when I didn't find a line a mile long waiting outside. I pushed through the door to see three stalls. The room was surprisingly clean for a nightclub, for which I was grateful.

I took one step toward the middle stall before I heard a voice behind me. A wrong voice because it belonged to a man.

"I've been waiting for you to come in here."

Spinning on my heels, I tripped and felt myself going down. The only thing that stopped me was the sink beside me. Unfortunately, because of the alcohol running through my veins, my reaction time was slow. Instead of bracing myself against the sink, I crashed against it, clipping my wrist against it.

I hissed in pain.

I looked up to see the man approaching me. Blinking, I looked up into his light blue eyes, trying to figure out what was happening. He wore a sardonic smile as if he knew me, but for the life of me, I couldn't figure out who the hell he was.

"I've been waiting for you," he'd said.

"I think you've mistaken me for someone else," I told him, my words coming out slower than normal and slurred.

"Oh no." His mouth tightened. "I have the right person. That motherfucker made me lose everything!" the man seethed, baring his teeth. "I'm blacklisted, can't get a job, my wife fucking left me." He became more frantic by the second. "And because he caused me to lose everything, I'm going to cause him to lose what's precious to him," the stranger hissed.

It took a few beats for my mind to process what he was saying. When my cognitive function finally caught on, I gasped. "It was you." I pointed at him while backing away. "You tried to break into my shop."

He cackled. "That was just the start of what I planned to do to you to make him suffer."

The gleam in his eyes was demonic. It terrified me, and I opened my mouth to scream for help, but before I could, I felt the first strike across my face.

CHAPTER 33

Brutus

I surveyed the club around us. People had begun to file out of the club even though there was about an hour until it closed. Nothing was off from what I could see, but there was a twisting in my gut that kept me vigilant.

Since Mia told me that her sister and friend wanted to take her out for a bachelorette party before Carlene's wedding, everything in me protested it. I still hadn't figured out who the fuck was behind her shop's vandalism. It wasn't Vincent.

And there wasn't another soul who had any sort of vendetta against Mia.

With one final sweep of the club, I pulled out my cell phone. I had a text from Jameson that I hadn't had a chance to check earlier.

Jameson: **Congratulations on the upcoming nuptials! You know I'll be there. Just give me a time and place. Listen, about a month ago, one of my employers heard from a Taggert Billings. Said he worked for you and the Townsends. He tried to get a job with my employer.**

A cold chill ran down my spine.

Me: **Thanks. You didn't hire him, did you?**

A strange feeling overcame me. I peered over my shoulder in the direction of the woman's bathroom. Everything seemed calm. It'd only been about two minutes since Mia went to the restroom.

Jameson: Not at all. I had my guy contact your staff for a reference and learned all I needed to know. It took less than half a day to find out you blacklisted his ass.

I started to type a reply, but another text came in from Jameson before I could finish.

Jameson: When I told him he wouldn't get the job with me or any other security staff, he lost it, though. Said how you ruined his fucking life. I've heard other guys we've fired say shit like that, so I didn't think much of it. I've been out of town on a sensitive op for the past three weeks, which is why I'm just telling you all of this now.

Another one of those chills ran down my spine. Yeah, guys in my line of work often talked shit, but finding this out from Jameson made something snap into place for me like the missing piece of a puzzle.

"Where's Mia?" Kayla asked, with Joshua standing beside her. "We're about to head out."

Mia.

I didn't bother answering her or Jameson's last text. Instead, I took off toward the women's restroom. Before I even reached the door, I heard a woman's shrill scream.

"Get off of me!"

My head snapped in the direction of the scream. There, I saw Mia flailing her one free arm while someone dragged her toward the door at the end of the hallway. The man who had her was towering over her. His back was to me, but I didn't need to see his fucking face.

"Taggert!" I yelled, rushing toward them.

He peered over his shoulder, a cold gleam in his eyes and a smirk before he pushed through the door, dragging Mia along with him.

"Fuck out of my way," I barked at the man who had just emerged from the men's room, standing between me and the end of the hallway. He jumped out of my way right before I barreled through his ass.

I chased after Taggert and Mia, bumrushing the door just before it closed in my face. It slammed against the outside of the club.

"Brutus!" Mia's voice carried, calling for me.

I chased in the direction, seeing Taggert pushing her into a dark sedan. She fought to get free, but it was useless. Taggert overpowered her by slamming his fist into the side of her face. When her body went limp, a sound came out of my mouth that I'd never heard before.

It was a mix of a growl, a curse, and a plea. I was going to kill that motherfucker, rip him from limb to limb. And then I'd mail his body parts, piece by piece, to anyone who loved him.

Taggert hopped over the roof of the car and was able to get into the driver's seat right as I made it to within inches of the passenger door. I reached for it, but he peeled off, almost running over my foot.

"Fuck!" I bellowed, feeling more helpless than I'd ever felt in my damn life. My heart pounded in my ears as I started to search my pockets for my car keys. When I found them empty, I racked my mind to figure out where they were. That's when I remembered that I'd left them along with my wallet up in the VIP lounge.

"Son of a ..." I started to take off to head back inside to get my keys, cursing myself for letting Taggert get a head start on me.

"Brutus!"

I spun to find Joshua standing a few feet away. He tossed me my keys, which I easily caught.

"Go. We'll follow."

I didn't wait for him to finish his before I was in a full-on sprint to my car. Though it felt like hours had passed, it must've been only a few seconds because right as I reached my SUV, I saw the dark sedan that Taggert drove pass right in front of me.

I jumped in my car and peeled out of the parking lot, hitting the curb on my way out. I pressed the palm of my hand against the steering, letting Taggert know I was on his ass. He hit the gas and sped up, blowing through a red light. I narrowly missed a head-on collision as I kept on his ass.

My only focus was the car in front of me. I would chase this dumb fuck all over the city and beyond to get Mia back. And then I'd bring all the havoc and rage I felt in my body down on his head.

He turned off the main road and led us down more isolated streets. A few of them were pedestrian roads. Due to the late night, however, most of them were empty. I thought about ramming the back of his car, but there was too much of a chance of injuring Mia.

I tried to play this out to figure out where the hell he was going. If I could figure that out, maybe I could get ahead of him somehow. But Taggert didn't have any property out this way. We were close to exiting the city limits. An area that was slightly more rural.

Right when I was about to make a move to pull up on Taggert's driver's side to force him over, I saw Mia leap across the center console and attack Taggert. That made my heart leap into my throat. She was up and fighting, which had to be a good sign.

Yet, from behind them, I could see that her distraction caused Taggert to swerve all over the road. He drove up on a curb and just narrowly missed hitting a fire hydrant. I wanted to yell and tell Mia that I was right there. She didn't have to fight. I would do it for her. But also, I was proud of her for not going down without a fight.

I honked the horn again. At the same time, Taggert came up on a side street with more empty lots than actual houses. Much of the road was overgrown.

"Where the fuc— *No!*" I yelled when Taggert swerved in what looked like an attempt to regain control of the situation in the car. He overcorrected and ended up driving right into a tree head-on.

I slammed on my brakes and screamed again, seeing how still the car was. My entire body shook in fear. Somehow, I managed to get out of my car. As I ran to the passenger side, I could only think how much this was my fault.

It was my job, my fucking business, that had put Mia's life in danger. The past month I'd been questioning Mia about who could have something against her, but I never stopped to think that it was someone with a beef against me that put her in harm's way.

"Mia, baby," I cried as I tried to yank the door open. It didn't budge. Realizing the door must've been locked, I put my elbow through it. The glass shattered and allowed me to unlock it from the inside. As soon as the door opened, I heard Mia groaning.

"No, no, no," I repeated when I saw a trace of blood across her forehead. "Baby, please be awake."

"Brutus," she mumble-whispered.

"I'm here," I consoled. "I'm here."

I didn't want to move her due to possible spine injuries, but smoke rose from the front of the car, and I could hear and see sparks flying. We were in danger of an explosion. I had no choice but to pull her out.

"You're okay," I told her as I carried her feet away from the car.

"Brutus," I heard Carter call as I knelt to the ground. I hated to place her on the street, but I needed to check over her injuries.

Carter was by my side, checking her pulse. "She's alive. Her pulse is strong."

I heard his words but couldn't respond because emotions clogged my throat.

"The ambulance is on its way," he assured.

"Don't leave her," I demanded, rising to my feet.

I had Mia, but she wasn't safe just yet. She wouldn't be until I took care of the bastard in the driver's seat—if the accident hadn't already done that. I heard other cars pull up, but I didn't bother to see who or what they were.

When I made it to the driver's side of the car, I found Taggert pushing open the door in an attempt to flee.

"Get the fuck back here." I grabbed his shirt and yanked him backward, making him stumble and fall on his ass.

Immediately, I went down on top of him, whaling on his ass. He threw up his arms in a pathetic attempt to cover his face.

A scream accompanied the first crunching sound I heard.

"Yeah, scream like the bitch you are!" I yelled. All I could hear was the sound of Mia yelling for help as he dragged her out of that nightclub. All I saw was the way he'd hit her right before pushing her into his car. I pounded his face, skull, and chest. Anywhere I could find, I punched it.

It was like an out-of-body experience, watching myself destroy him the way he'd tried to kill me. Because whatever he planned to do to Mia would've destroyed me. As it stood, I was a wreck, not knowing the extent of her injuries.

"Brutus!" a voice called. I knew the voice but was powerless to respond to it.

One.

Two.

Three more hits, I thought, *will satisfy me.* But I kept punching.

"Brutus, the ambulance is getting close," someone said next to my ear.

Aaron.

"We have to get him back in the car. Go take care of Mia."

Joshua and Aaron placed their hands underneath either of my arms, helping me to stand. By the time I rose to my feet, Taggert wasn't moving at all. The stillness of his body indicated only one thing.

The bastard rested in hell where he belonged.

"Go," Joshua said. "Mia's calling for you."

I turned and ran back over to Mia, collapsing by her side.

"Brutus," she whimpered.

I hated to see how swollen her face was. Either from the accident or from Taggert's hit.

"I'm here," I told her, taking her hand in mine and pressing a kiss to it. I knew I probably looked like a mess, covered in Taggert's blood, but I couldn't leave her long enough to wipe it away. "I'm here," was all I could get out.

The paramedics soon arrived, and I insisted on riding in the back with her. I wasn't about to let her out of my sight. I must've looked crazy enough for them not to argue because they didn't.

The entire ride to the hospital, I thought this was all my fault. And that if anything happened to Mia, I wouldn't survive.

CHAPTER 34

Mia

I sat up in bed and stretched my arms overhead before smothering my yawn. As usual, when I looked over to Brutus' side of the bed, it was already made up. Empty.

The alarm clock at the side of my bed read one minute before eight.

"Three ... two ... one," I counted down the seconds on the clock until it ticked eight o'clock. And not even a beat later, the bedroom door burst open.

In walked Brutus, carrying a tray with my breakfast on top. This morning routine had been since I left the hospital two weeks earlier. I had only been in the hospital for a day for observation. All in all, I'd gotten off easy. I sustained a concussion, sprained wrist, and some cuts and bruises. Relatively minor compared to what had transpired, but to Brutus, you would've thought I had been on my deathbed.

"Ah, ah, ah," he warned. "Don't you dare get up." He placed the tray over my lap.

My shoulders slumped. "You still don't think you're overdoing it?"

He frowned. "I'm not doing enough," he replied. "As far as I'm concerned, this isn't enough compared to what happened to you." He brushed his fingers across my cheek.

I let out a small moan and my body hummed for his touch. I reached my arms up, beckoning for a hug. When I turned my lips to meet his, he gave me a chaste kiss before pulling away.

"You need to eat." He pointed at the plate of scrambled eggs, pancakes, and sausage. On the side, he'd filled a bowl with berries and had fixed a cup of my shop's vanilla flavored coffee.

It all looked great, as usual. But I wasn't hungry for what was on my plate.

"I don't want food right now." I yanked at his hand, tugging him to me.

His lips twitched, but he clamped them together tightly before saying, "No. You're still heal—"

"I'm healed." I threw out my arms in frustration. "You haven't touched me in the two weeks I've been home."

His forehead wrinkled. "I touch you all of the time."

Sucking my teeth, I tossed my head back. "Babe, as much as I appreciate your foot rubs and cuddling with you every night, you know that's not what the hell I mean." I started to lift the tray of food to place it away from me, but Brutus took it from my hands.

I stood and stripped out of the long, white nightgown I'd worn to bed. "Take me," I demanded, standing there in all my naked glory.

His eyes traced up the length of my body. They heated with telltale desire. In response, my nipples hardened. His hold on the tray tightened, as indicated by his reddening knuckles. But he didn't move.

"Mia." My name came out as a hoarse whisper.

"My fiancé doesn't want to fuck me," I said before climbing onto the bed and planting my feet on the mattress. "I guess I'll have to find my own pleasure." I let out a deep, regretful sigh while spreading my legs, to let him see my pussy, glistening wet and ready for him.

"This …" I trailed off as I glided my fingers down my belly, through the short hairs below, and directly over my clit, "could've been yours for the taking."

I moaned as I rubbed circles into my clit and down farther, letting one finger sink inside. "Instead, I'll have to do it myself," I purred and then moaned as the heat in my body started to build.

"Fuck." The curse sounded tortured coming out of Brutus' mouth. It almost made me laugh, but then I heard a loud thud as something hit the floor.

My eyes popped open to find that he'd dropped the food tray. Uncaring about the mess on the floor, he barged over to the bed before ripping the T-shirt he wore off.

"Stop this shit," he demanded, grabbing my hand by the wrist. He bared his teeth, his grip on my wrist firm while his chest heaved up and down. His restraint was paper thin.

To push him over the edge, I teased some more.

"Stop what?" I asked innocently, batting my eyes and opening my thighs even more.

His answer was to bring the two fingers that were just inside of me to his mouth. He licked them free of my juices. Brutus quickly stripped out of the sweatpants he had on. I was relieved to find that he'd gone commando underneath the sweats.

I gasped when he climbed on the bed and bulldozed his body between my legs. His dick thumped against my sex, stealing my breath.

"You need to heal," he said, his voice cracking under the weight of trying to hold himself back.

"I need your dick," I replied.

His nostrils flared, but he didn't move.

I started to reach for his hard cock to guide it to where I knew we both wanted it, but Brutus stopped me. He wrapped his hand around my throat, forcing me back to the bed. That only served to make me grow wetter.

"Please," I begged. He hadn't touched me in weeks. Every damn night he'd ended our night with a chaste kiss to my forehead or, if I was lucky, my lips. I loved him for showing restraint while I was injured and vulnerable, but I was fucking over it.

I also knew he felt guilty for what happened. Because it had been one of his former employees who attacked me to get to him. But enough was enough.

I needed him. His touch. His everything.

"Mia." His voice sounded so haunted. He laid his forehead against mine. "What happened to you was my fault."

"No." I clamped my thighs around his waist. "It wasn't your fault." This was a conversation we'd had many times in the past two weeks. "It's his and he's gone," I reminded him. "Dead. But we're not. And if you don't fuck me right now, I'm going to get up, lock myself in that bathroom with my vibrator, and make myself come so hard, the walls will shake. And you'll be on the other side, forced to listen to it all."

"I'll fucking break the door down," he replied.

"Or you can just fuck me now." I squeezed my thighs again and lifted my hips slightly, rubbing my pussy against his hardness.

"Fuck, woman!" He groaned simultaneously, pulling his hips back, lining his cock with my entrance, and then surged inside.

His hand around my throat tightened, heightening the feel of his length inside of me. It felt like a homecoming to have him inside of me again.

"You're so tight," he murmured against my lips.

"You're so damn big," I groaned, wiggling my hips. "Take me, Brutus."

He pulled almost all of the way out before surging in again. He alternated the movement of his hips with his hand squeezing around my throat.

Having had to wait two weeks for this feeling again, it didn't take long before I came all over his cock.

"That's it, baby," Brutus praised. "Milk me. Take all of me," he said as he came inside of me, my pussy still convulsing and squeezing him.

"I love you so much," he said over and over, pressing kisses all over my face.

"I know," I panted. "I love you." Satiated, I started to get up, but his hand on my stomach stopped me.

"Where the hell are you going?"

I blinked. "I have to get to work."

I'd returned to work at Cup of Joy a week earlier but had two of my employees opening early for me.

"Hell no." Brutus shook his head. "My father can handle business at the shop for the morning."

Yeah, Rick had come to work at Cup of Joy with me. He'd gone from security to working as my assistant manager. It turned out he loved it and was great at it. Plus, I loved having him there. It also made Brutus less worried when he went back to work for the Townsends the week before also.

"I can't let Rick work by himself all morning."

Brutus gave me a warning look. "You should've thought of that before you spread your legs, baby. Your ass is mine for the next few hours."

While I felt a little guilty about leaving Rick to fend for himself for a couple hours, when Brutus flipped me onto all fours and slid into me from behind, I couldn't feel anything but pleasure.

EPILOGUE

Brutus
One year later

"She's glowing, son," my father said as he slapped the back of my shoulder. We stood at the head of the dance floor, watching as Mia and Ray had their father-daughter dance to Luther Vandross' "Dance with My Father".

Our wedding reception was held at the sprawling estate of Townsend Manor. I hadn't wanted to wait a full year to marry Mia, but she insisted on an outdoor wedding. And the elder Townsends all but insisted that their home would be the perfect location for the event.

Next to me, Jameson chuckled. "You've finally tied the knot. About fucking time. Don't let her get away."

I never took my eyes off of my wife. "I won't," I promised.

"Good," my friend replied. "I see a brunette over there who looks a little lonely. Maybe I'll find wife number four tonight."

"Thank you." I squeezed his shoulder in gratitude.

He nodded, understanding that I still wasn't a man of too many words when it came to others besides my wife.

"Thank you," he replied, jokingly. "I'm about to get lucky tonight because of you." He wiggled his eyebrows.

With a shake of my head, I wrapped an arm around Jameson and slapped him on the shoulder before watching him go off.

I surveyed the over a hundred guests who came to celebrate with us. Most of them were focused on the dance floor, watching Mia and her father. I dipped my head at Damon Richmond who sat with his wife, Sandra. He'd become a friend as well through his friendship with Joshua and his underground fighting club. Beside Damon and his wife, sat Connor O'Brien and his wife, Resha. Both also an important part of the Townsend extended family.

At the same table as Connor and Damon was Connor's younger brother, Mark, with his wife. I raised my champagne flute at the table and all of the men did the same to me.

Family.

I once thought the Townsends were just a job—the family I worked for. But they'd become my family.

I let that sink in before I turned my attention back to my wife and father-in-law. My father was right, she was glowing. And it had nothing to do with the spotlight on her. She shined naturally. But in the white, floor-length, satin gown, with her hair swept up in an intricate braided crown around her head, and the ebullient smile on her face, she appeared as if she floated in mid-air.

There was another reason for her glow as well. One we had yet to confess to our families. But it was the glow that came with a bundle of joy at the end of nine months. Just thinking about Mia carrying my child had my smile growing wider.

"You look like the cat who ate the rabbit," Tyler said as he and his brothers strolled up beside me.

"The canary," Carter corrected his younger brother with a roll of his eyes.

"What the fuck ever."

Chuckling, I shook my head but kept my eyes on Mia. I couldn't tear them away.

"He's not going to tell us," Joshua said.

"We know anyway," Aaron added.

That caught my attention. I spared them a look. "Know what?"

Carter chuckled, and Aaron's lips twitched, which was as much of a smile I'd get out of him.

"We're all familiar with that glow." Tyler dipped his head toward Mia.

"Looks like the ladies will have another baby shower to plan," Joshua said.

"No shit!" my father said, surprised. "Is she really—"

"Shshsh, shut up," I bark-whispered at him. "If she finds out anyone knows before we tell them, she'll wring my damn neck."

"Our lips are sealed," Carter promised. "God knows we've kept a hell of a lot worse secrets than a pregnancy," he murmured.

All of the men snorted in agreement, including me. I'd kept theirs for years, and they held on to mine.

The night Taggert kidnapped Mia, Aaron and Joshua had somehow gotten his beaten and battered dead body back into the car. Within seconds of them doing so, the vehicle erupted in flames. The ambulance had arrived before the police and fire departments. By the time they came, flames had engulfed Taggert's car with his body inside, and Mia and I were in the ambulance to the hospital.

Taggert had blamed me for the downfall of his life. Not only had he lost his livelihood, but the numerous affairs he had came to light in addition to the fact that he'd driven his family into hundreds of dollars' worth of debt, trying to keep up his fake lifestyle for his mistresses.

His wife left him and took their children. As she should have. All of that was his doing, but he failed to hold himself responsible for any of it. And the bitch paid with his life.

As far as the police knew and could prove, a disturbed former employee of mine attempted to kidnap Mia for revenge, got into an accident, and died in the car. It was close enough to the truth.

My only regret over the situation was that I hadn't had more time to make the bastard suffer before he took his last breath. The guilt of not figuring out that it was that son of a bitch behind the break-in before he had a chance to get anywhere near Mia continued to weigh on me.

Mia, of course, never blamed me. Yet, I still vowed to never let anything like that happen to her again.

"To family," Joshua said, holding up his glass of champagne with his free hand on my shoulder.

I looked at all of them, holding up their champagne flutes. I held mine up as well.

"To family," I repeated. We clinked glasses and downed our drinks.

As soon as I swallowed, the song faded, and I locked eyes with Mia. My heart skipped a beat, and before I could say 'excuse me,' my feet were carrying me to her.

"Take care of her," her father said as he placed her hand in mine.

I kissed the back of her palm before telling him, "Always."

I scooped her into my arms and spun us around in a couple of circles, making her laugh. The sound never failed to light up my body.

"What were the five of you over there talking about?" She jutted her head toward where I had stood with the Townsend brothers.

I kissed the tip of her nose.

"Family."

She stopped dancing, almost making me trip. "You didn't tell them, did you?" she whispered angrily.

"Baby, there are fifteen kids between the four of them. They can damn near sniff out a pregnant woman by now."

She pouted. "I wanted it to be a surprise."

I tugged on her chin. "It will be. They won't tell anyone. But I should warn you, if they've figured it out, Patience, Kayla, Michelle, and Destiny are probably chomping at the bit to plan the shower. They definitely know already, too."

Mia's face took on a thoughtful expression. After a moment, she shrugged. "There are worse problems to have."

"Exactly." I spun her again, right as an upbeat song started to play. More and more of our family and friends joined us on the dance floor.

"I can't wait to have this baby dressed in a Cup of Joy onesie," Mia squealed with love and happiness shining in her eyes.

"Trust me, they've probably ordered them already." I dipped my head to the Townsend wives.

Mia giggled. "I'm so glad I quit my job and decided to pursue my dreams. I got so much more than I could've ever asked for."

"You are so much more than I could've asked for."

She hummed and leaned against my chest, even though it was a fast song. "Thanks for being my favorite personal protection specialist," she said with a smile.

"Until my dying day," I said before brushing my lips against her temple.

* * *

KEEP IN TOUCH WITH TIFFANY

Looking for updates on future releases? I can be found around the web at the following locations:

Newsletter: Tiffany Patterson Writes Newsletter

Patreon: https://www.patreon.com/tiffanypattersonwrites

Website: TiffanyPattersonWrites.com

FaceBook Page: Author Tiffany Patterson

Email: TiffanyPattersonWrites@gmail.com

MORE TITLES BY TIFFANY PATTERSON

The Black Burles Series
Black Pearl
Black Dahlia
Black Butterfly

FOREVER SERIES

7 DEGREES OF ALPHA (COLLECTION)

Forever
Safe Space Series
Safe Space (Book 1)
Safe Space (Book 2)
Rescue Four Series
Eric's Inferno
Carter's Flame
Emanuel's Heat
Don's Blaze

NON-SERIES TITLES
THIS IS WHERE I SLEEP

My Storm
Miles & Mistletoe (Holiday Novella)
Just Say the Word
Jacob's Song
No Coincidence
The Townsend Brothers Series
Aaron's Patience
Meant to Be
For Keeps
Until My Last Breath

TIFFANY PATTERSON WEBSITE EXCLUSIVES

LOCKED DOORS

Bella
Remember Me
Breaking the Rules
Broken Pieces
The Townsends of Texas Series
For You
All of Me
My Forever

THE NIGHTWOLF SERIES
CHOSEN

The Ahole Club Series (Collaboration)**
Luke